Roma Wells is a Sri Lankan and Irish writer with a family heritage entwined with wild animals and sectarian conflict. Roma studied International Relations at Cambridge University and has worked in journalism, foreign affairs and international development. She's happiest scribbling under trees and at home you will find her bonding with an array of local wildlife. Seek The Singing Fish is Roma's debut novel.

seek the singing fish

ROMA WELLS

époque press

Published by époque press in 2022
www.epoquepress.com

Typeset in Proforma Light/Light Italic/Book Italic/Medium/
Medium Italic, Samarkan Normal, Fertigo Pro Regular
Typesetting & cover design by Ten Storeys®

Printed and bound in Great Britain by Clays Ltd,
Elcograf S.p.A.

British Library Cataloguing-in-Publication Data
A catalogue record for this book is available from
the British Library

ISBN 978-1-9998960-9-6 (Paperback edition)

*For all the creatures
and wounded souls*

prologue

Before I plunge you into the dripping labyrinth of my mind, dear reader, it feels like you should have a name. We will be squelching through sweat and grit, blistering trauma and blood drenched betrayal and that's no journey for the nameless. If you are kind enough to lend me your eyes and beating compass for a while, then the very least I can do is give you a label.

What to call you then? Language stirs trouble and clumps in hues of rotting flesh, the soil of my island whispers this hot and clear. So, let's take it way back, dip our toes in ancient waters and find you a gem in the sunken treasure chest of Sumerian cuneiform codes, the very first language of civilisation.

You are Shi, breath of life, my trusted companion through these pages. Although I say this is my story, it's not really, this tale simmers in shades far darker, oozes with curiosities more scrumptious and teems with creatures vastly more dazzling than you or I.

Now, before we begin, I should mention three things. If you're coming on this twisted voyage with me, it's only common decency to share a little about the hands steering the ship.

Firstly, I am plagued by a relentless curiosity, crippled by an exhausting intrigue about the world. I have an unquenchable thirst to understand things, writhing about until I've wrapped my mind around it and digested it like a ravenous boa. Take this very instant; when I should be soaking us into this story I'm instead thinking about you, Shi. I'm conjuring an image of what life you lead, what elixirs you slurp and what home pot marinade you ripened in. I want to know what tickles a smile to your lips and which vices invigorate your bones. This curious appetite of mine is vast, an insatiable creature condemned to an endless hunt, but I mustn't complain; this creature has kept me sane in the darkest of hours.

Secondly, I live and breathe in the animal kingdom, so melted and tangled in its splendour that my reality purrs, chirps and rumbles. Iridescent birds swoop, marine life dance and majestic creatures pant and prowl in footprints beside my own. I've always felt more comfortable around animals, Shi, humbled and nourished in the hypnotic grace of their world. In the stride of the species, I slip into my most natural rhythm. In the wild beat of their hearts, I've found the most honest home.

Thirdly, I adore words, for which I have my father, my appa, Edward De Zilwa to thank. I spent most of my childhood in his study, nestling in word thickets and weaving between a jungle of spines. It was there I curled up in the velvety ink folds and let sentences swell and stroke me. I inhaled their floral elegance, bled on their barbed edges and let their buttery curves lull me like wise honey. In appa's library I learnt to feel words, and now my bones tremble with a story that needs to be told, so

I've decided to unleash it here for you, Shi. Not a polished little tale wrapped neatly in a bow but an untamed eruption. I can't promise you'll be moved, stirred or woken in any way. You may return this to the shelf and never think of me again. But for now, I have you, so let's wade in my world for a while.

Oh, there is one more thing I should mention. I have a mangled face. I hate that it defines me, yet it does, unquestionably. Not an intriguing little lightening scar or a quirky imperfection but a grisly disfigurement that makes people squirm in my presence. I wasn't born with it, in fact people used to compliment my appearance before shrapnel sliced through my cheek with jagged claws, leaving bone and chewed flesh on display for all the world to gawp at. I'm lucky, the doctors trumpeted, I could easily have been blinded. In all honesty, Shi, I sometimes crave blindness, long for the cool embrace of darkness, void of pity glazed eyes and horror-spiced unease.

In better moods I feel a gratitude bubbling for the scar, which gifted me a liberating solitude as I grew up. Whilst other teens indulged in crushes, hormones and parties, I feasted on an inky banquet of books, filling my head with flavours that lodged deep and stained vivid. It has also granted me a unique vantage point to observe humans. As people desperately avert their gaze from the monstrous gravity of my cheek, I am free to study them. The cloak of their discomfort falls snugly, allowing me to digest their tone, body language and conversational masks, unshackled from the constraints of eye contact. Sadly, Shi, this has made it all too clear just how underwhelming we are as a species. Well, not all of us.

In the pattering slosh of monsoon afternoons, I often

wonder why my scar provokes such discomfort. Why are people so quickly repulsed by the flesh turned inside out? Perhaps I disturb people most because I remind them of how insignificant we all are; vulnerable hunks of flesh, bone and tissue masquerading behind these special identities we craft.

No, it's more personal than that.

To fellow Sri Lankans I'm a living, breathing reminder of the war. My face conjures up the loved ones slaughtered, the violence which shredded, maimed and tore our island just as it did my cheek.

I am beauty spoilt; Lanka corrupted.

I suppose now you're probably wondering how I got this grisly thing. Well, Shi, we will get to that shortly.

It emerges from the sweltering lagoons under the glow of a bloated mango moon. Listen closely and you might just hear it. As quiet dusk cloaks Kallady Bridge and the swollen moonlight settles, dip an oar in the water and listen. A mystic croaking. An enchanting siren song. A mythical hum might just meander to your hungry eardrums. Through the velvet rippling of the water and the feverish chirping of the crickets, you might just hear the singing fish.

part 1

false tigers, sham lions

The girl wouldn't stop shuddering, a sodden heap convulsing on the dirt.

'They m..m..made me watch.'

Salt snakes slithered down her cheeks, glistening in the lime shards peeping through the leaves. The breeze swayed with sweat and sea salt.

'They p..p..peeled his skin...rubbed pepper in the gashes... ripped his f..f..fingernails off one by one.'

A wild grief glazed her eyes, mucus bubbling from tattered nostrils.

'He...he didn't do anything, didn't know anything. They just wouldn't stop la..la..laughing.'

I slumped to the ground to join her, stifling a sigh for the jackfruit curry I knew I wouldn't make it back in time for. I imagined the tender fruit simmering in pepper and cinnamon, swirling in chilli kissed coconut milk, dancing garlic strides with the sour goraka beneath a canopy of bubbling pandan leaves. My taste buds tingled in longing. Why on earth did

9

I stop?

You're probably thinking I seem pretty heartless at this point, Shi, and perhaps you're not wrong. Weeping hordes of these broken souls had been pouring into our town for quite some time. While the Sri Lankan Army and Tamil Tigers shredded our island's luscious tapestry, the displaced began seeping in from all over. Everywhere you looked, traumatized crowds filled the local churches, temples and schools, dripping devastation, teeming in sweaty heaps under the palm trees. Limbless, homeless, hopeless; the living debris chewed up and spat out by the war.

At first, heart strings and curiosity would lead me straight into the folds of the sobbing huddles; I couldn't help but approach the sari-drenched agony, the raw grief and rocking bones, the irresistible siren songs of sadness. Lonely seeks lonely, I guess. But when the stories got particularly gruesome, I soon learnt to subtly tune myself away behind a convincing glaze of nods and concerned mm hmms. I looked beyond their faces and focused on the sand lizards scampering about for their supper. I listened to the flies gorging on rotting guava flesh and the motorbikes purring in the heat. When the weeping got really intense I'd watch those serpents slithering down their salt flat cheeks, etching faces into ghost maps of grief, wondering where those snakes evaporated to, what clouds they'd join, what wind currents they'd ride and what calmer soil they'd patter down and escape to. Their molten eyes would peer into my own, tragedies rolling from their quivering lips, as they sought some fragment of sympathy that I simply couldn't provide.

You see, Shi, when you've lived through so much barbarism

you start to lose all feeling; nothing shocks you anymore. So, when these trembling saris told me of their heartache, I felt nothing. When they wept stories of sons burned and husbands maimed, I felt nothing. When they choked out the pain of daughters who were torn and raped, I felt nothing. It had taken me so long to tightly lock my own trauma away I wasn't going to let them swoop in and loosen those hard-earned nuts and bolts. So, I tried to avoid them at all costs. The palm trees' new fruits were not to be tasted.

The shuddering girl was a moment of weakness; she seemed so alone, sitting detached from all of the others, her perfect cheekbones glistening as she stared serenely at the ground. Captivated, I dusted off the blushing pomegranate Mr. Ananda had given me earlier at the market and approached. Big mistake. As soon as I offered it to her, her crinkle bread nose went wobbling into a teary stew of tragedy.

She told me of how the soldiers had poured petrol on her father and disfigured her screeching brother piece-by-piece, and as she spoke, through the dust and blubbering, a colourful mosaic danced to life before my eyes. Her swollen papaya lips, cornflower sari and wet hazel eyes iridescent in the warm, mango dusk. Splendour soaring from sludge, beauty rising through darkness.

The art of distraction.

When cruelty is as common as coconuts, you have no choice but to focus on the little things, find comfort in the neglected, wade in the beauty of the in-between.

My childhood is a case in point. Even before the palm trees bore these sobbing fruits, Batticaloa was a tortured place. The soil and spirits of our lagoon-side fishing town had endured quite the beating. The fog of conflict was inescapable, looming over our every move, seeping its crimson gravy into every paddy field and cooking pot. That said, there was a delicious charm to be found in Batti if you knew where to look. Sure, newcomers flocked to colonial landmarks like the peeling lighthouse and the crumbling Dutch fort but Batti's true intrigue rumbled in the teeming natural life it sheltered.

It's mighty fitting the word nature comes from the Latin word for birth, because nature was where I felt most alive, Shi. Under the cloak of a sticky humidity and a whispering sea salt breeze, pockets of scrumptious beauty blossomed for those present enough to breathe it in. Glimpsing dolphins frolicking on sun-drenched waves as hermit crabs dodge toes nestled in hot sand, tracing striped rasbora weaving through the mangroves while sea-eagles glide currents in the vast cerulean pool above, watching bulbuls craft their nests in the kumbuk trees as bloodtail dragonflies flit past earlobes in the moist breath of evening; this was my Batti.

It wasn't friendship I sought in the animal world, though my introversion probably made most think this was the case, it was more of an infatuation. I revelled in the symphony. The erratic crescendo of squirrels as they spiralled around ancient trunks, wrapping the bark momentarily in striped cocoa ribbons. The frenzied tempo of ants as they marched through the mangroves. The stillness of archer fish lurking beneath the lagoon surface. Crocodiles hissing and huffing their base chords, mouths agape to release heat from their armoured bodies. Did you know, Shi, that crocodile teeth can grow back up to fifty times in one lifetime.

In my creature muses I found a serenity missing from my

two-legged neighbours, a purity at odds with the sickly local malaise. People could slash and seethe over who owned what chunk of land all they wanted but I understood it wasn't theirs to begin with. All that hacking and yacking was pointless in the grand scheme of things; our land, all land, belongs to creatures far greater than us. So as war, grief and resentment festered all around, I escaped with the butterflies and soared with the hornbills and babblers. Watching these ancient masters of soil, sea and sky, I fell snugly into the grooves of fascination, content with a respect garnered from a distance. Respect from a distance was a habit hard to find amongst the opposable thumbs.

You know, Shi, our teardrop island has wildlife to rival an entire continent. It's a natural laboratory of enchanting adaption, from its jungle lungs and mountainous heart to the sprawling ocean on its coastal curves. From the winged beauties soaring above mist-cloaked forests to the bejewelled beetles, trapeze artists and majestic coats lurking on the jungle floors. As night casts its quilt of stars across the canopies, porcupines, leopards and sloth bears emerge from the shadows while slender lorises pluck fruits from moonlit branches glistening with silk threads. Far beneath Lanka's shores, a tropical crossroads for migrating marine marvels, shoals of yellow striped fusilias and reef fish mingle near coral cities as blue whale bellies heave overhead. Life teems in the shipwrecks littering the coastal floor, creatures hunkering down in the ruins of trawlers and cargo ships, feasting on algae bursting from tattered hulls, reclaiming a little territory back from the scraps of human folly.

I loved nothing more than to spend an afternoon by the

lagoon, cocooned in its humid lattice, a dripping limbo between land and water. Most locals thought the mangroves were an overgrown mess, a tangle of roots rasping to the earth like dead men's fingers. But I saw them for what they truly were, a nursery for young fish, a larder for flamingos who sifted shrimp from algae as they wiggled their toes in the mud. You know, Shi, it's the shrimp and brine that make flamingos pink and the weaker hunters can be spotted by their paler hues. I always liked the idea of the shrimp living on through the flamingos, immortalised in their feathers in vibrant defiance. I'd watch the cormorants there, drying their wings in the sun, a cluster of jet-black wings toasting in the heat. Overhead, white-bellied sea eagles would soar elegantly, waiting to swoop for their scaly snacks. They mate in pairs for life, Shi, performing synchronised acrobatic dances to renew the bonds with their beloveds. Graceful doesn't quite capture it.

My favourite rabbit hole though was dragonfly watching. For hours I'd study the striped threadtails, blue perchers and yellow waxtails flitting across the water. I'd lose all sense of time tracking pintails, scarlet baskers, blue sprites and bloodtails. I craved dragonfly vision to experience the full flavour of their movements, because while the human eye processes sixty images a second the dragonfly manages around two hundred. Still, even with the feebler human eye I was hypnotised by the dancing dropwings, entranced by the infinity patterns of the foggy-winged twisters and bedazzled by the shimmering gold patches of the wandering gliders. With over one hundred and twenty different species flitting around the island, people take these winged wonders for granted. Their heritage is one thing, being one of the first insect species to inhabit the planet over three hundred million years ago, their near 360-degree vision and ability to see vastly more dazzling colours than us, is another. But most neglected of all is the fact dragonflies are the most successful hunters in the animal kingdom. Honestly, while we trumpet about the hunting skills of sharks, lions and tigers, dragonflies are the creatures with the highest success rate. They pre-empt where prey will move to and then catch it mid-air in a calculated ambush before shredding it with their serrated mandibles. I reckon people would tremble more, Shi, if griffenflies, their gigantic precursors, were still around today. Pretty hard to ignore a hunter with a two-foot wingspan.

The life cycle of a dragonfly is also unusual. When a larva hauls itself out of the water and splits its skin, a complete adult emerges from inside. These newly hatched adults were always peppered around the lips of the lagoon, waiting vulnerably for their wings to strengthen before mastery of the air could begin. They reminded me a little of Batti's children; forced to mature early, condemned to a vulnerable limbo state between childhood and adulthood, predator and prey.

I often zoned out simply staring at the surface of the lagoon, entranced by the branches and clouds reflected in the ripples. It's breath-taking, Shi, to see earth, sky and water fused all together like that, a mirror of everything that is, was and will be. Problem was, the curfews would always shake me from my cocoon and force me back to reality. The war was a possessive kind of monster and I always knew when something atrocious had happened around town. I heard the whispers rush through the branches of the trees and saw the leaves trembling with what they'd heard. The trunks witnessed, creased and ached, and beneath my soles I could feel the hot panicked murmurs rumbling between the chattering roots. Sometimes it even sounded like the air itself was screaming, swelling with the weight of some terrible thing, desperate to escape what it had seen.

Locals referred to the war as the prachanai, the problem, which always seemed a vast understatement to me. A lazy brother or a flat tyre would be a problem, a mutilated brother shoved through a burning tyre is something else entirely. Now, far greater minds and more impressive pens than mine have traced the deep roots of the conflict, Shi, so I'll just paint a few inferior strokes for you to set the scene.

The civil war was fought between the Sri Lankan Government and the Liberation Tigers of Tamil Eelam, better known as the Tamil Tigers. The Tigers wanted an independent homeland in the north and east of the island for Sri Lanka's Tamil minority. From their perspective, decades of state discrimination against Tamil people and blatant favouritism for the majority Sinhalese population confirmed the political machine was a useless tool for achieving this homeland. Two thorns cut particularly deep; the Sinhala Only Act in 1956 which made Sinhalese the only official language and forced countless Tamils out of work, and the 1970s standardisation policy which forced a dramatic fall in the number of Tamil students entering universities. Violence was necessary, the Tigers growled, their homeland must be demanded from behind the barrel of a gun.

A fiery turning point arrived with the burning of the Jaffna library. As countless books and historic palm leaf scrolls were devoured by flames, many Tamil people felt the Government could no longer protect them or their cultural heritage. This, along with numerous anti-Tamil pogroms that had simmered since the 1950s, made the Tigers' roar for a separate state all the more appealing. The Government, on the other hand, cast themselves as the sword-wielding lions from Lanka's flag, tackling centuries of colonial injustice with flowing manes and roaring might. The English-speaking Tamil minority had enjoyed disproportionate privileges under British rule so with independence in 1948 came a chance to tackle this inequality. Through language, education and a firm military grip, it was time to raise up the Sinhalese majority and knock the privileged Tamils down a few pegs. To them the Tigers were terrorists, vicious scoundrels hell-bent on shredding the fabric of a newly liberated Lanka. It was their duty to protect her, at all costs.

Then in 1983 came Black July. After a Tiger ambush killed thirteen army soldiers a brutal massacre of thousands of Tamils erupted across Colombo. There, from the blood-soaked, ash-caked streets, an all-out civil war belched forth. For the Sinhala Lions and Tamil Tigers, it was now an all claws, all jaws fight to the death.

Both predators claimed a moral high ground that didn't exist. The only ground was the trampled, blood-drenched wastelands left in their wake. Inevitably, it was the civilians who suffered most, trapped in the middle and slaughtered in the crossfire for almost three decades.

The misuse of lion and tiger imagery really frustrated me, Shi. These majestic creatures shouldn't be emblems of such darkness, their coats shouldn't be rolled in the crimson filth of war. Tigers and lions are quite humane killers, snapping the spinal cord or major artery of their prey for a speedy death before dragging it to a secluded spot. The butchery of the two-legged predators was quite different, maximising pain and leaving mutilated bodies on display as warning signs. While real tigers mark their territory with buttery, popcorn scented urine, the human ones marked theirs with limbs and landmines. While real lions spend most of their day resting, the army lions were always on the hunt. And while a lion's whisker holes and a tiger's striped skin both bear a pattern as unique as a fingerprint, the two-legged predators all blended into a homogenous blob of brutality.

Batti was ravaged by the predators on both sides. By day, the Lions gripped the streets, prowling through their patchwork of checkpoints, but as night fell the Tigers emerged from pockets of jungle, lurking through the largely Tamil town they considered their own. Batti was a carcass ripped by both sets of Kalashnikov claws. Inevitably, the maggots began to fester from its rotting flesh.

Beneath the bitter shadow of this conflict lived my family.

❖　　　　　　　❖　　　　　　　❖

My amma, you could say, was exactly what you needed in a mother; encouraging, respectful of your personal space and stern when required. She was beautiful in a delicate way, self-effacing and relished a juicy gossip over a glass of sweet lime. She loved me, I knew that, but it never felt like she actually liked me. I was a girl to be guided, not a daughter to be cherished.

Amma was also a magician. With any handful of spices and a little coconut milk, she could whip up a banquet to induce tears from the gods. She was a true alchemist of the scrumptious;

humming around steaming pots, sprinkling herbs like pixie dust and crafting dishes that would replenish your very soul. Like a conductor she'd prance around her kitchen orchestra, tasting, spicing, dabbling and dancing with all manner of flavours. In the mornings you'd find her steaming pittu inside bamboo, drizzling treacle on buffalo curd and smothering hoppers with coconut gravy. Come evening, she'd be tempering parippu dhal with cumin seeds, marinating jackfruit in chilli-ginger stew and pickling veggies for her sour achcharu. She had such a knack for flavour, Shi, pairing sweet and sour into surprising gems. I remember her chuckling as our frowns morphed to smiles as we gobbled down her mustard sugar olives and vinegar-soaked mangos. Without words she taught us opposites could make the best of pairings.

On my ninth birthday she showed me how to make lamprais. For hours we infused cutlets with clove and cinnamon, soaked rice in stock and drenched chilli sambol with lime and salt. As we steamed our packets in banana leaves, I remember thinking how unfair it all seemed. So much time spent slaving away for everything to be gobbled up in mere moments. Why should women put in all this hidden effort with no lasting results to show?

'All pleasure demands preparation Mila, patience is the best marinade,' she had said as she fed me a spoonful of sweet rice. 'You see? The dedication comes through in the flavour, its rewards are felt in the bones.'

Amma's unusual choice of husband certainly embodied her cooking philosophies. Hard-earned pleasure and the splendour of opposites made sense for a woman disowned for pursuing a love marriage to a chorus of scorn all round. Rather than pick one of the good Tamil men her mother had selected for her in a frenzy of astrological charting, amma fell defiantly in love with my father, a Burgher.

The Burgher minority are a layered hotchpotch of western ingredients, a small Eurasian ethnic group descended from Portuguese, Dutch, British, German, Italian and other European men who slept with native Sri Lankan women. Privileged under British rule for their English tongue, many islanders resented these living reminders of colonial meddling. Thus, despite Burghers also being targeted by the Sinhalese government's policies, most of amma's relatives saw a Burgher husband as a corruption of their family line.

So, my appa, Edward De Zilwa, wasn't even given a chance. Their bloody loss. I stand by my belief that if anyone spent just five minutes in a room with appa, they'd be enchanted. He was simply a different kind of soul; a bundle of intrigue, humour and delightful weirdness wrapped in colourful trousers and cedarwood cologne. In a flurry of peppermint toffee breath, he'd bewitch you with his facts and fancies and engulf you in his marvellous mind maze of metaphors and musings.

Appa would get lost in his study for hours, flitting between book spines and scrambling through soaring piles of paper with pots of steaming tea. His study was more like a little library, an oaky cocoon drenched in every genre you could imagine. Academic journals spiralled up like wild thickets, periodicals sprawled like knotweed and yellowing scrunched paper burst like creeping buttercups. I adored that forest of reworked trees. He always joked that his career as an English professor was chosen only to fuel his real passion of book collecting. And what a collection it was. His inky jungle catered to every taste. Voltaire, Rousseau and Aristotle beckoned from Philosophy Alley. Marx, Foucault and Durkheim whispered social observations by the window. Orwell and Woolf bustled on the Empire shelves, Xueqin and Guanzhong called from China Corner, and Chekhov and Dostoyevsky mingled on Russia Row. Religious tomes, philosophical classics, sociological gems, historical greats and collectables brimmed from every surface. The room was hypnotic; cross the threshold and your senses were marinated in that delicious old book smell, dazed by the patchwork of spines and drenched in the sepia splendour oozing from the wall maps.

I enjoyed looking at those wall maps a lot as a child. I'd conjure animal shapes in the curves of the continents; canine snouts, elephant ears, wingspans and horns all nestled amidst the canvas of the world. When the sunlight faded and the lamps went on, those animals came to life in the glow. A hound leaping downwards in Baffin Island and a tadpole wiggling in Norway. A trout dangling in Kamchatka island and a dolphin's head lunging landwards in the Kara sea. On days when the bullet thunder was heaviest, I'd sit there tracing those creatures over and over until I'd lulled myself into calm. My island was so tiny compared to the rest of the sprawling shapes, and the more I looked at Lanka on the map, the more it seemed like a jackfruit. Its prickly skin putting people off from discovering the glory nestled deeper; it's latex sap which can work like glue, the nutritious bulbs and seeds bursting within, the vitamins and the nourishment right there beaming if you took the time to look. But people saw the bumps, got a whiff of the war rot and turned their backs on it. I hoped that one day people would see our Lanka fruit for the delight it truly was.

With so much energy bursting between its walls, appa's study had its very own pulse. Bones of shelves, red-penned arteries of research and veins of blue teaching folders all encasing the beating heart of his desk. The floorboards moaned in the heat and the breeze hummed through the window cracks. I'm telling you, Shi, that room was alive. Appa would select his favourite books from the shelves, and we'd sit discussing them for hours with sweet kalu dodol pinched from the kitchen when amma wasn't looking. Under a square of loose floorboards, he helped build my reading den. With cushions and a good deal of cleaning we padded the alcove into my own cosy burrow, a secret library within a library.

As I sat in my literary hot box, inhaling the intoxicating oaky scents, I'd often wonder what trees those books started out life as. I wondered about the contours of their bark, the spread of their roots and the creatures that once nestled in their branches. When I walked through a dense thicket of trees, I sometimes had the thought in reverse. I wondered what stories they may one day hold, what words might be immortalised in their splendid, sacrificial skin. When our time comes to return to the earth and our bodies feed the soil, perhaps we revive again in the trees, set to turn into untold stories held between unborn palms. Maybe one day, Shi, my body will become bound in the pages of a story your great grandchild holds.

Through the cracks in the floorboard ceiling, I'd watch appa working away at his desk, and I would feel like a sapling bursting through the forest floor, striving up towards the vast canopies flourishing overhead, craving to join the master trunk as it reached further into the sky.

To feed my love of wildlife, appa began amassing a special

stack of nature books just for me. Every evening I'd dissolve in those pages, feasting on creature intrigues, running my fingers over the decadent pictures and absorbing everything until my head began to thump. Behaviours, features, Latin names and geographical spreads of all kinds of species soon seared the contours of my mind. I even began dreaming in wildlife.

On restless nights, I'd sneak down to the light of the library and rather than force me back to bed, appa would let me read with him under the citrus glow of his lamp.

'Our little secret, La' he'd whisper through toffee tea breath.

My eyelids would soon grow heavy and I'd drift off to the gentle scrunch-whirring of his eyelashes, opening and closing in step with his ticking brain; the sound of appa thinking was the best kind of lullaby. With my welling curiosity and burgeoning love of books, appa had found his kindred spirit. In the time he made for me and the way he looked at me, there was an unspoken understanding that I, not Ravi, was his favourite.

❖　　　　　　❖　　　　　　❖

My relationship with Ravi has always been a strange one. I wish the syrupy warmth of sibling comradery was all that coursed through my veins at the thought of my little brother. But the truth is, Shi, my affection for Ravi was tainted in ways that quite frankly embarrass me. I hid it well, of course. To the outside world I was the doting sister, brimming with a protective love, enviably pure. And this affection was pure at first bloom. Appa and amma gushed often about how attached I was to my baby brother. 'Wouldn't stop cuddling him, men! Always rubbing his cheeks like they housed the magic of a genie's lamp.'

Hazy memories still swirl in sepia strokes of how I'd climb into his cot at night. Pulling the blanket into a tent above us I'd stroke his velvet earlobes until he'd drift into tropical oblivion. Watching his tiny chest rising and falling in harmony with the sighing waves, a sharp jab of protectiveness lodged in my own little chest. I was his lokku akka, big sister, and those toes and tiny fingers were my responsibility to protect.

As we grew up, new feelings began their corruption. I soon realised amma's love for Ravi far exceeded what she felt for me. It was subtle, but in those lingering stares, the school sport events never missed, the soft Thallatu lullabies she'd hum whilst stroking his curls, it was clear golden boy was the apple of her eye. She loved and liked Ravi.

Ravi's striking resemblance to her father certainly helped. Appappa Nimal and amma were close and he was the only one who had accepted her bold marriage choice. Where others saw a betrayal of her Tamil brethren, appappa saw only his little girl dancing bravely to the beat of her own heart. When he died, bludgeoned in Wellawatte's 1983 tide of anti-Tamil riots, amma lost her only family. As his legs were slashed and his bloodied torso dragged through the streets, amma's banishment was sealed. Her mother and siblings, vicious in bitter grief, forbade her from attending his funeral. It was her selfishness, they hissed, the bad karma she'd brewed that was to blame for their misfortune, her actions that had fuelled the fire of the bloodthirsty mob. And just like that, amma was cast out from the Colombo lot for good.

So, in Ravi's dark curls and chocolate eyes, amma found her father again. Reviving appappa effortlessly with each glance, smile and laugh, I knew Ravi would always be her favourite. It was impossible to contend with. No matter what I did, said or achieved, my place as her eternal other-child was sealed. Ravi took this bias for granted. He grew increasingly despondent with amma's stifling attention and brushed off her kisses like dirt from his shoes.

All that said though, Ravi and I still shared a special bond and in the sunset of our childhood years, while violence mounted and fear seized Batti's bones, we found a calm in each other. Before the currents of puberty came lashing, we paddled together in those simpler shallows of childhood. When curfews tightened and the rains came drenching, we'd craft our own entertainment at home. Ravi didn't care much for books but there were some stories which tickled him. Invariably tales laden with intrepid pirates, brave knights and fierce warriors sparked his boisterous intrigue and I read them to him with relish. *The Three Musketeers* was his favourite and time and time again he'd ask me to read it aloud to him.

Between the talons of curfew, we'd race our bikes to the lighthouse playground, lap the lagoons and cruise in the salt spray of the lake roads. We'd inspect rockpools with sticks, skim pebbles on the water and sketch shapes in the scorching sand. Abuzz with the sugar of our favourite cinnamon kokis, we'd do impressions of local characters and collapse in dazed giggling heaps at our creations. Ravi's impression of Mrs Pradeepa was uncanny, his snobby pouting and finger wagging always reduced us to gleeful foetuses writhing in the sand.

Although Ravi didn't share my unfettered love of animals, he still enjoyed some of our encounters with them. On one sweltering beach visit, we tried carving our names in the rocks and when we stopped to rest from our wobbly RA and MI attempts, we spotted a few streaks diving in and out of the distant water.

'Spinner dolphins.' I beamed, my pointed finger shaking with elation.

'Why are they called spinner dolphins?' Ravi asked, squinting at the shapes.

I explained what I knew of the acrobatic creatures from appa's nature book, how they rotate and spin metres in the air as they chase schools of juicy tuna and scour the sea for bounty.

'But why do they spin?' Ravi pressed.

'Some say it's a way to send messages to each other. Others think it's to remove parasites or sea gunk stuck to their skin. Truth is, no one really knows Rav. I like to think they do it just because they can.'

Ravi smiled warmly.

'I like that idea too.'

The sun's rays were gently stroking his dark cheeks, eyes glistening in the citrus glow. In silence, we admired the distant spinners with an envious flavoured delight. An unspoken understanding lingered on those rocks with us; how wonderful that spinning must be, how precious that freedom to do things whenever you want, just because you can. We kept watching until the curfew crawled up and forced us home.

The bond that drew us closest, though, was our feverish pursuit of the singing fish. Locals rave about Batticaloa's mysterious scaly singers but very few have actually heard them. For those who say they have, perhaps it was just the hum of crazy Chittu they heard as he lapped the lagoon collecting rubbish in his pockets. Chittu lost his mind after an incident with a landmine he planted. The army vehicle was delayed that day and the Jony mine hit a bus instead, a bus with his wife and daughter on board.

The fishermen say your best chance of hearing the singing fish is in the stillness of a full moon night, near where the lagoon laps Kallady Bridge. Dip your oar in the water, hold one end to your ear and listen closely. If you're lucky, an ethereal plucking, a mystical croaking or a ghostly humming might rise to your eardrums. The sound could just be water flowing between the rocks, or perhaps, the siren song of mermaids. Truth is, no one knows for sure. This elusive watery wonder is a genuine mystery and Ravi and I revelled in it. While locals grappled with the darker mysteries of identifying charred remains and countless family disappearances, we'd sneak off to Kallady Bridge and sit listening intently by the lagoon. We dipped rotting oars, shells and crumpled bottles in the water, desperate to find this other world, to taste the magical realm rippling just beneath. Sometimes we convinced ourselves we'd heard it, but we knew deep down we were deluding ourselves. We remained shut out, forever on the painful cusp of understanding.

owl fever,
curious krait

As you know, Shi, I revel in the company of animals. No point beating around the bush. Their eclectic charm entices me far more than the predictable arrogance of us lot. Do we have three hearts and nine brains like the octopus, horns of hair like the rhino, regenerate limbs like the axolotl? Can we regrow cartilage like the spiny mouse, breathe through our bum like the turtle or secrete an antibiotic sunscreen like the hippo? Animals enthral me, humans rarely do. That said, there are a few humans who do enthral, a few people who can uplift the spirit with such an infectious energy one is left mildly dazed in their company.

My appa was one such rare gem. A gem more dazzling than the azure blue sapphires nestled in Ratnapura's mines. While most just survived or existed, appa lived. He was a patchwork of delights; there was his treasure trove of a brain, his flair for metaphorical language and of course that living library of his. But one of my very favourite traits was his humbling appreciation of the stuff most of us take for granted. He truly savoured the little things; the smell of an old book, the curves of the moon, the journey wrinkles of washed-up rocks and only appa could extract such genuine joy from listening to rainfall in the middle of a warzone. All held value to him. While the bloodshed around us seeped a darkness into most souls, appa preserved an unwavering light, a light he would share and nurture tenderly in other people. He watered the seeds of our passions and helped them flourish into branching beauties.

He nurtured amma's love of cooking, encouraging her experiments and finding spices for her to dabble with. He nurtured Ravi's cricket passion, helping refine his bowling technique on the beach until even the sun had had enough. But with me, he was the most attentive. My endless questions, which he'd never dismiss, and our sprawling reading sessions were one thing, but appa truly fanned the flames of my animal obsession. It was he who had persuaded amma to call me Artemila, a compromise on Artemis the Greek goddess of wild animals and with a name like that, perhaps my passion was inevitable.

I loved sitting with him on the lagoon banks after a drenching rainfall. We'd watch the way the mud squelched and oozed with nutrients, a sprawling tapestry of tiny brown lakes. If you listened closely, you could hear the water sinking into the soil, the roots feasting and slurping minerals deep into the earth. If you looked closely, you could see the teeming insects and amphibians, trace the tracks to their tunnels and hideouts lodged beneath. On the edges of the water, where the swaying reeds wore the shape of the currents, we'd watch the brown slosh glistening in the sunlight, twinkling and shimmering like smoky quartz. You know that well-worn saying, Shi, about finding a diamond in the rough? Well, down by my lagoon, often the rough was the diamond, a thriving treasure trove encrusted with a thousand gleaming gems.

Before long, I was pointing out mudskippers in the rockpools, green whip snakes in the shrubbery as jezebel butterflies sipped our nutritious sweat with their feet. I showed him brown-capped babblers in the wood apple trees, sand lizards darting by our toes and rock skinks peeping through the leaf litter. I told him how spider silk is stronger than steel, how the slow loris secretes poison from its elbow and how the sloth bear has no front teeth so it can suck up termites like a vacuum. I loved to surprise him by exposing animal myths. He stopped in his tracks when I told him fruit bats actually have great vision. We really do get so much wrong about animals, Shi, we go on believing these easy myths, too careless to check for the truth of it. As I would ramble on about mating habits, quirky adaptations and life cycles, appa would always give me his full attention, his interest further spurring on my own. I was encouraged in ways only the march of time has allowed me to fully appreciate. Without realising, I would digest field guides and facts with an eye on how to explain things to appa later, absorbing information in a translatable way and conjuring metaphors to bring it to life. Without instruction, he taught me to learn in a way one could share and to live in a way that was generous.

When the claws of curfew retracted, we'd escape for moonlit strolls between the stars and the crickets. I loved that time of night, cool and laden with scrumptious possibility. One evening, distant owls began hooting in a fervour. Appa said he always found the sound comforting, the soft pulse of the twilight hours, as he put it. He told me that in Greek mythology a flying owl was a sign of impending victory and that the goddess of wisdom, Athena, was always accompanied by one.

'Do you think we can spot one La?' he chirped.

'Maybe if we had their ears.' I was attempting to be cryptic. I really wanted to impress.

'Their ears? Don't you mean their big eyes?'

'Nope, their ears appa. Many owls have different sized ears placed at different points on their heads. That way, each ear receives sound at slightly different times and allows them to pinpoint the location of the noise perfectly. It's why they're such great hunters.'

'No way! Good thing amma doesn't have those ears, ey? But what about their eyes, don't those big saucer eyes help?'

'They're actually eye tubes, appa. They can't see things very well close up, so they use tiny feathers on their beaks and feet to feel out their food instead. They also have not one, not two, but three sets of eyelids. One for blinking, one for sleeping and one for keeping their eyes clean.'

Appa quizzed me all the way home about the hooting wonders. We talked about how their stealthy feathers reduce turbulence and how the whopping fourteen vertebrae in their necks allow them to twist it 270 degrees. I told him how great horned owls hunt other owls and how barn owls swallow their prey whole, regurgitating the fur and bones later in little balls. I swelled with pride at the thought of having taught him something. The morning after, I dug out the owl chapter from the wildlife book in his library to see what I'd forgotten, and in the margin I noticed appa's familiar handwriting etched in fading pencil marks. I was starting to understand, Shi, that it was my passion that delighted him so much and not the facts themselves.

You see, appa valued curiosity above all else. In everything we did together he made sure to stoke the flames of my intrigue. One conversation in particular has stuck with me, sparked by a black and white photograph labelled Sabine Weiss, Paris, 1953, that he had framed in his study. The photo was of a woman running down a park pathway lined with trees, but because of the shadows, I couldn't tell whether she was running towards the camera or away to the sunlight yawning in the distance. Appa caught me gazing at it as I slurped my lime juice.

'Magnificent isn't it La? I've always loved that picture.'

I nodded, slurped and continued to stare.

'But I don't get it appa. Is she running towards us or the light?'

'Ah, well there you are, you do get it.'

'Get what?'

'The beauty of it' he said, as he smiled at the creases appearing on my face. 'The fact you don't know which way she is running is the beauty of it, La.'

'But don't you want to know the answer?'

'Of course. But sometimes it's better not to know.'

'Why?'

'Because that way you get to both want and feel more.'

'What do you mean, feel more?'

'Well, let's suppose she's running towards us. You could say the photo feels more intimate that way, more personal somehow, like she's connected to you in some way.'

'Like she knows us?'

'Right, now suppose she's actually running away to the sun. That feels more poetic doesn't it? She is leaving the darkness for the light. It's precisely because you don't know the answer that you get to experience it both ways. She is running both towards you and away from you so it feels both intimate and poetic. That magnificent blend of emotions is all thanks to our uncertainty. The answer is out of reach and the unreachable is enchanting.'

I stood staring at the picture as I digested his words. 'The most important thing is wanting to know La, it's not the knowing itself. The curiosity is important in its own right, it's our fuel. Remember what Plutarch said, our minds are not vessels to be filled but fires to be kindled. Don't forget that La. Less filling and more kindling.'

Truth is, Shi, despite appa's words, I still couldn't help wanting to know for certain which way the woman was running.

❖   ❖   ❖

I wish I'd known more about appa's take on the war. Aside muffled conversations gleaned through door cracks after bedtime, those discussions were purposefully kept out of earshot. When I asked about the curfews and blackouts, the bullet thunder and the funerals, I was fed child-proofed messages about islanders being peaceful and bad eggs causing problems that most people didn't want. I know he meant well. He wanted to shelter me for as long as possible, preserve what slither of childhood he could. But no amount of sheltering could keep the war out. The way I saw it, the adults were the ones creating the mess so at the very least us children deserved to know why. I realise now, that why was increasingly an enigma to all ages.

One soggy afternoon by the lagoon I tripped on a piece of wire gauze the soldiers had left out. My palms were grazed and appa had to untangle my hair from the mesh. He cleaned the dirt from my throbbing palms with a tissue as I winced.

'At times like this, La, you've got to channel the patience of our island, be like Lanka. You've already got her green heart and a belly full of gems and spices, but now you need her patience. You may feel a little pain now, but it'll pass, you will heal. Do you know why they call Lanka the pearl of the Indian Ocean?'

I shook my head as he gently brushed away the little stones stuck to my skin.

'Well, a pearl is formed when an irritation like a grain of sand slips in between the shells of an oyster. In order to protect itself, the oyster covers the visitor with layers and layers of nacre until the beautiful gem is formed. Friction transformed into beauty, that's what our Lanka does best. You just need a little patience.'

He kissed my hands and moved on to untangling my hair.

'Stop fidgeting, La. The hairs tangle more with each struggle.'

He sat down in the sludge and muttered away as he worked at my release.

'With a knot like this, we must consider our options carefully. A sharp yank may be the easiest path, but this rarely solves the problem. If it's really bad we may need to cut the entire knot out, get rid of all the nuisance strands for the sake of your beautiful head. Or there's the third option, the best option, which just requires a little patience. We can study the strands, really look at the knot and bit-by-bit we can undo the layers of tangles. They flowed in harmony from the same scalp before and they will again, La.'

He sat untangling that knot for ages, unravelling the mess until I was free. At the time it seemed like a lot of effort. Why waste so much time overthinking, who cares about a few lost hairs in the grand scheme of things, why was he rambling on so much about it all? Only later did I grasp that he was referring to a different knot entirely.

He was always doing that, the metaphors. He had a habit of conjuring scenes with his words and wrapping you up in their folds. Amma teased him for doing it but I know she enjoyed it too. We all craved a fleeting stroll through those vibrant windows he opened. I wondered why he did it so much, it didn't seem like escapism for him. I liked to think he was just a colourful soul who approached the canvas of the world with a rainbow palette in hand, word painting away in vivid strokes. Whatever the reasoning, I enjoyed appa's conversational art greatly and strived to follow in his brush strokes.

The morning after appa untangled my hair, I went back to the lagoon and removed all the chunks of wire and harmful tat I could find. Exhausted in the moist heat, I sat down to rest and breathe in the wildlife carnival. As the sweat beads trickled down my temples, I noticed something quivering in the long grass not far from my toes. Peering closer, I spotted white striped scales slithering and glinting in the morning dew. I stood up immediately and stepped back. I knew to be extra careful of snakes, exquisite creatures, but dangerous. Not all of them of course, but enough for me not to get complacent. This one was a beautiful krait, bluish black in colour with chalk crossbars striping its skin like slices of amma's cashew aluwa, but as it slithered onwards I noticed something all the stranger about this fellow in particular. It had two heads, Shi.

In appa's encyclopaedia entry on serpents, I had read about a rare disorder called dicephaly, where snakes are born with two heads, each with separate brains. The two heads, with their separate personalities, fail to realise they share a body so end up fighting each other to death over food, and as they fight they make the whole organism more vulnerable to larger predatory talons and claws.

As I watched the krait slither away into the thickets, I couldn't stop thinking about the missed potential of the doomed creature. Double the eyes, double the fangs and double the brain power. If those heads could work together, coordinate instead of clash, just imagine the spectacular feats it could accomplish.

❖   ❖   ❖

Between all the metaphors, rocks and toffees, there was still one thing appa adored more; the rain. I'd often catch him just staring out of the window, completely lost in a downpour, a soft smile glazing his features. The heavier the drenching, the more fixated he'd become. It always poured brightest in the reflection of his eyes.

'Isn't it spectacular La? Here we are floating in a galaxy on a spinning chunk of matter with a mist field that comes drenching and washing us as we go looping around a giant burning star. The rain reminds us just how tiny a blip we are in this great, big concerto.'

Whenever I'd find him rain gazing, he'd gather me under his arm and teach me to listen to the different instruments of the rain symphony. The pitter pattering on the leaves, the tinkling on car roofs and the deep sloshing under tyres. The quiver plunge of the big droplets, the wet slapping of the soil and the soft hiss humming all around.

'The warmth wins out La, rises above the chill and comes replenishing us all. The heavier the clouds, the more refreshing when they burst.'

During one magnificent monsoon downpour, appa was more animated than usual. With dramatic hand gestures, he explained how the cooler moist air from the Indian ocean was being pulled up into a vacuum created by hot air rising from the land. But then he dropped his arms and stopped his explanation quite abruptly. Crouching down, he sighed deeply and gently held my shoulders with both hands.

'But some things need to be felt La, not explained'.

A smile glistened from his pupils, he didn't have to say what he was thinking, his face was screaming it.

We rushed to the hallway, scrambled into our gum boots and went feverishly zipping coats with glee. When he opened the door, with a triumphant yank, we were greeted with thunderous curtains drenching everything in sight. It was roaring out there. He turned back towards me.

'Ready?'

I nodded frantically like a flame-backed woodpecker.

'Good, because the rain waits for no one!'

And with that, he went lunging into the waterfall. I plunged after him, soaked to the skin, slapped and smattered by the weeping skies. The water was deafening. So heavy and boisterous, kissing and bruising us, hissing and numbing us, filling our nostrils, ears and eyes until we couldn't see, hear or feel anything else. It was glorious. Exhilarating. Intoxicating. We were part of the downpour, one with the water, swimming in the skies. The crashing curtains were so thick I could barely see appa, he was trying to say something, but his words were swallowed in the onslaught. It sounded like he was laughing. I began to laugh too and soon I couldn't stop. Hysterical laughter pouring out with the rain, washed with the sonorous rivers. Right there, drenched in monsoon laughter in the sodden haze, I've never felt so free, Shi.

Amma was fuming when we eventually dripped back in, she wrapped us in towels and scolded with roughly dried hair. Still, it was worth it. Not a shadow of a doubt. I'd endure a thousand years of amma's scolding for such an intoxicating cleanse. Glancing over to appa, I caught the same knowing smile, the same delicious sense of freedom glistening in his eyes.

humpback hope, bruised petals

Around town, appa was a popular man. It was impossible to keep momentum on a Sunday stroll with all the people stopping him to chat, smoke and share a cup of tea. The fishermen resting on the catamarans, the traders at the fruit market, the locals peppered around Gandhi Park; all bustled for their dose of appa. The calls of 'machan! machan!' became somewhat of a theme tune as we walked. He always gave them the time, listening to their stories and rocking his concerned head at their latest strife. In all honesty, it irritated me, Shi, I wanted him all to myself.

Yet despite his popularity, appa was a private man; he shared little of himself, instead indulging others with questions about their own lives. Fidgeting near his hip, I soon learnt how much people love to talk about themselves. It seemed few knew how to do much else. I saw how even the routine enquiries directed at appa, about the family and life at the teaching college, were a mere precursor to launch into an account of their own life. Of course, appa knew how to expertly perform the public role they sought, slap on that social smile and give them the ear they craved. The rising fuel prices, earlier curfews, declining prawn yields, the wife's bad back, the kitchen damp; he absorbed it all graciously. Yet despite all the smiles and backslaps, I don't think appa had many real friends. Comfort came to appa in the quiet of his books, the crevices of his small family and the companionable silence with a few old pals.

One such pal was Raja uncle. He and appa grew up in the Wellawatte district of Colombo together and while appa pursued his teaching positions around the island and settled east to start a family, Raja stayed drinking and gambling, a lone wolf in the very same square mile. When the money ran out, he ventured south to Mirissa and began fishing to ensure the flow of arrack continued. Ravi and I loved when Raja came to visit. His wonky moustache wobbled when he laughed and he'd hurl us into the sofa while beating his chest like a silverback gorilla. Appa glowed when he was around, like a big kid with extra bounce in his step. Amma felt quite differently and arguments bubbled whenever Raja visited. His sour liquor stench, boisterous table manners and wheezy talk of women clearly disagreed. One summer visit, amma caught Ravi fiddling with a pocketknife Raja had given him and he was never invited back after that.

Appa would occasionally still go to visit Raja though, and the spring after my eighth birthday he took me with him as a treat. Raja met us at the station, swung me around four times in the air and announced he had a surprise. The anticipation was like a rash and it had me itching all day. Each plea was met with, 'patience little one, you'll find out soon enough', chuckled through hot sour breath. At first I thought it was the dessert he bought me after lunch. That Avocado Crazy was creamier than anything I'd tasted before and my taste buds danced in its sugary pulp. Then I thought it was the view at Mirissa harbour. Boats and sails of all shapes and sizes bobbed and glimmered in the sunshine like a rainbow quilt. Finally, as we climbed aboard his boat, all was revealed.

'How would you like to go whale watching little one?' Raja winked.

I couldn't contain my excitement. It was prime season to spot the blue whales migrating from the Arabian Sea to the Horn of Africa and Raja knew just where to find them. We coursed through the water as the pictures from my wildlife books rushed to life before me. Sooty shearwaters and skuas swooped overhead while bridled terns swayed in the wind currents, an olive ridley turtle passed right next to the boat and moments later a kerfuffle of striped dolphins went gliding just ahead. Appa gasped as he spotted two shark fins. It made me think about how powerful sudden fear can be, how strongly a shape can be associated with danger, just like how the little wooden Jony boxes around Batti made my bones seize up. Would I always tremble at the shape of tiny wooden boxes in the dirt?

Hours passed with more dolphins, tuna, seabirds and turtles gracing us with their presence. Enchanting though they were, I was desperate to see a whale. Did you know, Shi, blue whales have hearts the size of cars, arteries large enough to swim through and tongues that weigh as much as elephants?

Raja was getting restless. The beers were finished and he was itching to head back.

'You know little one, the whales are overly cautious of the

boats, after all remember how they used to come hunting them. Our luck may have run out today, but you've seen a lot, no?'

As the sun began to sink, we headed back to shore. Disappointment lingered but I understood and respected the leviathans' choice to stay hidden; how horrible it must be for those old enough to remember the whaling boats. I wondered about how long such a fear would last. Then, I saw it. Shimmering just in front of where the sky met the sea. For just a second, a beautiful, perfect fluke rising from the water before plunging back beneath. A shape of fleeting hope, surprising courage, seared in my mind forever.

At dinner, it was all I could think about; I barely noticed the tension rising in appa and Raja's voices. As Raja barked about 'means justifying ends' and 'helping the brotherhood', my mind fixated on that dripping curve. As appa argued back about 'human shields' and 'means corrupting ends', all I could hear was that momentous splash.

We left in a hurry. It hardly registered that Raja didn't shake appa's hand. All I could see was that resplendent humpback tail, that fluke of glory shimmering undisturbed in my mind's eye.

We never saw Raja again after that.

❖   ❖   ❖

I often wonder about appa's childhood; what kind of hands, walls and rules raised him, what home pot stew he ripened in. He never told us much. Whenever I asked about his mum and dad, he'd find a clever way to change the subject and slide seamlessly into softer territory. Before I knew it, I'd be feasting on his latest story with my original question all but forgotten. From the little I gleaned, grandpa was an esteemed music professor who taught classical piano to Wellawatte's elite. Grandma was the chief seamstress of the suburbs. I liked to imagine little appa engrossed in his books, grandma stitching decadent gowns at his side to the backdrop of whirring concertos. In my imagination cave they were all smiling away in suburban bliss, swaying in currents of sweet bougainvillea and fine tea.

Unfortunately, I now know the less idyllic reality. Appa's parents were well-to-do Burghers, staunchly Catholic and crippled by an obsession about what others thought. Social standing was everything; each thread, each note, each strategically planted flower served to upkeep the reputation they had so meticulously crafted. Spontaneity and passion were a fool's errand; it was the gold-laced altar of class one must kneel to. The direction of appa's beating heart was an affront to this altar. His choice of wife was an insult, a slur on their good standing and estrangement curdled up from his defiance. So, as appa opened his heart and horizons, the Wellawatte house gates were locked shut behind him. No number of teaching accolades or plump-cheeked grandchildren could coax the key.

It must create a sad sort of burden to be rejected by the hands that once rocked you, to be cut out so ruthlessly like that. Amma and appa had only each other and risked everything to swirl off in that bubble of theirs. You'd think it would create a real pressure, an unimaginable strain to prove it was all worth it. If there was such a strain, they hid it well. From the glances, the laughs, the symbiotic rhythm of their company, it was clear amma and appa adored each other. Occasional arguments were mere peppercorns dwarfed in the tender soup of their marriage. Perhaps I'm rose-tinting, perhaps I was just oblivious, but I choose to believe they had figured it out. They had the kind of partnership that conjures poetry, immortalises ballads and cultivates emerald fields of envy.

Appa was not a religious man, at least not in the conventional sense, but he was gripped by the idea of belief and the dark and beautiful ripples it could spread in heart, soil and psyche. What other force has you weeping, chanting and killing with such raw conviction? What other force can bend knees, spark wars and tickle feet to dance with such passion? No particular religious cave sheltered appa; no one shrine, temple or alter commanded his loyalty. It was the floating mystique of faith itself that enthralled him. Growing up in a stern Catholic household, teaching in largely Buddhist schools and raising kids with a Hindu wife; appa perched on the rooftop of these powerful caves. While most cave-dwellers saw only entrenched stone walls surrounding them, appa saw the wider tunnels they were carved from, the rocks that underpinned all.

One sodden Sunday in his library, I caught him engrossed in the TipiTaka. Curtains of hot rain lashed at the windo panes and our bellies were full from amma's kiri bath and jackfruit curry.

'Are you becoming a Buddhist, appa?' I asked.

'No, no, just smelling the eight-fold flowers.'

His eyes were glistening, I could sense one of his metaphors coming along.

'You see La, these things we call religions are in their essence, flowers. Just as beautiful petals encase the pollen sprinkled stigma, vibrant rituals encase a spiritually nutrient core. Just as filaments and anthers soar beside the ovary, scriptures and prayers rise from a religion's womb. Each flower attracts insects to its nectar cave with different colours, smells and shapes, just as miracles, deities and teachings entice us to sap nectar at the altar of temples, churches and mosques.'

The puzzled creases in my face spurred him to continue.

'Think about it, La, each of them promise to replenish us with vital sap as we venture on our journey, be we bees or believers. Each requires our time and tender attention to flourish. A flower must be nourished with gentle distance and trusted to grow, just as faith is about trusting its resilience through every terrain life throws at us. And if bitterness festers in the soil, the faith flower wilts, shrivels and dies. But with tenderness and respect, the roses of religion rise resplendent.'

He pointed to the frangipani bush blooming just beyond the window, its milky lemon petals shivering rhythmically in the downpour.

'Sadly, La, we all too often forget the common roots of these flowers. When we gaze at indigo water lilies, scorpion orchids or lava buttered hibiscus, it's easy to see only their differences. We see coral vine candles, shrines of scarlet flame beans and magnificent mimosa minarets. Holy water of hydrangea, poppy blushing pandals, communion bread of carnations. Their pigments distract us, lull us into considering them separately when they in fact bloom with united purpose. In the very same way, we look for differences in the Vedas, the Quran, the Bible and the Sutras when their ink runs with the same intent. After all, the very word religion means to bind in its Latin origin.'

He took a sip of his tea and began softly drumming his fingers on the desk.

'Think of it this way, the beat of the Bhajans at the temple are infectious, aren't they?'

I nodded.

'Well, if you listen closely to them, along with the rousing rumble of the call to Prayer, the hymns rising from the pews and the chants of the saffron-robed, you'll hear the same tone ebbing through all of them. Each ear may digest them differently but the underlying rhythm, that universal pulse of purpose, persists right there in the music.'

He looked at the dripping flowers beyond the window.

'So, as frangipani, roses and bougainvillea bloom, we must remember the common ingredients they all depend on to thrive. Water and sunlight dictate their lives just as blind faith and compassion thump through the bloodstream of the religious.'

'But don't they pray in different ways appa? And to different gods?' I was a tad baffled by the floral frenzy of his latest word painting.

'Absolutely, La. But they are just different dances swaying to the very same rhythm. Think about giving to the poor. Christians and Buddhists collect alms for the needy just as Hindus give Dana, Muslims give Zakah and Jews give Tzedakah. Think of sacrifice. Abraham commanded to sacrifice his son, Jesus sacrificed on the cross, Buddhists' self-sacrifice for personal liberation, Hindus releasing the soul through Yajna and Muslims celebrating Eid al-Adha, the festival of sacrifice. And of course, nowhere is it clearer than the Golden Rule. Do to others as you would have them do to you is the glorious beat thumping through the Bible, the Hadiths, the Mahabharata and the Udana-Varga, even if wrapped up in slightly different lyrics.'

Appa taught me that you didn't need to have religious belief to appreciate it. Religion itself was remarkable; not in its scriptures or deities but in its ability to move people in such profound ways. In each church, mosque and temple appa took me to, I felt it. The silences there were never really silent. The air was heavy with emotion and bursting with a hope so tangible you could cut and serve it with dollop of cream. Given its inescapable ripples, I guess you could say we are all in some way religious. Some are drawn to the flowers directly, others like to rip at their petals, while many simply stroll amongst the colours and appreciate the scent in the breeze.

Of course, this all sounds whimsically lovely in theory but it's far too forgiving. Not just in the obvious sense of how destructive religion can be, how flowers compete for resources and can devour landing insects with predatory relish, no, my issue is with the way those of full flower faith can twist and shed petals purely to suit their own agendas.

Take the two main religions of Sri Lanka, Shi. Buddhists talk of following a noble eight-fold path of thought and action, and of transcending suffering through detachment from desires. Yet these same Buddhists called for crushing the dissident Tamils and securing the island's desirable land at all costs. Hell, even the island's monks went picking up Kalashnikovs and hiding grenades under their robes in the name of the greater good. So much for that sacred first precept of not taking life. Hindus, meanwhile, seek to re-join Brahman, the true reality of things, and awaken to the oneness of the universe. Yet these same Hindus turned to butchery to pursue separateness at all costs. Both religions provided thick sauce for the meat of warfare, a sauce spiced full of mental trickery. Other islanders were no longer seen as brothers capable of salvation, they were no longer even seen as human. They were beasts, aliens, dogs and vermin; the filthy nuisance other. Piece by piece, their humanity was hacked away until nothing remained but a cardboard target with fangs and claws. The killing became easier that way, smoother, common sense.

Another contradiction thrums loud in my eardrums; the relationship between religion and nature. Didn't Buddha find enlightenment under a tree, Mohammad find God on a mountain and Moses find Him in a bush? The natural world appears an integral canvas for divine inspiration. But let's take animals more specifically. Hindu gods often manifest in animal hybrids, such as the elephant-headed God of Obstacles Ganesha, Hanuman the monkey God and Kamadhenu the miraculous mother of cows. Countless others travel with fauna, such as the Fire God Agni astride his ram, Brahma the Creator with his swan and the Water God Varuna traversing waves with his crocodile. On our sporadic family visits to the temple, I remember my focus always wandering to the animals. While farmers asked Indra to nourish their crops, I studied his white elephant. As struggling businessmen sought fortune from Lakshmi, I focused on her owl. While worshippers sought guidance from Kartikeya about the war, I gazed at the feathers of his magnificent peacock.

In Christian scripture, respect and compassion for animals is weaved throughout. Humans are to serve a stewardship role, respecting creatures and learning from their humility. From the dove that guides Noah's Ark, Balaam's talking donkey, the lions who don't harm Daniel, the ravens who supply food to the prophet Elijah; creatures teem in biblical proportions. And didn't Jesus enter Jerusalem astride a donkey?

Buddhism enshrines respect for animals clearer still, considering them sentient beings capable of reaching enlightenment. Such fair treatment makes sense given their rebirth doctrine holds that any animal could be a dead relative or friend reincarnated. Would you risk squashing a spider, Shi, if it might be your dear brother?

In the Islamic teachings Muhammad chastises those who mistreat animals and teaches them the value of mercy. The Hadiths are peppered with compassion; *Whoever is merciful even to a sparrow, Allah will be merciful to him on the Day of Judgement... An act of cruelty to an animal is as bad as cruelty to a human being...Fear Allah in these beasts that cannot speak.* Once again, kindness bleeds through the ink.

Yet despite such clear instruction, respect and compassion for our fellow creatures crumbles at the human altar. Christian's see ownership, not stewardship, in their role while Muslims persist with their ritual slaughtering. Hindus see basal desires symbolised in the animals their Gods ride while Buddhists see animal rebirth as signalling karmic misdeeds. Basic compassionate teachings are twisted too readily under the snobbery of our opposable thumbs. People will always see what they want to see, feast with an eye that serves them. For this reason, the faith flowers have never magnetised me in the way they dazzled appa. In those vibrant petals, I've come to see only more colourfully decorated tools for human cruelty.

All that said, as a child, I found appa's enthusiasm for religious celebration infectious. The gleeful spirit nestled beneath his skin could be coaxed easily with an antique book or some treacle toffees, yet nothing awoke him faster than the incense-soaked, petal-strewn religious festivals. Temple, church, mosque; it didn't matter, appa would relish any chance to dip into the celebratory fervour and dabble in the fleeting pockets of colour. I loved going with him; any chance to ride on appa's shoulders through the babbling crowds and sparkling lights was a treat.

'Wait until you see the pandal' he beamed, one sweltering Wednesday afternoon as he swept ten-year-old me along to the Vesak festival at the Temple. 'I hear it's a real beauty this year La.'

The ground was blistering dry like an elephant's hide and the trees dripped with heat.

'This is a day of generosity, La. A day when all the good instincts come out.'

His words swirled with the scent of fried chickpeas and sizzling coconut milk, and as we neared the temple, smiling ladies stirred pots of steaming curry and humming vendors tossed hot kottu roti. Appa scooped up a vadai lentil fritter and handed it to me, offering only a smile to the cook.

'Aren't you going to pay her appa?'

'It's free little one,' he chuckled 'The dansal stalls give food out to everyone, a day of generosity remember.'

I'll never forget how delicious that vadai tasted, and as the spices melted on my tongue I absorbed the unfolding fervour. The winding streams of white-clothed Buddhists, the lava-glow of the window lanterns and the calming Bhakti Gheeta songs filled my ears and eyes with their flavours.

Appa insisted we get a good look at the pandal, a huge colourful structure of blinking lights depicting a story from one of Buddha's previous lives. Everyone clearly had the same idea and as the crowds became denser, appa scooped me out of the sweat folds and onto his shoulders to survey the patchwork below.

There was such a rhythm to the crowd; a heaving, weaving, smiling energy, even the soldiers looked relaxed. I had the best view from my throne on appa's shoulders. I spotted swallows flitting overhead, squirrels scurrying around a tree trunk and two bedraggled dogs panting near the roadside. A plump lady was beating a carpet on a rooftop in sync with the music and a lime motorbike pulled up with an ice box. I remember hoping he had ice lollies, hoping appa would let me get one on the way home. The thought of a cooling mango lolly was the last thing I remember before that blinding flash.

❖ ❖ ❖

When I opened my eyes, devastation stared back. A blur of crimson puddles, jagged glass and crumpled fabric flickered in the smoke plumes. Limbs and marigold petals were strewn across the street, chunks of flesh scattered in the dirt like confetti.

My temples throbbed.

Ambulance lights flickered as wailing women rocked in the dirt, holding crumpled heaps, screeching into the sky with wet faces. I felt their cries in my bones.

Ash flakes cascaded like bruised petals.

Agony oozed from every angle.

Appa. Where was appa? I needed to find appa. The thought charged through my arteries as I willed my legs to move, but with each heave a searing pain surged through my insides. *He'd be looking for me, helping the medics, helping the injured. Where was appa?* My temples pulsated, shaking my organs with each thump and a metallic bitterness flooded my mouth as I tried to swallow. Again, I tried to drag my body forward. Nothing. As I raised my head, a blinding pain announced itself in my right cheek. I raised a hand to touch it and felt an unfamiliar hardness, not skin but bone. Wet bone. A needle-sharp sting erupted as I withdrew my fingertips. I still remember that red, that deep dripping crimson streaming down my nails before I plunged back into darkness.

When I stirred again the nightmare was unfolding from a different angle. I was on a stretcher, a medic rolling me through the chaos towards the flashing vehicles. More crumpled heaps and blood-caked faces whirred past in the ash haze, a strange sweetness choking the air. Not the meandering jasmine incense from before or the aroma wafting from the vendor carts. No, it was a different kind of sweetness, a sweetness so sickly, so vicious, that it curdles in your stomach, lodges under your skin and pollutes your bones. A sweetness you can never forget.

From the cluster of moaning stretchers I scanned frantically for appa. The faces and shapes were blurring, the stinging in my cheek growing more intense. Blurred Khaki shapes were barking orders, shirts hurrying past, wailing women being pulled away from the heaps. The carcass of a lime motorbike was being surrounded with tape, the charred remnants of an ice box beside it.

Then I saw him.

Through the flickering chaos I saw those unmistakable pistachio trousers. Amma always complained they were garish and silly, but he stood his ground, insisting they were lucky. On my fifth birthday he'd told me they were magical. He said that on the right day, at the right time, they could make the legs inside dance with the passion of a thousand poets.

'It's happening. I can't stop them. La, help, I can't control my dancing legs!' he gasped and hopped as I giggled with delight.

And there they were, those magic, pistachio trousers, vibrant as ever. Yet the legs weren't dancing this time. Above them, chunks of intestine poured from his body and his eyes stared vacantly from a dark puddle.

When we turn our eyes and look at something, anything, it fills our whole world for just a moment. For that one moment, that split second, it is everything. And so it was when I saw appa lying there. That last glimpse filled me, emptied me and was everything. Problem was, Shi, that moment never ended.

golden paws, parakeet greens

For months, appa's mutilated body was all I could picture. Scattered petals conjured his shredded flesh, the moon his vacant eyes. Nets tumbling from the catamarans, intestines spilling from his torso. Rain pooling in potholes, thick puddles of his blood. With each whiff of a lentil fritter a sudden queasiness would curdle my stomach. Each glimpse of a child with a lolly would send currents gushing to my eyes. So many paths led to panic. Everything ached.

We began to lose amma too. In the gaping abyss of appa's absence she plunged to depths where no one could reach her. The kitchen orchestra fell silent, her smile crawled away and the darkened bedroom consumed her. For the first few months she rarely stirred, her hours were spent drifting between feverish sleep and staring at the shadows on the wall. Even Ravi couldn't bring her back.

Only now do I understand how truly broken she must have been, the desolation that must have choked her. She had lost the love for which she had abandoned everything she'd ever known. Amma had dared to swirl bravely to the thrumming of her heart but when the music stopped her heart was left shattered in the deafening silence. Amma was decaying. At the time, however, I thought she was being selfish. Appa was closest to me, not her, and she was a terrible mother for not helping me through it. She didn't see his body. She didn't have those sickening images seared in her mind. With appa gone, I lost my best friend, the only person who really understood me. I was alone and my own mother didn't seem to care. Why was I the one bringing her food, washing her clothes and scrubbing the grime from her skin? What kind of mother allows that to happen? I resented this new shell of a woman and wished she'd been the one to go.

It wasn't just what was going on in my head either, for my internal agony was paired with a new monstrosity on the outside. My cheek. My soft, dainty cheek now a mesh of chewed flesh and protruding bone. I was revolting, frightening, a mutilated wreckage. Every time I looked in the mirror I erupted into tears, tears that dripped stinging salt in my wound. In all honesty, I began to crave that feeling, I felt I deserved it. Still, the way the salt throbbed along the crevices of my torn flesh was nothing compared to the wound gaping within; the one so deep and dark and all-consuming that salt and sense couldn't reach it. As the tears slithered around the wreckage of my cheek and dribbled down to my chin, I felt my own body leaking sorrow, dripping and dissolving in the absence of him. It wasn't the ugliness itself that made me cry, it was the reminder. The vivid nightmares were one thing but now every glimpse of my own face brought that day screaming to the forefront. The ash, the flames, the heaps, the limbs, his eyes; swirling sour chaos tearing through me once again. I was branded by the day, smeared with the brutality, stamped with the tragedy. The scar made me more aware of myself than I'd ever been, with each throb I was constantly reminded that I was alive, that I had survived; that appa hadn't.

I knew amma thought this too. It's why she wouldn't look at me anymore. I was just a source of more torment. As I'd brush her hair, I'd catch her wincing at my reflection in the dresser mirror, her eyes watering and her nose crinkling at each glimpse of her mangled child, her debris daughter. I expected this unease from the locals, their pity and poorly veiled disgust was unpleasant but unsurprising, but from my own mother? Why wouldn't she console me, reassure me, protect me like I needed her to? She shut me out, Shi, when I needed her the most and it stung like an executioner wasp.

Ravi wasn't much better. He handled appa's death in a way that appeared dismissive. He was still young, and I'm sure this shielded him from the gravity of it, but he became colder and quieter, avoiding both amma and I as much as he could. I'd catch him stealing glances at my cheek, gawping like one would at a zoo creature, and when I'd turn to look at him embarrassment would flush his face. When I'd join him for breakfast and try asking him about school, he quite literally couldn't stomach the sight of me. He'd stop, mid chew, and interrupt me with a wince.

'Mila, do you mind?'

'Mind what?'

He nodded to my cheek, sheepishly and without eye contact. 'I'm just trying to eat. It's hard to, with you know...that.'

I turned away towards the window with welling eyes and

as he continued eating, I felt my heart being chewed to shreds with each mouthful.

Perhaps to keep his connection to appa alive, or perhaps just to escape the gloom, Ravi immersed himself in cricket with a renewed passion. He also started spending more and more time with the sweaty boy packs around town that I knew were no good for him. It didn't matter; he barely made time to see me, let alone listen to what I thought. As the years passed, the boy packs grew rowdier and with anger and testosterone a'bubbling, they reminded me of the bull elephants during musth, a period of heightened aggression when the mammals are turbo-charged with hormones. Though the boys may not have had sticky dark liquid oozing from behind their ears or urine dribbling down their legs, they had their very own distinct odour all the same.

With amma broken and Ravi distant, I hid myself away and escaped between the spines in appa's library. His presence still lingered there. Sometimes I'd read new wildlife facts aloud to him and other times, as the breeze whistled at the windows, I was sure I could hear his voice. I'd stick my nose in his desk drawers and inhale; toffee and cedarwood still lingered in the creases. He was a part of that room, nestled in its bones. As I sat there, tucked in my alcove, I kept going over the details of the Vesak day. What I'd had for breakfast, which novel I was buried in and how long I dawdled with my shoelaces when appa said we should leave. I thought about how long I had paused for that fritter and how many times I stopped to look at squirrels on the stroll into town. I figured if I had all the information in front of me, all the details at my fingertips, I could somehow make more sense of it. I wanted to understand what led us to be near the bike at that exact moment. If dragonflies can pre-empt where their prey move to, I thought maybe I could have pre-empted where that bike was going to be.

I thought about the trip appa and I had taken to Kottawa rainforest the week after my seventh birthday. For hours we explored that living maze, spotting kangaroo lizards scaling the vines, whip snakes slithering through the leaf litter and giant wood spiders crafting webs on the horas. Purple-faced leaf monkeys swung overhead as we crossed streams teeming with paradise combtails. Appa pointed out the gal karandha plant and carefully split the node to reveal a teeming ant colony inside.

'Didn't expect that did you, La? They work together you see, ants help the plant and the plant helps the ants hide from the world.'

I liked this idea of hidden alliances forged in unexpected places. I'd seen the grey langur monkeys and spotted deer do it too; the deer gobble the fruits dropped by the langurs while the langurs benefit from the extra eyes on predator watch. Same goes for crocodiles and plover birds; the crocs sit patiently open-mouthed and allow the birds to pick leftovers stuck between their teeth. Surprising harmony in an unpredictable world. Animals yet again mastering techniques that islanders seemed incapable of.

So many memories came throbbing, there were so many little things I ached to do with him one more time. One more dance tiptoeing on his shoes. One more cocoapaedia session - encyclopaedia and hot cocoa - under the glow of his study lamp. One more winding bike ride past the paddy fields alight with insect chatter. One more of his rock collection lectures that I used to roll my eyes at. One more chance to hear him loudly chewing his toffees. One more inhale of the tobacco fug wafting from his pipe. I'd give up everything I had for just one of those one mores.

Then there was the torturous stream of first times. I really hated those. The first time I spotted a new bug and realised I wouldn't get to show him. The first time I found a deep-wrinkled pebble and realised he'd never get to trace the lines. The first time I saw a full moon without him grinning there beside me. The first time I heard classical music and realised I'd never again turn to find him conducting an invisible orchestra with his pen. Those firsts were unbearable, Shi. Swimming back through memories was one thing but I couldn't bring myself to face a future without him. I just couldn't. Mine and appa's story just didn't feel finished. It had barely begun to unfold. Like a river that never reaches the ocean, a seed that never quite germinates or a sentence that stops before you've reached the...

Books helped. Those sprawling word trunks and tangled sentences formed a helpful barrier between me and my own thoughts and provided me with an inky jungle to melt into. I'd read anything; fact, fiction, nonsense, it didn't matter. I just needed something to percolate, to distract, to drown that screaming space in my mind chamber. I'd bury myself so deep in the pages, so close up to the words, that even the very shape of the letters began to slice. Take happy, for example. A gentle word, light on the palate and soft on lips. But for me, the h became jagged, the y leaked like an open gash and the heads of the p's began to look like vacant eyes. That's how far gone I was, Shi. That's how deeply the pain was lodged and I knew that if I gave it an inch it'd come up devouring me from the inside.

Some pain is better padlocked and dumped deep in the oceans of ourselves. Maybe it wasn't the healthiest approach. Maybe I should have processed it more openly and wholesomely, but it worked for me and we've all got to do what we need to do to get through the day. Right, Shi?

On my darker days, I would escape down to the lagoon but even there I could feel the pulse of appa whispering through the breeze of my outdoor study. The sticky tide of grief would come lashing up so uncontrollably that I figured the only way not to get washed away was to anchor my thoughts to something else I loved. I'd trace the delicate patterns of the dragonfly wings and observe geckos darting through the grass blades. I'd watch the little stints pecking at old coconut husks, breathe in time with the rhythmic heaving of the toads' chests and flutter off with the ballet of the butterflies. I remembered the diagram in appa's encyclopaedia showing their life cycle; how before caterpillars became butterflies, they turn to enzyme soup in the cocoon. I liked to think that's where I was, stuck in a gloopy soup, dissolving and disintegrating and each time the grief wave came gushing I told myself it was simply the soup doing its work. I just needed to stay patient in my cocoon and eventually I might flourish.

As darkness would descend, I found I could no longer look up at the stars. When we gaze up at the night sky, Shi, we are actually looking into the past, making wishes on something that died long ago. Each twinkle began to feel like a sham, a painful reminder of a beauty I could never reach and a brightness long since snuffed out.

Life in the pit of appa's death was bleak. But in that bleak pit, I found comfort in the company of two souls: Ashwina and

Pericles. It's time I told you about them.

❖   ❖   ❖

Pericles, I should clarify, was not the great Greek statesman and orator from Athens' Golden Age. My Peri was a wiry, golden stray I found panting near the lagoon. Through hazelnut puddles he'd watch me closely, filled with a caution refined through years of dealing with stick-wielding bullies. With each visit, he'd venture a little closer and before long he'd sit close enough for me to see his protruding ribcage rising and falling in the heat.

Even though we know animals feel pain, it's often difficult to recognise it but in Peri's puddles I could see it lurking unmistakably, that familiar torment rippling like dark, stained silk. I sensed he could feel my pain too and when the wound inside me throbbed hardest, he'd edge nearer and gaze at me. It was like he knew, like he could sense my immense strain at trying to hold in all that agony, sense every fibre within me struggling not to rupture under the weight.

I began to sneak scraps of roti bread from home to share with him, which he devoured with relish, and I pinched a bowl from the kitchen, filled it with water and watched as he drank with the thirst of a lifetime. Before long, I'd find him eagerly waiting for my visits, golden paws stretched out before him, tail wagging as I approached. As I watched the wildlife circus by the mangroves he would lie comfortably by my side, his wiry coat grazing my arms in the sun. I loved watching him dream, the way his paws and eyelids would twitch sporadically and his mouth would curl up in little smile spasms. I craved a haven like that, a place to go bounding off unseen and undisturbed.

Soon Peri began following me home and I wanted to bring him inside more than anything. In the past amma had always forbidden me from bringing animals into the house, but I figured she wouldn't notice from her new dwelling in the bedroom shadows. Ravi, though, thwarted my plan. He caught me trying to sneak Peri into the study and insisted I keep him outside or else he'd get rid of the 'grubby thing' himself. Resentfully, I kept the peace and with cushions, an old sari, some tarpaulin and a few driftwood branches, I built Peri a small shelter in the garden. He was confused by it at first, but soon grew to appreciate it when the rains came lashing.

With each lagoon stroll, each cycle, each reading session under the casuarina trees, a new shadow appeared beside my own; Peri would follow me everywhere. Of course, it's all too easy to project our own emotions on to animals and see them as mere canvases for our own feelings, yet with Peri, in those entrancing puddles and that restless tail, I'm certain a companionship blossomed. We were two strays coaxing each other out of a loneliness that had become all-consuming, and it felt good to be needed again. Sitting down at the lagoon with Peri, a new sense of purpose came to nourish me, for just as the soil beneath our feet interconnects and nourishes plants through an underground network of fungi, in a similar way, Shi, it felt like Peri grounded and reconnected me back to reality itself.

Dogs are remarkable creatures; twelve separate muscles control their ear's movements and they can hear things about four times as far away as we can. But their noses are even better. Did you know, Shi, a dog's sense of smell can be up to one hundred thousand times better than ours? Some breeds have up to three hundred million scent glands in their nose, we have about six million, and the part of a dog's brain devoted to analysing smells is about forty times bigger than ours. This superior sniffer enables them to do wondrous things. Sure, old Peri could detect my snacks a mile off, but bloodhounds can trace scents that are over three hundred hours old. There are even diabetic alert dogs that can pick up on a special scent released when their owner's insulin level drops, while others can detect subtle scent changes before an epileptic has a seizure. This marvellous nose also enables dogs to detect certain diseases before doctors, figure out which household members are pregnant and even tell when you're anxious, depending on your perspiratory fragrances. No wonder Peri and the Batti strays were so exhausted. The smell of our blood drenched, fear crippled warzone was overwhelming for even the weakest of human nostrils.

With the new confidence Peri had buttered within me, I ventured once again to Batti's bustling pockets. The deluge of pitiful smiles and whispers somehow felt more bearable with golden paws by my side. Still, there were more eyes on me than a scallop. Behind cupped hands and teacups, the usual commentary choir continued. 'Poor little Edward's daughter', 'Aiyo, such a shame- pretty thing before', 'Fancy living with that? Sin men', 'God knows where that mother of hers is.' Yet amongst the gossiping winds, in the heart of the fruit market, I found Ashwina.

It was fitting that I heard Ash before I saw her. Amidst the barking traders and clinking scales, a grainy voice was humming an off key Bhajan tune. I scoured for the source, compelled towards the haunting softness, fixated on finding the lips that conjured such a strange soup. It was no easy task; the market was a labyrinth, a simmering tapestry of colour, sound, smell and spice. Cashew apples, avocados, and sweet citrus carambola oozed beside guavas, pineapples and spiky rambutan. Possum purple passionfruit jostled with jackfruit, plump mangos beamed by breadfruit while red lady papayas sang sweetly to passing nostrils. Corridors of sweaty traders beckoned beneath jangling scales while women fanned themselves beside baskets of blood chillies, counting rupees opposite crates bursting with limes. Cabbage, onions and carrots heaved between banana flowers, while gold-ringed fingers rummaged between spice packets of ginger, cinnamon and saffron. Despite the import blocks and the struggling yields the traders moaned about, Batti's fruit market was a teeming cauldron of kerfuffle.

Yet amidst all the commotion, that haunting melody swirled in mesmerising defiance. My ears hungered towards it, enchanted as if it were Orpheus's lyre, until at last I spotted her. Beneath Mr. Ananda's stacks of blushing pomegranates and drooping vine plaits of bananas, a small shape sat swaying on the floor. Her sari was ragged and pale, the colour of pomelo drained in the sun. A tattered rug lay beneath her. Puffs of hot dust swirled by its edges with each footstep that passed, Aladdin's carpet wheezing through its final throws. On the rug, shells and crumpled flowers teemed from coconut husks beside a mesh of threads. I edged closer and watched as she wove the pieces into necklaces, her fingers aglow with saffron and marigold petal stains. Her thread moved in rhythm with her humming and I hadn't realised just how much I was staring until the humming stopped abruptly.

'Chi! Didn't your amma teach you it's rude to stare?' she barked, not lifting her eyes from her thread work.

'Sorry. I didn't mean to... I heard your voice...its...'

Curious now, she looked up. Her face carved by deep creases like the trunk of some ancient fig tree. Squinting at me, she chuckled through a soft wheeze.

'Aiyo, I guess you do know all about rude staring then, don't you child?' She nodded to my cheek. 'Does it hurt?'

No one had ever been this direct before. People either avoided mentioning it at all costs or skirted around the subject with vague questions about how I was feeling. This new bluntness was surprisingly refreshing.

'Sometimes. I'm used to it now. It throbs when I stay in the sun too long and saltwater stings like crazy.'

Peri began sniffing around her rug. She raised a hand as if to shoo him away, but to my surprise she opened her palm and he cautiously approached, sniffed her hand and relaxed as she scratched his neck.

'Nice fellow you have here. Come sit down child, give my neck a break.'

Without hesitation, I sat down beside her. There was something compelling about Ash, like one of the crumbling spines on appa's top shelf, an enchanting treasure trove, one of those books you know is going to be special before you've even opened it.

'I used to see you with that father of yours. God knows how he didn't get annoyed with everyone pestering him. Chi! I'd have screamed at them. Patient man. Nice man. Most of the nice ones are dead.'

She paused to clear her throat.

'No point wallowing child, it's all gone to shit. You can be a victim if you want, everyone here's a bloody victim, but it's an ugly cloth to wear. Weak stitching, itchy fabric. Don't wear it. Try find some peace, fill your tum and keep going. Only thing to do.'

There was that refreshing bluntness once again. At last, someone who just said it as it was, someone who didn't fill my ears with sugar coated sympathy and shove spiritual platitudes down my throat. She understood.

Close up I could see the network of wrinkles bending around her leathery skin, patches of swollen pigment forming shadows beneath her eyes, yet her pupils were a vibrant parakeet green, glazed with an energy at odds with her exhausted skin. Ancient trunks often sprout the freshest figs, after all. She spoke through rotting teeth, crooked enamel stumps soaked in brown and I soon learnt that Mr Ananda's supply of fruit-on-the-turn was the reason. He allowed Ash to perch by his stall in exchange for her sweeping the peel scraps each evening. He was a religious man who felt such kindness accrued bonus karma points, but he was a good man all the same. As my visits to Ash increased he'd cut me all sorts of fruits to try, sliced with a knife of pity no doubt but scrumptious nonetheless.

Perched beneath the bustle of the market on Ash's magic carpet, we would watch the world go by, gossiping about the traders or just nattering nonsense, our companionship blossoming amidst the fruit peel and dust. Ash's blunt charm was therapeutic and I began to think about my situation a little differently. At first, I figured I was a bit like the sweet wrappers that littered the floor around us. Long after the treat inside had gone, those wrappers lay there, holding the shape of the missing piece. It was like the emptiness had created a shape in and of itself and the wrapper was stuck cradling it. Yet as time marched on I tried to think of myself more like Ash's husk bowls. The coconut had been split, its fleshy goodness hacked out leaving just a shell, but that didn't mean the shell was useless. With a little creativity the shell could serve a new purpose and find other things to fill it up.

Though stubborn to the cartilage, there was an openness about Ash, she was enamoured with my animal ramblings and was always keen to hear more. She definitely wasn't just indulging me either because she wasn't the sort; if something bored her, she'd tell you straight. Yet my wildlife musings seemed to genuinely evoke interest, her parakeet greens twinkling as I'd explain quirky habits and identify the creatures scampering around us. I got the impression she too was underwhelmed and exhausted with humans, grateful to hear something beyond the usual cricket-poverty-war spiel lacing most lips.

On slow days at the market, when fear of army searches or rumours of an impending attack deterred the crowds, Mr Ananda would cut up fresh pomegranates for us to enjoy. As we sat feasting in the heat I thought about how mine and Ash's relationship was a bit like a pomegranate. Bitter peel was curling all around us but we nestled close and replenished each other with juicy nuggets of interest. Appa had told me that pomegranates were considered the fruit of the dead in Greek mythology, believed to have sprung from the blood of Adonis, and that the Babylonians believed chewing the seeds before battle would make them invincible. Gobbling invincibility gems atop a magic carpet in a fruit circus was a nice thought and so, with mouths bursting with seeds, Ash and I set about conjuring animal identities for all of the traders.

Mr Kohan was soft as syrup on the surface but if anyone tried pinching his egg plants a tide of hot profanities erupted with a vengeance. He became Kohan the moray eel to mark the hidden set of jaws that extended from his throat. Mr Pulavar and Mr Achari were always bickering about missing scale weights, sour armpit sweat gushing with each shake of their hands. They became the ring-tailed lemurs to mark the nauseating stink-fighting that went wafting between their stalls. Mrs. Servai became shoebill Servai. Her jolly face and big nose distracted from her vicious temper, just like the shoe-beaked ambush predator of the African swamps. We'd even seen her snap at a young soldier once, just as shoebills try their luck with baby crocodiles.

Geethan made us chuckle the most. He was a cheery bundle of noise, rumbling the entire market with chants about his mangos and rosy jambu. 'Come watch the sunset in my marvellous mangos!', 'Jambu so juicy you can take a swim!'. But it wasn't Geethan's poetic selling techniques that tickled us most, it was his unique way of mimicking everyone he spoke to. With the browsing grandmas, Geethan's shoulders would hunch, his head rocking side to side as he'd moan of aching joints. When the workers swung by, he'd puff out his chest and blurt predictions about the upcoming cricket match. When the soldiers patrolled, he'd light their cigarettes and make small talk about the rainfall. When the fishermen sauntered through, he'd offer betel quid and sigh about the septic discharge in the lagoon. He was a stubbly plump reflection of every browser, mirroring their gestures and postures in an effortless flurry of entertainment. So, for his shapeshifting mastery, Geethan became our mimic octopus. Just as the mimic octopus can change its pattern and shape to imitate floating coral, stingrays, jellyfish or sea snakes, Geethan too had developed a brilliant survival tactic. Charismatic camouflage right there amidst the mangos and jambu.

snapping turtle, flying fox

While gossip and nonsense came easy, Ash rarely shared anything about her own life. I was curious but didn't want to pry; I understood some things are better kept locked away. That said, one May evening as the traders packed away, Ash's cheeks flushed with a sadness I'd never seen before. She'd been sullen all afternoon and had barely weaved a single necklace. She'd shrugged it off as fatigue, so I hadn't pressed. It was only when I was getting ready to cycle home that she finally blurted something that stopped me in my tracks.

'He would have been forty-five today.'

With a twig she was carving the letter T in the dirt. I'd seen her do this before but this time the carving was much deeper.

'Who, Ash? Who would have been forty-five?'

'My boy, my beautiful baby boy. Thaya.'

She gripped the twig tighter and rocked softly back and forth, whispering his name over and over as she deepened the contours of the T. Pain oozed in her voice. I could see the name was crushing her with its weight.

I placed my hand gently on her forearm and we sat in silence, the air throbbing with sorrow. After three geckos had scampered past, she wiped her face on her sari, took a deep breath and continued.

'They say it gets easier with time, but time just changes the wound. Some things cut too deep for healing.'

A resentment slithered into her voice.

'I never even knew him. My own son. How can you hurt so much for someone you never knew? Someone whose voice you never heard?'

Her eyes were molten. She stared at the dirt where the droplets were falling.

'He came out so quietly. No screaming, no crying, just blood. So much blood. I thought if I held him close, kept him warm, he might wake up, come back to me. Stupid, stupid woman.'

She paused, clenching her jaw so tightly I thought her teeth might shatter.

'I wish I hadn't touched him. Hadn't seen that nose, those lips. I wish I'd left him in the blood and walked away. Chi! What good was to come from cradling my dead son? Why did I burn his face in my skull like that? Stupid, stupid woman.'

Her knuckles whitened around the twig, as if she were willing it to snap, but she snapped first.

'Enough. No more child, go home. These things are not to be talked about. Stupid woman bringing it all back up. Thaya...no good, no good, no good. Go home child! Find me tomorrow.' She continued muttering to herself, kicking up the dirt until the T was all but gone.

The following day, when Peri and I came to the market, Ash was nowhere to be found. Mr Ananda took me aside and handed me a cup of lumpy papaya juice.

'She'll be back tomorrow, she just needs some space, that's all.'

It was then he shared with me the bones of the Thaya story.

I feel torn about sharing Ash's trauma with you, Shi. She chose to keep it locked up and my loyalty inclines me to guard the box for her. That said, with time I have learnt how fundamentally pain defines us. The way we deal with pain demonstrates the very essence of our character, the raw fibres of this thing we call the soul. So, to really understand Ash, I must tell you of her trauma and the resilience with which she faced it.

For that reason, I will briefly share the broad strokes of her story.

❖ ❖ ❖

Ash and her sister Sita enjoyed a particularly shiny upbringing. Their parents sold gemstones from a small but dazzling shop paved with the most precious garnets, lime zircon, quartz and lava hessonite. Ash's father had friends at the Ratnapura mines and developed a knack for sourcing the finest of pieces. Their shop housed the amethysts Marco Polo raved about, the sapphires of Ptolemy's dreams and the rubies ancient Arab explorers pined for. People would travel miles to glimpse their stones, gawping between walls encrusted with rosy tourmalines, aquamarines and warming lemon topaz. The family did well and were proud of their jewelled trade. But the jewels soon dimmed when malaria paid a visit. Sita was ravaged painfully by the disease until all that remained were sweat drenched sheets, a bony carcass and her two-year-old son. Terrified and not-yet-twenty, the toddler's father quickly disappeared leaving Ash and her parents to care for little Thaya.

Thaya found both playmate and mother in his aunty while his aunty found her sister in him. The two became inseparable, almost. For Thaya's fourth birthday they took a trip to the beach and Ash did not see Thaya leave his sandcastle for the sea, did not see the tide pull him under, did not see him drowning that day. Ash grieved ferociously, screamed as if the waves had ripped him from her own womb. The grief chewed and consumed her like the fever which had gutted her sister.

She struggled on as best she could and four winters later, Amaran brought hope. Goofy, rugged and kind, he returned a smile long forgotten to Ash's lips and they were married within the year. For a while, Ash found peace. Her parents' shop was doing well, and she was happily married with a baby on the way, a baby to be named Thaya. Then came 1956. Anti-Tamil riots tore through the town leaving crimson devastation in its wake. The family gems were looted and the shop burned to the ground with Ash's parents inside. In the throes of grief and shock, liquid garnet poured down Ash's thighs and Thaya was lost again. The dark fever returned and Ash's lips lost her smile once again.

Hope glimmered again with the second swelling of Ash's belly. She clung desperately to thoughts of May, a May that would bring light again, a May that would bring Thaya into the world at last.

And so came May of '58. But it wasn't hope it brought. Mobs shredded through the town once again with glinting blades and burning rubber. Trapped inside as the chaos swirled outside, Ash was forced to squeeze her gem out early. In sweaty terror, she heaved and pushed and squirmed and squeezed, but her little topaz did not shine. In streams of liquid ruby her darling Thaya lay still and cold. As she wept and cradled those tiny fingers, she was yet to learn Amaran wouldn't be grieving with her. For as she sat there with Thaya's blood congealing on her skin, her Amaran was just two roads away, hacked to pieces in his own ruby stream.

❖   ❖   ❖

New information alters our lens in striking ways, Shi. Let's say I asked you to observe some stranger walking down the street and report back. You might mention their carefree saunter, their whistling or their smile. Nothing of it. But what if I told you that stranger was in fact a serial killer? I bet you'd start seeing things differently. Their saunter might look suspicious, their whistle somehow devious and that smile somewhat predatory. My point is that new information comes with a pigment; we start to shade the contours of what we see.

After learning of Ash's trauma I began spotting things I hadn't seen before. I noticed how intently she stared at the shell fragments, running her fingers over the shiny ones as if they were sapphires. I noticed how the birthmark on her arm looked a lot more like three interlaced Ts. I noticed how sometimes she'd rub her belly as if soothing a phantom child. I noticed how the market traders looked at her with the same pitiful glaze dished out on me. But I refused to pity Ash, not that her suffering didn't deserve it by the tanker load, I just felt I should do better. Pity is a cruel syrup; the sickly slush trickles on its targets, well-meaning but impossible to remove. You become defined by the stuff and if the stickiness pours both internally and externally, you'll be trapped in its glue forever. So, for Ash, I chose respect instead. She kept going and that was what mattered.

The more time spent with her, the thicker my skin grew and given the rising violence this was a necessary and helpful armour. Reports of bombings and assassinations were as common as the morning bird calls and the regular stream of funerals around town conjured little surprise. But no matter how thick my skin grew, the fresh red puddles around town still seeped through my armour and plunged my thoughts back to the passage on minerals appa had once read to me.

'Metals and minerals are what give the earth colour, La, the archaic crayons of our planet, all derived from the dust of ancient stars.'

I used to love the thought of bygone stars still beaming inside us and all around us. But with appa gone and the war beast gnashing harder, I just found the thought depressing. Each time I saw those red puddles, I couldn't help but feel ashamed. Ashamed that this was what those ancient stars had been reduced to. Ashamed that I was part of a species that goes squandering stardust.

❖   ❖   ❖

The aggression of the soldiers and Tigers mounted with sickening force. At night the Tigers left their warnings and by day the soldiers unleashed their payback. Bullets scattered the soil like hot seeds and purple limbs peeped from the mud like strange vegetables.

Tamil families were expected to relinquish a child for the Tiger cause and despite the soldiers' clamp down, young Tamil boys began disappearing all over town. But it wasn't all forced; many boys seemed raring to join the fight, turbocharged with anger and hungry for vigilante justice. The Tigers propaganda was alluring, a true brotherhood in arms promising sweet justice, a romantic fraternity out to carve a future for their people. They dangled a sense of adventure, a higher purpose, a grand calling, entrancing young ears like the snake charmers with their haunting punji music. Actually, Shi, the snake charmer and the cobra is a poor comparison. Unlike the Tigers and their recruits, the charmer and the cobra are in opposition from the start. Charming is the opposite of what goes on. Snakes lack the outer ears to hear the punji music so their swaying is a standard response to the charmer's movements as if they were any predator. And while the Tamil Tigers encouraged the violence of their young recruits, the snake charmers disable the cobras from the very start. Sadly, Shi, those basket cobras the tourists flock to have usually had their fangs ripped out, their venom glands gouged and even their mouths sewn shut.

So, the way the Tigers lured their young recruits was more like a bandura pitcher plant, or perhaps an alligator snapping turtle. It's all about deception, alluring with the promise of something wonderful in a way that shrouds the darker reality. The snapping turtle, for example, has a pink extension on its tongue resembling a worm which it wriggles around to entice hungry fish. Then it snaps its jaws shut around the unsuspecting prey. The carnivorous bandura plant, meanwhile, attracts insects to a sugary fluid at the bottom of its pitcher and its slippery walls ensure the critters cannot climb back up. The insects are doomed to drown while the plant drains the nitrates from their bodies. In a similar way, the Tigers drew in their recruits with sugary promises of justice and the scrumptious wriggling worm of an independent homeland. Ravenous young creatures were enticed without noticing the snapping jaws and slippery walls that surrounded them. The Tigers sapped the useful ingredients from their young bodies, snapping bones and cyanide capsules when they'd served their utility. And most recruits didn't even realise they were being deceived, just as the insects and fish don't realise they're done for until it's too late. Swimming in the sugar syrup and grasping at the juicy worm is the very last thing they remember; they die thinking they're the feaster when really they're the food.

Occasionally the madness imprinted itself in ways which were harder to shrug off. One morning as I cycled to the market, I noticed a cluster of people gathered near the paddy field. The cluster was gasping and growing with peculiar speed, so I detoured over to inspect. Have you ever seen the Buddhist dharma wheel symbol, Shi? It has a circular centre with eight spokes representing the noble eightfold path Buddhists must follow to reach enlightenment. It's a symmetrical design you see at all the temples and many people use it to anchor themselves as they settle into meditation. Well, as I weaved through the cluster of shirts and saris that day, the wheel appeared in a way I'd never seen before. It was anchoring the focus of the crowd for sure, but in quite a different way. At the centre lay a blackened tyre with what looked like kerosene bottles shrivelled inside but the eight spokes around the tyre weren't so symmetrical, they were charred bodies. The Tigers warning was loud and clear; the eightfold path was not a safe one.

Two days later the soldiers presented their revenge. From the limbs of the banyan trees, nine bodies swung limply in the breeze. Stripped, lashed and crusted with flies, the stench of those rotting fruits was eye watering. Most were Tiger fighters, cyanide capsules still dangling from crumpled necks, but a few locals were strung up there too. I recognised Mr. Mohini, our old school caretaker. He was known for speaking more openly to kids about the prachanai. While most teachers fell in line with the soldiers' script on the terrorist scourge, Mohini spoke about the need to be islanders first, drop labels, put down guns and all work to improve our country together. It was all very vanilla, but he didn't follow the script.

Watching him swinging there, I thought of how Mr. Mohini was a bit like a flying fox. Just as flying foxes are the caretakers of Lanka's forests, Mr. Mohini mopped our hallways and classrooms. Just as flying foxes carry seeds and help the forest to regenerate, Mr. Mohini planted seeds in young minds, willing them to rejuvenate our island. And just as flying foxes sleep hanging from the branches like dark fruits, there was Mr. Mohini, dangling in the breeze.

When it couldn't be clearer who'd executed such crimes, somehow mythical tales crept their way into the gossiping soup. The devil bird cropped up reliably, as it did that day under the trees. 'They must have heard the devil bird', 'I'm sure I heard that devil bird last night', 'Devil bird had her way once again, men', people whispered to each other. I suppose I can't mention the devil bird that many times, Shi, and not give you some context.

The cry of the devil bird is a bone-chilling scream that shudders the forests of Lanka and is considered an omen of death. As the story goes, a man suspected his wife of cheating so murdered her infant son while she was away. On her return, he served her a curry simmering with the infant's flesh. The woman ate it with relish, oblivious until she spotted the finger of her beloved child dripping in the sauce. In a frenzy of horrified grief she ran screaming into the forest and was transformed into the devil bird. Her anguished screech still echoes through the forest, bringing doom to those who hear it.

Now, because no one has ever seen the creature which makes this haunting wail, there's an added air of mystery which has fattened the folklore. Three things irk me about this, Shi. Firstly, the mystery is exaggerated; it's probably an eagle-owl, nightjar or buzzard living deep in the dense forest. Secondly, the folklore seems flagrantly unfair. Even if the wife did cheat, is the murder of her child and eternal agony in the forests a fair comeuppance? Surely the larger worry is the man who goes cooking children. Isn't the guy who calmly wipes his child's flesh from the cutlery the one we should be trembling about? Thirdly, how can people shift responsibility to folklore so easily? It couldn't be clearer who'd committed such crimes, the soldiers and Tigers practically signed their names on the flesh, so why shift blame to some mythical nonsense, why sidestep reality so ridiculously?

Locals coped with violence in various ways; suppression, distraction and religion being the usual contenders. Burying it deep within, focusing on the little comforts or pinning it to some higher purpose or karmic justice made sense when trying to get through the day. But the turn to folklore sort of sums it all up. The barbarism was so rife that nonsense tales became warranted. The brutality so surreal that colourful myths felt reasonable.

When neighbours hang from trees, devil birds become plausible.

watery jaws, strange squid

Water is a marvellous matter. I find it both humbling and mysterious. It's humbling as a reminder of how intertwined everything is. The water cycle has kept the same supply moving on earth for millions of years. Imagine that for a second, Shi. The water in your cuppa may be the same water Tutankhamun bathed in, the Titanic sank in and a Tyrannosaurus drowned in. It covers seventy percent of the planet's surface and makes up two thirds of our bodies. All life started within it and it allows all life to continue within us. Splendidly simple, vitally humble; water is the scaffolding of life itself.

Water is also deeply mysterious. Its puzzling heat capacity and surface tension are one thing, but for me, the mysteries of the deep blue unknown beckons louder than the chemistry. The ocean is the largest habitat in the world, a mystifying abyss riddled with creatures beyond our wildest imagination. Dragons and blue tangs weave through kelp forests towards reefs bustling with pom pom urchins. Flamingo-tongue snails dodge harlequin crabs on wrecks teeming with algae delights, while clown fish peep between lollipop sea squirts and anemone bursting like stinging sunflowers. Hawksbill turtles ride currents past schools of whirling tuna as humpbacks rumble ancient songs through the great azure tapestry. Far beneath, deep sea critters roam the darkest pockets of human nightmares. Anglerfish gnash their fangs at slithering gulper eels, while ghost sharks lurk above bone-chilling snaggletooths. Beneath the huge blood eyes of skulking vampire squids, the jaws of stargazers glint from the sand.

There are millions of life forms yet to be found, labelled and utilised, a swelling universe beyond human reach, a swirling secret sphere sheltered from our greedy nets, bustling in cryptic defiance. I've always been comforted by this, Shi. Our planet needs places that humans never get to conquer, mysteries they never get to solve.

On Kallady Beach I would watch the sea for hours, entranced by the watery lullaby, ebbing and flowing, rushing and receding, frothing and bubbling in my eardrums. There was such a beguiling rhythm to it. Enchanting, yet foreboding. Serene, yet daunting. Still, yet in constant motion. The tide became a therapy for me. When thoughts of appa got really intense I'd cycle out to the shore and sit listening to the rhythm of those waves. I'd lie in the warm sand feeling the vast potential of the endless blue fill my lungs. The cool salt wind which came whooshing inwards with the waves made me feel like I could breathe again. It was so much fresher and cleaner than the air around town which clotted thick with agony, gunpowder and the sharp sour pulse of animosity.

I remember appa telling me, Shi, that Lanka was defined by its love of the ocean. As we'd watch the water cradle the shoreline, he taught me how changing sea levels and cyclones had caused Adam's Bridge, the causeway connecting us to India, to be submerged and swallowed up by water.

'We can find our answers in geology, La, but really I like to think our Lanka just adores the water. She fell in love with the ocean's beating blue heart long ago and just wants to drift back into its arms.'

I liked to think the ocean loved Lanka too, Shi, lulling her closer and closer into its embrace. Sitting on the shore, watching land and water hand in hand, felt like witnessing an ancient and eternal love story.

Even when sitting in appa's study during curfews, I'd try to recreate the rhythm of the currents by running my fingers back and forth across the pages of whatever book I was reading, clenching my eyes shut and imagining the tide rushing and receding with each whisper of the paper. While the war shook everything into disarray, the waves remained constant. While bullets thundered and rockets wailed, the water remained indifferent. The tide licked the shores of chaos with a soothing kind of consistency. It was nice to have something reliable, something you could trust.

But then one December morning that trust was shattered.

❖   ❖   ❖

It began at breakfast. We were in Sasni aunty's kitchen with a mouth-watering feast spread out before us, the sort of banquet that makes you gawp a while before you tuck in, the sort of breakfast amma used to make. It was our fifth Christmas at Sas's since appa had passed and it was her way of honouring him, her way of providing a little escapism for her dear friend's widow and children.

Sas was a private woman who had worked with appa at the teaching college and become an aunty to us in the affectionate sense. She didn't talk much and most of the time when people knocked at her door, she'd pretend not to be there. I'm not sure what she did in that house all alone but if our Christmas trips were any indication, it involved a lot of staring out the window, cooking and listening to old vinyls whilst drinking milky tea. Her husband, Thirun uncle, died just before I was born. They had spent countless nights worrying about the sporadic Tamil massacres, but it was cancer that got him in the end. Appa had told me that Sas was different before Thirun passed. He talked of her infectious whooping laugh and how she would be the life and soul of parties; twisting, jiving, drinking and giggling until the early hours. It was hard to connect this oozing charisma he had spoken of to the quiet lady in the dark house that I knew. I really liked Sas, particularly her cooking, but it never felt like she was really with us in the room. A smile would flicker across her lips here and there, but it never reached her eyes. I got the distinct impression she wasn't hiding something but rather hiding nothing. Behind those thin smiles and appropriate gestures, she was empty. I think this is why amma and Sas tried to avoid each other as much as possible; each pair of eyes was an uncomfortable mirror.

Dark introspection aside, Sas was a sublime cook, almost as good as amma. There were always countless pots and pans simmering on the stove and sweet and spicy aromas waltzing with the salt breeze through the kitchen. Amma moaned that she was fattening us up during these Christmas feasts, but Ravi and I couldn't get enough. We gorged and waded through her dishes until the seams of our bellies ached us to stop.

That Boxing Day morning, I awoke to the smell of kiri bath meandering from the kitchen, the aroma teasing my nostrils as I yawned my way downstairs. Ravi was already at the table, shards of pale sunlight striping his face as he gleefully inspected the banquet. Egg hoppers glistened with coconut gravy while fresh passionfruit juice beckoned beside the sambal. Treacle-drizzled curd shimmered tantalizingly beyond the stacks of steaming pittu, and at the end of the table a golden kevum cake sat cooling by the window, wafting hot cinnamon breath across the whole scrumptious mosaic.

'Where's amma and Sas?' I asked Ravi, hardly caring.

'Sas is in the garden, I think. Amma's getting dressed.'

Ravi's eyes were fixed on the cake. I sat down to join him and poured us both a glass of juice. I couldn't wait to see Peri's face later on, a third day of delicious scraps in row for him.

'Where to start? You thinking savoury or sweet?'

'Both', Ravi grinned. He was always in a better mood at Sas's.

As I reached for a hopper, that's when the birds began; a sudden flurry of shrieking blistered the air with alarm. I dropped my fork and headed to the window. The sky was swollen with winged chaos; darting, flapping, screeching clusters cutting the air with panic. Next came the rumble; a thunderous roar getting louder and louder, drowning out the cries of the birds as they fled. I saw people running, screaming, horror drenching their voices. They were diving into buildings, climbing up trees and scrambling on to rooftops. I snapped into action.

'Ravi, get to the roof!'

He was dazed, paralysed by the unfolding mania beyond the window. I grabbed his arm and shook him hard.

'Now Ravi! Get to the roof, find amma and get to the roof!'

Raising a pointed finger to the window, he moved his lips as if to speak. I grabbed his shoulders and shook him.

'Now Ravi, there's no time, get amma and get to the roof!'

He raced up the stairs as I darted into the garden shouting for Sas. My voice was drowned by the sounds of screeching and wailing. The rumble was getting louder, closer. There was no time.

I screamed for Ravi and his voice quivered back from the bathroom. Inside I found him wrapping amma in a dressing gown as she reached to pull the plug from the tub.

'Leave it amma! Get on the roof!'

The alarm in my voice shook her to attention. I flung open the bathroom window, climbed onto the ledge and looked up to the tiles. It was steep but reachable. I pulled Ravi out on to the ledge. He placed one foot on the gutter, grabbed the tile ridges and heaved himself up with ease. Next I helped amma out onto the ledge, she shook her head frantically when she saw the distance but I shouted her to stillness. I lifted her up by the waist as she scrambled hopelessly for a grip on the tiles. I grabbed hold of window frame and ordered her to step on my shoulder. As the rumbling swirled louder, I raised her up and Ravi hauled her on to the tiles beside him. I clambered up behind, straining and grasping until finally I fell panting on the roof.

There was no time for relief, Shi. From the rooftop, the roaring thing revealed itself with vicious clarity; a raging wall of bubbling brown talons gushing through the streets, lapping up buildings and devouring everything in its path. People were running, climbing and yelling as their bodies were dragged into its watery jaws. It surged closer, slower but still hungry. We tucked our heads down and clung to the tiles with all the strength we could muster as its jaws closed around us, drenching and lashing, chewing and pulling, soaking and battering. I clung to that roof with everything I had.

Seeing and feeling nature in full force like that, Shi, is something you can never forget. How can something be so beautiful yet so horrifying? How can wonder and terror mesh together so closely? I never once imagined nature could be so destructive, so powerful...no...powerful is too human, too weak a word to capture it. To be honest, no words will ever capture what nature did that day.

❖   ❖   ❖

Sas should have been my first thought as we climbed back through the hole where the window used to be. Inside, clothes, pots, photo frames, lamps, plates and furniture floated solemnly in the murky soup ruins of her home. We shouted and called for her until our throats ached, but in all honesty, Shi, Peri was the one on my mind.

We left the wreckage of the house and waded through the crumpled streets. The air clogged stagnant, sludge dripped from trees, brown soup dribbled from brick carcasses; everywhere you looked a sodden wasteland stared back. We weaved through the litter, the sobbing, the wilted buildings and shattered families, waded through the twisted tree limbs, jagged planks and the throbbing stench. Remnants of lives floated past solemnly, a toothbrush, a green sari, a toddler's glittery sandal.

People pulled at bloated limbs protruding from the wreckage, stopping to vomit, brown water spewing from their lungs. Some clutched wrinkled photographs and wept as they looked desperately for loved ones, whilst others roamed silently with chunks of wood lodged in open wounds. Corpses were wrapped in sarongs and placed in rows at the roadsides, colourful ladders with new rungs regularly deposited. Mothers sat wailing on the debris, rocking back and forth with palms open to the sky. Fathers crouched blubbering into the rubble, clutching their heads in their hands. Rubbish cluttered endlessly but Batti had never felt so empty.

Pain oozed from every crevice; agony poured from every pore.

Our house had been left surprisingly intact. The lagoon had absorbed most of the direct impact and the skirting lake roads had shielded much of the inner suburbs. The watery jaws had still reached our street but had taken bites rather than consumed it whole. Our windows had been smashed, fragments of glass, plates and wood swirled in brown puddles and a carpet of stagnant water lined the floors; but we had been lucky.

In appa's library only the bottom shelves had been damaged, his tomes were safe, but my den had been drenched. In the garden, chunks of netting, plastic and other people's furniture were piled in the place where Peri's shelter had been. He was old but his instincts were sharp. He had to have made it, he was a survivor.

Relatively few animals had been reported dead in the

aftermath, leading some to conclude they possessed some kind of sixth-sense which enabled them to foresee the disaster. Truth is, Shi, it's not some extra sense they possess, they just have far keener senses than us and a far greater awareness of their surroundings. When the sea receded moments before the tsunami struck, animals would have fled immediately rather than standing transfixed by curiosity. Flamingos would have flown from their low-lying breeding areas and elephants would have felt the seismic shuddering using the onion layers of nerves on their feet. So, I had to believe that Peri had made it, that he'd scampered off elsewhere.

❖ ❖ ❖

In the days that followed, once most of the bodies had been dug out, locals still waited hopefully by the shore. The outgoing current had dragged people far out to sea and the waves were still spitting out the occasional corpse. I recognised a few of the swollen blue faces. Mrs Vasanta, the maths teacher at Ravi's school. Alagar, the proudest prawn farmer on the east coast. Jolly Geethan from the market, who looked oddly peaceful lying there. His final hue was a fitting blue, just like the octopus with its copper-based blood; one final mimicry immortalised there in his skin.

A large ruptured squid, with long tentacles and a bright mantle, had washed up next to Geethan. I wondered how far it had travelled, how deep beneath the water it had once lurked, how strange it was that two heartbeats which had spent their entire lives beating so far apart, in such different worlds, had now fallen silent together in the very same spot.

The few boats that had survived the onslaught were taken out for human fishing. Families clustered on the beach, waiting for their latest haul with an anticipation drenched in dread. The day's catch offered only raw closure or more aching uncertainty. I think uncertainty was the better option. I see why most craved to find their loved ones' bodies; to pray, kiss, bury and burn them with ceremonious finality. But with uncertainty, you don't get that searing final image in your head, you don't get their vacant eyes burned into your retina. With uncertainty they never have to die at all. Their living moments can dance unimpeded in the chambers of your mind where some extravagant exit can be conjured. They can dissolve softly in some peaceful swirl of your own choosing instead of decaying bluntly in pistachio trousers.

That is why I stopped looking for Sas and Peri, why I stopped willing that final grisly reveal. Instead, I settled into the grooves of my own conclusion. Sas went drifting gracefully on a tide of vinyls and milky tea to rest with Thirun once again. And as for Peri? Well, he went bounding off through the indigo hills, tongue and tail lolling as he rolled into some roti filled oasis. He was in that secret heaven he dreamed in. Maybe it was a tad childish, but it worked for me. It made it a little easier to stomach the creeping realisation that I'd never see either of them again.

vulture clean,
puffa dirty

Even when Batti began to dry up, the currents didn't stop coming. Salt water streamed down faces instead of streets, soaking the wreckages of the loved ones left behind, chewing and submerging our town of debris hearts. In the month that followed, the monsoon rains drenched heavier from the fattened clouds, as if the tragedy was falling all over us again.

Although the island was awash with generous global aid, it struggled to reach the neediest thanks to the government's stifling bureaucratic hoops. Thousands lost their homes and were forced to live in flimsy tents and transition shelters. The angriest amongst them were the hundred metre refugees. Their homes had been swallowed by the sea leaving them forced to live in sodden limbo; barred from rebuilding in the hundred metre buffer zone, they watched enviously, under dripping tarpaulin, as their neighbours rebuilt their houses just metres away.

Inevitably, dark human nature festered and looting curdled up amidst the chaos. It became a staple of conversation and it was unusual not to hear people cursing about those dirty vultures who went callously picking through the carcasses of old lives. But their comparison to vultures bugged me, Shi, as vultures are very misunderstood. These frightening looking birds are actually vital guardians of public health, highly adept scavengers who help prevent the spread of disease. They have adapted to clean up carcasses with remarkable efficiency; hooked tongues help scoop flesh from bones, long necks help dig at organs from the inside and one species has even evolved to digest the bones themselves. Better yet, their poop is so acrid that it's actually a powerful disinfectant. So, while rat and dog scavengers rush off spreading rabies and the likes, these birds are hoovering up rot and passing hygienic cleanser out the rear. Lumping them in with looting human scavengers just seemed unfair. Of course, with tension simmering around town, I knew to shut up and keep this to myself.

Life moved on as best it could. They sent the children back to school to cope, the idea being to return us to a semblance of normality and anchor us to some continuity amidst the mayhem. But the countless empty chairs and missing classmates just proved a source of more trauma for most. Days since the wave turned into weeks, weeks crept into months and months crawled into years. Memorial plaques went up, bricks were lodged into new houses and life limped on as it had grown so used to doing. The sound of the sea had changed, though. If you listened closely, beneath the rushing of the waves, a soft whispering could be heard, the sea reminding us not to forget what it was capable off. The water was not to be trusted.

Talking of shattered trust, the fragile ceasefire came tumbling down too. President Rajapaksa rolled in with his tougher line against the Tigers, who in turn focused anew on civilian targets. Bus and train bombings erupted across the country, peace talks spluttered and bullets thundered through the skies once again. Hot metal poured from gunpowder skies upon the Tigers' human shields, and soon the eastern stronghold of Vakarai was captured amid lashing monsoon rains. The Tigers melted into the jungle pockets of Thoppigala and new army checkpoints scattered Batti's soil like peppercorns. Amidst our new khaki landscape yet another flood poured into our town; a tide of weeping refugees from all over the eastern province, clinging to the fragments of their butchered homes.

Ash and I returned to our usual rhythm, weaving necklaces and nattering amidst the cracks of the healing market. I never got to the bottom of exactly how Ash survived the wave. She insisted she'd scaled a palm tree with her bare hands and swung in the branches like a monkey until it was all over. Her voice beamed with such enthusiasm as she recounted her macaque-like grip, I really wanted it to be true, but I'm pretty sure Mr Ananda had invited her to his home for the Christmas weekend. Ash was far too proud to admit to being the recipient of any charity and so, the monkey-swing story stuck. Besides, I liked the idea of Ash up there in a tree swaying around above the turmoil with the purple faced langurs.

Ash told these sorts of stories quite a lot. She wasn't a dishonest person but every now and then she'd go spinning some ridiculous tale and just leave it hanging there. One time, she told me how she had wrestled two crocodiles in the lagoon with her bare hands. Another time, as we watched the outline of a jet disappearing into the clouds, she explained how she'd once landed a plane safely in a paddy field after the pilot suffered a stroke mid-air. On another occasion, she told me that she weaved coconut vine bras for women and that they had become so popular, a big international company had bought the idea from her. Whatever she spun, it was always amusing, but I still couldn't help wondering why she did it. Was it to add some excitement? Did she get a kick out of improvising? Was it just her little way of escaping reality? Whatever her reasoning, it seemed lie and truth had become so tightly woven in Ash's head that she herself couldn't tell them apart, and that was something we had all grown used to, after all, that was the bread and butter of the prachanai. It's easy to hide salt grains in sugar and sugar grains in salt.

Somehow, Ash's carpet had survived the wave. We found the old thing tangled in a boat carcass a few roads down; magical still, if not a little soggy. The carpet felt emptier though without Peri there, its pigment drained by his absence and whenever I thought of him, my guts and gums would ache and my chest muscles would bite tightly. When the echo of his fur grazed my skin I would turn and expect to see his hazel puddles staring back up at me. Ash could tell I missed him dearly and I knew she did too. Each time a stray crossed our path she squeezed my knee in unspoken solidarity. She also began demanding a lot more of my animal ramblings. Perhaps it was to distract me, perhaps to distract herself, either way, those chats were certainly a welcome diversion from the throes of Peri withdrawal and the army's tightening iron fist.

One scalding afternoon as the market emptied, she pointed out two dogs romping under the shade of a murunga tree. The scabbed female looked fed up as the male mounted her in a clumsy stagger of buzzing flies.

'Aiyo, look at this poor girl. These animals don't mess around ey? Straight in for the prize. At least we get a little spoiling when our men want their way. A little sweetness never goes amiss. Mind you, this war is turning them all into animals now, taking whatever they want, whenever they want it.'

'That's an insult to animals' I said, 'They have more charm than we like to think. I'll bet no man will ever seduce me like a bowerbird.'

'A what bird? What nonsense are you talking child?'

'When a bowerbird wants to impress a lady friend, he builds an extravagant structure out of twigs and lines the floor with shells and stones. He even decorates it with an array of flower petals and shiny objects to get her attention.'

'So, the best decorator gets the girl then?'

'Well, the best decorator entices the girl. And then there's the frigate bird, he doesn't need to go scouring the forest for dazzling décor. He is the package.'

'So, these free gates are handsome fellows?'

'The males have bright red throat pouches which they inflate like balloons to catch the eye of females gliding overhead. They drum on their magnificent red bosoms with clacking beaks to allure the females in with their throbbing love call.'

'Aiyo, seems our men could learn a thing or two from these winged fellows.'

'Yep. Once the female is interested, the male shimmies, shakes and charms her into choosing him. Don't see many men around Batti doing that.'

Ash's face sunk as she exhaled.

'Too arrogant to learn from our own neighbours, let

alone animals.'

Touching my knee, she widened her eyes with a smile.

'Now tell me child, tell me some more of these animal rituals.'

Our chatter sizzled for hours that evening, lacing the light breeze as dusk crept upon us. We gushed about the pebbles Adelie penguins collect for their nesting beloveds and I told her how nursery web spiders present silk-bundled parcels to their crushes. The pufferfish rituals intrigued Ash most. Her eyes widened as I described their elaborate sand art, the symmetrical ridges and valleys they craft, how they spend days decorating them with shell fragments before an impressed female chooses to lay her eggs at the centre. Inspired, Ash insisted we create our own, so with sticks we etched puffa patterns in the dust and decorated our works with fruit peel, seeds and bottlecaps. They were surprisingly good. From dirt and rubbish we created our own kind of beautiful. Splendour dancing through neglect.

Enwrapped in our craft, the curfew had slipped our minds. A group of patrolling soldiers appeared and panic punctured our bubble as we scrambled off in obedience. The next morning, our puffa patterns had gone. In their place, sat a clump of rotting fruit flesh.

❖   ❖   ❖

Now, Shi, it's probably time I told you about Kai. In nicer stories this is the part where you'd be enraptured by the blossoming of a romance, the pulsating sexual tension, an enchanting kiss and an epic love story to tickle your hungry heart. But I'm afraid I can't give you this, Shi, no matter how much I wish I could. Romance for me was a lofty impossibility, a plush fancy confined to the safe pages of my books. Don't get me wrong, it wasn't that I didn't get those feelings; I experienced the same hormonal cravings baffling teenagers everywhere. But such a thrill feeds off the possibility of it all, the potential for passion to dance to sensual life and sweep us into its lair, and for me, repulsively maimed little me, that was dead in the water. Any affection that tiptoed my way was a brand buttered thick with pity, an emotion adept at curdling the very core of passion. So, I ignored the cravings and this worked just fine.

Then came Kai.

He was older than me, three years older to be precise and he moved with a maturity far greater than his years suggested. I'd sneak lingering glimpses at him as he dragged in the day's haul, labouring away amidst the wrinkled fishermen under the blistering sun, sweat beads and salt spray glistening on his mahogany skin, the muscles of his biceps tensing rhythmically as he'd heave the nets along the sand. Yet it was his sadness that magnetised me most. If you looked closely, you could see a quiet torture lingering around him like a dark halo.

Of course, on our shattered island, you'd be hard placed to find someone who hadn't suffered. Yet Kai's wounds ran deeper than most. It was well known around town that Kaivan Selvadurai was a tsunami orphan. The waves had devoured the family home; his mum, dad, brother and grandma were all found gashed and bloated in the wreckage. His little sister's body was never found. The Selvadurai family seemed a genuinely close bunch and not just in the rose-tinted hindsight of tragedy. Cricket on the beach, picnics on Bone Island, loud Deepavali dinners amidst dancing tealights; a family who stirred envy amongst the gossiping town saris. Through mouthfuls of tea and jaggery, the same gossips could be heard speculating about why Kai wasn't with them that day: 'Out chasing that Sinhala temptress in the suburbs. Chi!', 'No men, he fought with his poor appa!', 'No, the boy went gallivanting up north to those nuisance cousins'. Wherever Kai had been, he had returned to the gutted carcass of his home, life as he knew it battered to sodden garbage protruding from the sludge.

With the flick of life's cruel tongue, Kai was sent to live with his uncle Mali; a gambler never seen without an arrack in his hand, a hulking fist of a man. His spitting temper was infamous and most knew to stay clear when that deep phlegmy wheeze trundled near. Kai became a means to fuel his lethargic greed, a working mule to keep his arrack and card games flowing. Higher education was out of the question, Kai was to man up and start earning the roof over his head.

I never saw Kai complain or raise his voice to Mali, he simply got on with his sentence. He reminded me of the elephants who'd undergone phajaan, the training regimen used to beat and starve them into submission for the tourist industries. He seemed to have that same despair hovering about his movements, that same dejection glazing his eyes, that same crushed spirit. I would often watch him pacing along the shore at dusk, his eyes scouring the sand intently beside the lapping waves. I couldn't shake the feeling he was out looking for some trace of his sister, some proof to allow him to give up hope completely.

I was drawn to him, Shi. It was an intense magnetism, raw and warm, unsettling and comforting all at once, and, like those dragonflies lacing the lips of the lagoon, I couldn't take my eyes off that boy.

chilli leaves, shrimp fists

Graffiti is a fascinating thing. Where some see crude vandalism, others see an outlet of creative expression for restless souls. While some see thuggish strokes, others see shapes galvanizing neighbourhoods to life. The human urge to leave a mark is an ancient one. Viking signatures in the Hagia Sophia, drought records in China's Quin Mountain caves, hieroglyphic tags in the Pyramid of Giza and prisoner farewells in the Tower of London; you name it, graffiti has etched the corridors of history in captivating ways.

The graffiti around Batti was odious. On walls and benches, lampposts and doorways, four big red letters, TMVP, became increasingly splurged everywhere. The letters may as well have been scribed in blood. You see, these were the markings of Colonel Karuna's clan, a breakaway faction of the Tamil Tigers. Colonel Karuna, hailing from a small village near Batti, pulled away from the Tigers on the grounds the eastern Tamils were laying down their lives in disproportionate numbers for the northern leadership. Karuna's group and the Tigers became sworn enemies, and the TMVP used extortion, abduction and assassination to cement their control in the east. It was also an open secret that Karuna's group were supported by the army. Everywhere you turned, Karuna's TMVP propaganda drenched our town, painting the Tigers as violent mercenaries far removed from their own peaceful approach of working within the political system. Their adjusted logo reflected just this. The Tigers' circle of bullets and crossed bayonets was replaced by rice flowers and a unifying handshake. They plastered the town with posters and blared their song, *Rising Flower of the East*, to stake their claim to Batti's soil.

You poured poison as milk into our mind.
Our hands that should carry books carried something else.
Our legs that should go towards the school went elsewhere.

I see in front of my eyes people who are suffering.
I am dismayed seeing life which is a mirage.
We don't want this. We don't want this any longer.

This all sounds very noble doesn't it, Shi? Swapping violence for dialogue, valuing education, condemning the Tigers' brutality; a refreshing change of approach at last. In reality, though, Karuna's boys only added more pockmarks to the walls and hurled more bodies on the pile. They poured blood, as milk, through our streets and slashed the hands and legs of suspected Tiger sympathisers. They were the new mirage.

In the spirit of appa's metaphors, Lanka's rain tree comes to mind. Karuna's messages pitter pattered with soft allure from a distance but close up the grimmer reality loomed. Just as the rain tree's soothing hum is really the gushing of defecating caterpillars, the letters of the TMVP's shiny slogans were really carved in rotting flesh. The same old filth wrapped in new ribbons.

As if the addition of Karuna's hungry pack wasn't enough, the machismo of the army soldiers around town grew ferociously. By Summer of '07 they'd attacked the last Tiger stronghold in the east; the jungle bastion of Thoppigala. Rocket grenades and tanks plundered the thick jungle caves, crushing the Tigers as they prowled their network of trenches and tunnels. Capturing Thoppigala peak meant they had secured the Eastern Province and arrogance wafted thick through the aftermath. The soldiers saw themselves as the dashing Buddhist warrior kings of the Mahavamsa epic, Duttagamani reborn, Ashoka awoken, fighting a just war to unify the island given to them by the Buddha himself. The Sinhalese may have made up seventy per cent of the population but they painted themselves as the minority. The talon of south India loomed just overhead, brimming with Tamils, a constant threat ready to swoop down on their homeland at any moment. They were the noble minority, the righteous Aryans, the honourable underdogs stamping out the Dravidian Tamils for good.

Drunk on their Thoppigala victory, the soldiers picked on Batti's locals as they pleased, bludgeoning bodies for the fun of it, making it clear who ruled the eastern roost. People were herded from their homes with gun snouts jabbed in their necks; hot teas left brewing, cigarettes still glowing, curries still simmering on the stoves.

You could spot the worst soldiers a mile off, the ones who thrived on cruelty and relished punishment as an end in itself.

Just as crocodiles have pointed V-shaped snouts and prefer saline water, the cruellest soldiers had sharper edges and craved the salty grit of a fight. And just as crocs' teeth stick out when their jaws are shut, the soldiers' lips had a jagged glint. Batti was infested with crocs and under their relentless gaze, life began to feel like a performance. Conversations, gestures and glances had to be sterilized and purged of anything that could appear even slightly suspicious. The stench of sour menace hung thick in the air and hot breath whispered peril down our necks. A disrespectful glance could set your flesh aching blue-black for weeks, an insolent sigh could beckon blades across your digits and a brazen comment could send you rotting in the soil.

Mrs Arachchi got a particularly raw deal. She was kindness incarnate, soft to the core and someone who wouldn't dare step an inch out of line. In fact, the only feisty thing about her was her infamous Jaffna curry. One spoonful of it would send chilli fire surging through your veins, blazing your capillaries with its flavour fever. There was nothing quite like it, Shi, and Mrs Arachchi always seemed to smell of the fiery blend, as if the spices were so strong they'd permeated her very skin. Aside from her curry, she was also known for having her husband and only son taken by the Tigers in the name of the cause. It was highly likely they were killed in the Battle of Thoppigala, or one of the eastern sieges, but she still carried her boys' picture and wore her red marital bindi with hope. The soldiers clearly weren't fans of such audacious optimism and Mrs Arachchi soon turned up sliced, gashed and swollen in a ditch near the old banyan tree. Crazy Chittu lay just beside her, soil caking the stumps where his limbs once were.

You could tell how long they'd been dead by the congestion

of flies that coated them like a quilt of buzzing raisins. As soil was shovelled atop the bodies, and the buzzing raisins scattered, I found myself wondering if the earth would taste Mrs Arachchi's curry. Perhaps the banyan's roots would savour her spiced skin, perhaps its leaves would tinge red with chilli fever, perhaps she would live on through the flavour of its branches.

Of course, Mrs Arachchi's son and husband were no unusual case. Men and boys disappeared so frequently all over town that it was hard to keep track. The Tigers demands had ramped up and every Tamil family were to give not just one, but as many children as possible for the fight. At night they came skulking by doors to collect their latest fodder. Resistance and heartfelt pleas were futile. If parents refused to cooperate, punishment followed and their offspring would disappear anyway.

The Tigers didn't just have to rely on this human tax though. All around town more and more of the younger boys were itching to join the fight. They couldn't wait until it was their time to train in the jungles, their turn to start firing Kalashnikovs for the freedom of their people. The Tigers filled their young heads with vitriol and convinced them that the only way to protect their families was to join the honourable brotherhood. The cruelty of the patrolling army soldiers only served to enforce such toxic nonsense. The whole affair made me think of the gruesome Cordyceps Fungus. Thriving in tropical rainforests, the fungus infects carpenter ants, drains their nutrients and manipulates their muscles like a puppeteer. The fungus compels the ants to leave their nest and ascend a nearby stem before piercing through their heads with a spore-laden stalk. The deadly spores then rain down on to the ant's colony starting the brutal madness all over again. In the same way, the Tigers infected the minds of islanders, swirled violent propaganda in their bones, drained their prospects and manipulated their muscles to shoot and slash as they saw fit. Then, from those mutilated corpses, they'd spin propaganda upon the siblings, infecting them with an outrage to be manipulated all over again.

The resentment simmering amongst so many local teenagers was pungent. I tried to avoid their bitter packs, they were always up to no good and my cheek was an easy target for their cruelty. I liked to tell myself I didn't care what they said, and I certainly acted like their words didn't hurt me, but truth is, Shi, it did hurt. Each insult stung like salt water.

One afternoon as I was cycling home round the Esplanade Lake Roads, I spotted a pack of them clustered at the fringes of Fort Park. I would have ridden straight past were it not for those yelping barks which sent me instinctively slamming on the brakes. Through the huddle of trousers, I glimpsed the trembling legs of a stray, its panicked yapping cut right through me and brought Peri bounding to the front of my mind. Without thinking, I ditched the bike on the roadside and stormed across the grass towards them. As I got closer, I saw the tallest one had his fingers wrapped around a chunk of wood with nails jutting out the end of it. He swung it and took a jab at the cowering dog while the boys around him sniggered in amusement. Rage flared through me.

'What the hell are you doing?' I shouted, my voice seething and frothing with the heat of a thousand cobra chillies.

The pack turned their heads and I recognised the tallest one, Inbam, from Ravi's school. He smirked and spat in my direction.

'Mind your own business freak. Do us a favour and go hide that face in some books.' He waved the nail-stick in a shooing motion as the boys beside him sneered.

'I'll go as soon as you leave that dog alone.'

Inbam shook his head slowly side to side.

'N'aw, beast loves the beast ey? Bitches united. Not today mongrel, get out of here or we're gonna have a problem.'

I stood my ground. Four against one was a tough hustle but if I could distract them long enough, I knew the stray might have a window to escape.

'Have you got nothing better to do? Are you really that bored? Does bullying defenceless animals make you feel big and strong?' I chided.

'Got a lot of balls, haven't you freak? Maybe we should see to that other cheek of yours, even out the ugliness a bit.'

He swung his nail-stick like a pendulum and took a step closer to me. The other boys laughed and behind them I could see the stray limping off. Inbam took another step closer and I realised I hadn't really thought my plan through.

Two steps closer. I could see his weapon in detail, rusty nails spiking menacingly between the splinters. Shivers rippled across my skin. This was going to hurt. Another step closer. My legs were rigid, refusing to budge. I swallowed, clenched my eyes shut and waited for his strike. Then, a deep voice came shouting through the darkness, refined, like strong coffee or dark chocolate. I listened to it pour and opened my eyes to find Inbam's pack thumping away across the grass. The chocolate voice spoke softly from behind me.

'Ignore those pests, too much time and too little sense. Are you ok?'

I turned. Chestnut eyes glistened back, flecks of amber scintillating at the edges. Kai. I wanted to say something cool, poignant, funny, something utterly dazzling to mark our first encounter, but no words came at all.

'You should be more careful, those morons are looking for any excuse to cause trouble. I saw what you did though, helping that dog like that. You like animals, right? I think I've seen you feeding birds down near the beach.'

I felt my face swell hot and watched his eyes shimmer as he studied my face. He was even more beautiful up close. I had to say something.

'Yes, I really like animals, adore them. Prefer them.'

Two dimples appeared beside his lips and the amber in his eyes beamed brighter. His whole face seemed to glow like molten cocoa. My insides tingled warmly. Clammy palms, fluttering tum, pulse fever; the old clichés erupted with gusto.

'I don't blame you. Shame we don't all have the same respect. The way people treat animals says a lot about their character. My mum liked animals, she was always watching the fishermen near the beach, said she felt sorry for the shrimps sloshing about in their buckets.'

I couldn't have fancied him more.

'Did your mum ever see a mantis shrimp?'

'Don't think so. Why, worth seeing?'

'Yes. They see the world in a psychedelic rainbow of pigments that we can't even begin to understand. Scientists call them the shrimps from Mars.'

'Why's that?'

'I think because they've evolved so independently and quirkily over time. They're ancient too, been around about four hundred million years, long before the dinosaurs were on the scene. Sorry, sorry, I must be boring you.'

He shook his head and smiled invitingly.

'Not at all. In fact, that's probably the most interesting thing I've heard all month. So, if these mantis shrimps are so great, why isn't everyone hunting them?'

'People try but they're pretty smart. They stay well hidden in their sandy burrows plus they're really fierce predators, fastest strikers in the animal kingdom. They smash and pummel prey with lightning speed using their wrecking ball fists. Can swing them at like fifty miles an hour.'

'Now I have to see one. Reckon the aquarium has one?'

'Unlikely. They can crack aquarium glass. In the time it takes us to blink once, they can deliver one hundred blows, each with three times the force of a professional boxer.'

I stopped to catch my breath. I was worried I was coming across like an arrogant little know-it-all.

'That's brilliant. Mohammad Ali eat your heart out. It's so cool you know all this stuff, makes a nice change from the usual drivel I hear down at the beach.'

The sun stroked his face with a tangerine glow and his cheek hairs shimmered delicately. I noticed an angry red mark by his elbow. He caught me looking and tapped it with his finger.

'Got stung yesterday when we were out on the water, a jellyfish, I think. Sneaky fellows, I'm sure they're getting closer to the shore you know. Tell me, are they as fierce as the Mantis Ali boxers?'

I smiled. There was no way that mark was a jellyfish sting. No doubt it was the sting of uncle Mali, but I wanted to keep him talking.

'Not quite. Strange creatures though, no brains, no blood, no bones and there's an immortal type too. Mostly made up of water hence why they pulse along so sneakily. Might have been a moon jelly that got you yesterday but just thank your lucky stars it wasn't an Irukandji. Their venom is a hundred times more powerful than a cobra, possibly the most dangerous animal toxin on the planet.'

'Wait, back up a second, did you say immortal? Are you telling me there's a jellyfish that can live forever?'

'Pretty much. When in crisis, there's a tiny jelly which can reverse the ageing process and revert from a medusa to a polyp. It essentially starts its life cycle all over again, so kinda like a frog turning back into a tadpole or a butterfly into a caterpillar, and it can theoretically keep doing this forever. Its cells undergo transdifferentiation.'

'Transdiffer what?'

'Transdifferentiation. Just a fancy way of saying they morph into all different forms; nerve cells turn to sperm cells, sperm cells to brain cells, brain cells to muscle cells and so on. It's remarkable and a grand mystery too because no one knows how they actually do it.'

Dark caterpillars arched above his eyes and his gaze settled on me in a way I wasn't used to. It's strange when this happens; when someone really looks, really sees you. I wonder if you also find it unsettling, Shi, does it make you feel vulnerable too? Like for that one moment you've given your whole self over to someone, laid yourself bare and dared them to see you for who you really are. Funny thing was, when Kai did it, I didn't find it unsettling at all. In fact, with our eyes locked like that, it was the most settled I'd felt in a long time.

I'm really not one for soppy gushing, Shi. I always hated the way the women in the books I read would get so caught up on men and lose all sense of themselves. It always seemed so unrelatable. But that evening with Kai, laughing and glowing there like that, I did sort of lose my bearings a bit. You know those conversations where it flows and fizzes so effortlessly that you lose track of time? Well, Kai and I glided through one of those that spring evening in Fort Park. It felt like I'd known him for centuries, Shi, and throughout it all I couldn't tear myself away from his eyes. The longer I looked, the more those amber flecks seemed like the quivering reflection of a lantern rising above water, or perhaps sinking beneath it, still alight but plunging deep below. Rising, sinking; I couldn't tell which way the light was going and that enraptured me all the more. Looking at Kai was both poetic and intimate all at once.

croc salt,
otter grief

My eighteenth birthday dripped along with an aching kind of happiness. Kai was coming for dinner in the evening and amma was making a real effort to be a mother; forcing a smile, dressing in her nice lemon sari with the sequins, hell, she had even baked a cashew butter cake for breakfast. As Ravi and I sat down for our morning treat, it almost felt like we were a regular family again. As we tucked into the cake, amma stood behind me and stroked my hair. It's an odd feeling when someone touches you again after so long, Shi, a shivery sort of familiarity. Her estranged fingertips sent goosebumps erupting across my skin. She had a glow that morning, the first sign of colour in a long while and in her eyes there were embers of warmth flickering faintly amidst the coal.

Ravi was being unusually nice too. He put the last piece of cake on my plate and insisted I stayed put while he cleared the table, a move as rare as spotting a pangolin in the midnight forests. He said he had a cricket match after school but would come straight home after to 'interrogate the boy trying to trap his sister'. Amma and him smiled at each other knowingly.

Such little flickers of warmth were all the more special to me, Shi, because I'd finally come to accept that Ravi would never again be the doting little brother I once knew. He was like a young dragonfly strengthening on a leaf at the lagoon, ready to take to the sky and begin mastering the air. It was his time to flourish and embrace the next stage of the life cycle.

The mood cloaking the kitchen that morning was unusually pleasant but despite how hard we tried to mask it, appa's absence thumped heavier than ever. He loved birthdays more than anyone, Shi. He had promised Ravi and I that we'd have the grandest parties when we reached eighteen, said we'd dance into adulthood with soul and style until everyone's legs were jelly. When I woke that morning, I glimpsed him in my bedroom doorway, beaming there in the morning light, wiggling a newly wrapped book in his palms. As I dressed, I heard him humming softly from the bathroom, muttering about how I'd grown faster than his beard hairs. At breakfast I smelt his cedarwood and toffee aroma wafting near the butter cake. I yearned for one of his hugs, to feel his arms wrap around me while I told him how excited I was about Kai coming round to meet him. But that was never going to happen and neither was the grand celebration he had envisaged, for the embargos, food shortages and sombre tension around town made a party out of the question. In all honesty, I was relieved. A party wouldn't have been the same without appa and I would have had to subject Kai to the forced grins and heavily laden questions from all the neighbours about his intentions. Having him grilled by amma and Ravi was going to be painful enough.

All day I swung between a bubbling excitement at Kai

coming to the house for the first time and a surge of anxiety at how amma and Ravi would treat him. I could think of nothing else. As the final bell screeched down the school corridors, I cycled down to the market to see Ash. I hadn't told her it was my birthday as I didn't want her to feel obliged to mark it somehow, or worse, to give up one of her beloved shells. The greatest gift was to hear her tut about the weather as we gobbled the mango chunks Mr Ananda had cut up for us.

When I got home, amma was cooking dinner. Coconut milk and cinnamon wafted from the kitchen, plunging my thoughts back to happier days. The house swelled with the aromas, as if the floorboards and walls were inhaling and savouring the long-missed flavours. I could tell amma was keen to meet Kai. 'What time will he be here? Will he arrive before Ravi gets back? You did tell him he doesn't need to bring us any gifts? How does he like his lamprais? Will he eat ash plantain?' The questions were darting thick and fast like a shoal of sardines, so I crept off to the study to escape them.

Appa felt more present than ever. The shelves seemed to ooze with him; the spines, maps and floorboards whispered with his energy and throbbed with his presence. He would have known not to bombard me with questions, he would have known I was nervous and would have done his best to distract me. Shards of fading sunset yawned through the window, illuminating *The Arabian Nights* spine. I retrieved it and sent a puff of dust waltzing in the sun splinters as I blew on the cover. It was as exquisite as the first time appa had showed it to me; intricate gold lattices and cerulean swirls, a tapestry of eastern tessellations stitched with calligraphy, the page edges laced in shimmering bronze. You shouldn't judge a book by its cover, Shi, but some covers judge other books and this one looked down on its neighbours, scoffed at the paperbacks that rubbed shoulders with its luxurious robes. As I stood there in the dappled motes of sun reflected dust, wondering where appa had sourced such a glorious tome, the sound of shattering glass came slicing through my thoughts.

A thunderous pounding boomed through the house. I shut the book, approached the door and as I reached for the handle a stampede of footsteps plundered into the hallway beyond, voices shouting and cursing in Sinhalese. I darted to the safety of my reading den and as I pulled the floorboard shut above my head, I heard the door smash open and heavy boots thump into the room. I held my breath as my heart thudded frantically against my ribcage. A gob of phlegm spattered hard as it hit the wood and a gravelly voice cursed.

'Not here. Find him. Upstairs, outback, tear the place apart until you find the little shit!'

The gravelly voice spat again and footsteps prowled closer above me.

'Look at all these books. Moan all day about food and oil shortages but these bastard hadi demalu are hiding libraries in their homes!'

'Sly Tamil bastards!' A younger voice chimed in.

I pressed my palm against my ribcage and tried to muffle the pulsating shudders of my heart.

'What do they need with all this shit men? Maybe we're due another Jaffna blaze ey? Should burn the lot.'

The gravelly voice was interrupted by shouting from beyond the door and the boots marched out to re-join the barking pack. My heart raced faster against my palm. Amma. *Was she hiding?*

Did she run? Had she made it out the back in time? I strained to hear what the voices were saying, but they blurred and chafed, the scuffled tension drowning beneath my thumping chest.

A piercing screech erupted from the kitchen.

Her scream tore through me like hot metal. Muffled laughter rose louder, swallowing her voice. I heard movement, struggle, ripping fabric, shards of her voice spluttering through the commotion, yelping fragments cutting through the frenzy.

Then it stopped.

I couldn't hear her anymore.

I wanted to run to her, help her, distract them, do something. I wanted to burst through the floorboards and chase them screaming out of the house. But I did nothing. I lay there paralyzed, shuddering uselessly under the floorboards.

The gravelly voice was barking again. 'Valuables, no time wasting...quickly...check for liquor...bring her...in the back...in the back...wrap the body first.'

The library door swung open again and more boots trundled in. Books began to slam to the floor by the shelf load. Then came a zipping noise and the sound of water trickling as a soldier chuckled.

A suffocating silence descended and swallowed all sense of time.

❖ ❖ ❖

As I climbed up through the floorboards and my pupils adjusted to the light, it wasn't my home that stared back. The library haven was gone, Shi. Ripped pages and crumpled books lay strewn across the floor, torn maps wept from the walls and empty shelves ached forlornly. Appa's cedarwood aroma and that glorious old book smell was gone, and in its place, a musty fug of ammonia wafted. Around my feet lay the battered remains of my childhood friends. Friends with more spine and honesty than most. Salt snakes streamed down my cheeks, poured into my wound, quivered at my chin and plunged onto the broken bodies of the books. That room no longer felt alive, Shi, its spirit had been stamped out.

I stumbled to the kitchen to find the cupboards gaping and all the cooking pots thrown from the stove. By the table, splatters of blood coated the floor and sequins glittered in its viscous embrace. I ran from room to room, eyes molten, chest tightening, agony swelling. The whole house had been ravaged in the looting frenzy and a salty sweetness choked the air. I could smell them in the kitchen, hear them in the hall, feel their bootsteps pressing into the floor. The very fabric of the house had been polluted; I had to get out.

The sunlight was searing as I went pedalling frantically down the streets with one thing driving me forward; Ravi. *Why hadn't he come home? Why were the soldiers looking for him? Where was he?* I had to find him. I couldn't let myself think about amma, the yelping, the ripping, those sequins, I just couldn't. I had to find Ravi.

I lapped the cricket fields, the beach, the lighthouse, the school and the lagoon to no avail. Panting in dazed desperation, I asked everyone I passed if they'd seen him. Blank faces stared back and heads shook uncomfortably. As I stopped to catch my breath, two ladies came walking past, fanning themselves and sneaking judgemental glances at me before continuing with their chatter. I got of my bike and quietly followed at a safe distance to listen in.

'Aiyo men, so many. Both of poor Vidya's boys, Arjala's daughter, Mr Prabakar's sons, it's just too many. What are these poor parents to do now?'

'Keep your voice down men. You don't know whose listening.'

'I know, I know but they were so bold this time, waiting right near the schools with their vans. I heard whole groups were bundled into the back like livestock. Sin men, so young, this is not their war to be fighting.'

I moved towards the women as the red sari began shushing the green sari again. Sweat shivered on my skin.

'Do you know which kids were taken?' I asked, 'what schools the vans were outside?'

The red sari shook her head.

'We don't know anything and we didn't see anything. Besides, you shouldn't be eavesdropping like that girl.'

'Sorry, Mannikkavum, I'm sorry. I'm just worried about my brother. He didn't come home and I can't find him anywhere. If you know anything that could help, please, I don't know where else to look, I don't know what else to do. Tayavu ceytu. Please.'

The green sari's face softened.

'When did you last see your brother?'

'Yesterday, I think. Wait, maybe the day before. What day is it today?' My head was swimming with exhaustion. 'Were the vans near St. Michael's school?' I blurted impatiently.

I didn't need to hear their answer, the wince on the green sari's face said it all.

It couldn't be; Ravi was smart, fast, he'd have found a way to avoid the Tigers, he wouldn't have been bundled into a van like that, he just wouldn't, not Ravi. Temples shuddering, I jumped back on my bike and pedalled as hard as my legs would let me, hoping the faster I fled the quicker I could erase their conversation from my head. Mr Ananda would know more than them, he could help me with my search and so I rammed the pedals harder and raced to the market. Ash might have seen something, she could reassure me that those fanning women were talking nonsense. I gripped the handlebars tighter. I just had to get to the market and everything would be fine. I could come up with a plan on Ash's carpet. Yes, I'd refuel with some pomegranate seeds and figure out how to find him, my baby brother, the only family I had left.

The market was winding down when I got there. A few traders lingered, stacking crates and wiping surfaces. Mr Ananda was always one of the last to leave so I had no doubt I'd find him carefully packing up his leftovers while Ash swept the floor peels, muttering away to herself as usual. But Mr Ananda wasn't there, and his stall was empty. Ash was nowhere to be seen. Where her magic carpet should have been, dark smears stained the concrete and crumpled petals quivered by my feet like torn wings.

❖　　　　　❖　　　　　❖

Do you look back fondly on your eighteenth birthday, Shi? Did the day roll in on a tide of new confidence, celebration and warm memories with loved ones? I hope so. I hope reflections on the day you entered adulthood evokes a dish, a drink and a dance that comes tumbling in gift-wrapped splendour and sparks a smile to your lips. My eighteenth was quite different. It came rolling in on a tide of new terror, ripping loved ones away with zeal. Confusion, anger and fear come tumbling in grief-wrapped nausea at the thought of it. It took me a while to piece together what happened that day and I'll spare you the further details of all the frantic pedalling, searching and questioning that occurred after the market and skip straight ahead.

The Tigers, in dire need of fighters, had launched a large sweep of the town. In a flurry of screeching tyres, they grabbed as many Tamil youth as they could and melted back into the jungles. The soldiers, incensed this had happened right under their noses, were convinced locals must have been in on the plan, so they embarked on their own retaliatory sweep to find the culprits. Thundering down streets and stampeding through houses, they etched their lesson loud, red and clear.

So, as I gained a year, I lost my life. From hushed slithers of conversation I was to learn both Ravi and Kai were amongst those taken by the Tigers. Ash and amma bore the brunt of the soldiers payback and as for Mr Ananda, he and his family packed up and fled West, one of the many families to join the mounting Tamil diaspora.

I was alone, Shi, and I truly felt it.

I could no longer stay in the house, that much I knew. The soldiers' smell was still there and the whole place ached with the absence of appa, amma and Ravi. So, I shoved a blanket, the few books I could salvage and some clothes in a bag and left without looking back.

But where to go? Where to scurry when your whole life has caved in around you? The thought of joining the refugee hordes in the temples made my stomach churn. I didn't want to melt into their sticky grief, I didn't want to be around anyone. The market was out of the question too; the absence of Ash and

Mr Ananda gaped like my wound and the thought of every missing laugh, wrinkle and tut sliced through my insides. So, alone and broken, I wandered aimlessly before ending up under the casuarina trees at the far end of the beach, far enough away from the fishing boats that would plunge my thoughts straight back to Kai. It was now just me, the creaking branches and a bag sagging with a few remnants of my old life.

I tried so hard not to think, Shi. I tried so damn hard not to think at all, to see and feel nothing but black. But it was impossible. No matter how hard I focused on the darkness of my inner eyelids those sequins still came glinting and those droplets still came pooling. Amma's yelping, the laughter, the ripping fabric; all swelled louder and louder, hotter and sharper, until I couldn't hear or breathe anything else. I kept picturing her mouth cupped, thighs spread, eyes streaming as they pierced her raw. I could feel it. Feel their filthy hot thumbs on her neck, grabbing at her breasts, pinning down her pelvis as she struggled. I felt their breath and sweat on her skin, their weight on her ribs, their grime squelching and spreading inside her. I felt them tear her, fill her, discard her. I felt the blade on her neck, the dripping silence they stole with their laughter. I was part of her, Shi, and I felt everything. My amma, the magician, broken and tossed away like eggshells.

Grief is a cruel disease, Shi, it's a plague of misery that comes crippling and draining everything you thought you were and corrupting everything you thought you loved. Even if you muster the strength to convince yourself things might get better, it still comes gnashing at you with renewed force when you least expect it. A slipper, a smell, a stone; anything could set it off, rising up from your insides and gushing through your nostrils, eyes and pores. You can't really fight it, you just have to let it drown you for a while.

It doesn't just infect humans either; animals fall prey to it too. Wolves, chimps, magpies, elephants, dolphins, otters, sea lions and countless others have been observed grieving family members in heart-wrenching displays. It erodes us all. When you experience it, you realise grief is not just one neatly packaged feeling. Oh no, grief is a malady that bundles a whole host of emotions in its vile sweep, leaving you aching with a hollowness that never quite goes away.

I don't want to hark on about how I felt under those trees, Shi. I could fill pages with the anger, the frustration and deep sadness that went broiling under my skin, but I'll spare both of us that uncomfortable detour down grief lane. Suffice to say, the raging emotions chewed and sapped me raw until I had nothing left to feel but empty.

At night I stared out at the waves breaking on the shore, their damp echo left glistening on the sand under the wash of moonlight. I listened to the push, break and pull and wished the waves inside me, the ones breaking and dragging me back and forth, could also leave behind such beauty. But the damp echo they created did anything but glisten.

I thought many times about walking into the sea, wading far into the water until it swallowed me whole and stopped my thoughts for good. But I was too cowardly for that, Shi and so my plan was to sit there under the casuarinas and decay unnoticed. At least my body could provide some sustenance for the creatures, some nourishment for the roots, prove of some use in the end.

But I didn't go unnoticed.

As I lay there hunched and wasting, a pair of eyes were watching me closely.

crouching dragon, hidden sloth

He was painfully skinny, that was the first thing I noticed. Sunken cheeks, protruding bones, collarbone jutting sharp as a blade; he was uncomfortable to look at. In fact, the very sight of him sent my tummy anxiously growling for food, demanding I spare it from morphing into such a sight.

I'd been under the trees for three nights when he first approached. There was no hello or introduction, he just thrust a plate on my lap, demanded I eat, and before I could refuse he was already striding off across the sand. My decaying strategy was proceeding as planned, but that plate of hot, buttered okra smelt so good I gave in. My taste buds tingled sharply in gratitude.

The next evening he turned up again, this time with two bowls in hand. He thrust one towards me and slumped down nearby. Together we sat, two strangers devouring chickpea curry without a word. It was a strangely comforting silence. Companionable, minus the companionship. As he finished, he lit a cigarette and stared silently out at the waves. With each inhale, his ribcage heaved beneath thin skin and as the molten glow dwindled between his fingertips, he flicked the stub, picked up the bowls and stared straight at me with unnerving calm.

'Good?'

'Yes. Nandri, thank you.'

'Good. Tomorrow we talk.'

The next night, belly full with lotus root stew, we did talk and I began to learn about Roshan Kandiah.

Rosh was not what I expected. Observing him on our dinner encounters gave the impression of a man of few words, a man who kept to himself and a man whom life had beaten down. Only one of these proved to be true. When I finally shared the brief strokes about what had happened to me, he didn't hound me with questions or interrogate like I'd imagined, instead he nodded and absorbed it in silence before sharing an entirely unrelated anecdote about his inability to tie nets. His unphased demeanour was oddly soothing. He made sure my trauma didn't get its way and greedily slurp all focus towards it. He saw it, put it on a shelf and carried on. I didn't know that could be done, that it could be controlled like that.

He told me it made no sense wallowing in self-pity with the mosquitos and that I should come to live in his home. I refused at first, but two rainy nights passed and the offer became more appealing, his badgering more insistent. Drenched, exhausted and covered in bites, I eventually accepted. What did I have left to lose?

His home was cloaked in neglect. Empty arrack bottles cluttered the floor, food-scabbed plates teemed from the sink and the windows were draped in dark rags. There was a whiff of homeliness lingering there, but the sort which had been left to stale. Photo frames, little elephant ornaments and trinkets on the windowsills all sat snoozing under a thick frosting of dust. I began to tidy, it felt like the least I could do, and as I pottered around, dusting and scrubbing through the mess I began uncovering little fragments of a life paused long ago. It felt oddly therapeutic, like each sweep and each swipe was helping to declutter my own mind. Dusting down the photos, I paused to admire the woman and toddler who smiled warmly from the frames. Rosh saw me looking but he didn't say a word; he kept his eyes averted from them at all times. In all honesty, Shi, I wasn't curious to know about them, it was just more trauma waiting to acquaint itself and I was quite frankly tired of its familiar face.

The little room I slept in felt clogged with sadness and no amount of tidying could get rid of the atmosphere staining that space. Dainty teddy stencils stretched around the skirting boards and the broken slats of a cot were slumped in one corner. A stuffed elephant sat beside the wooden bars, ears drooping, covered in cobwebs. The walls were bare except for one small clock and as I dusted down its tired lemon face, tiny cartoon sheep beamed back their frozen smiles.

I've always disliked clocks. Strapped to wrists, tucked in pockets, pinned to walls; why must that constant tick-tocking punctuate our lives so rigidly? Seconds, minutes, hours spent dreading school, work and curfews. Why do we slice time with such stifling precision? Things must have been so much freer before, when time was measured by the sun and the seasons, not the tick and the tock. The vaguer rhythms of the shadows and the flowers, the moon and the sun, sounds scrumptiously more spacious. Alas, schedules came creeping, from the obelisks of

Ancient Egypt to the time sticks of India, from Ancient Greek water clocks to sea faring hourglasses, from the candle clocks of Japan to astronomical sundials, gradually we slid towards ever more choking timekeeping. And as industrialisation flourished, the tick-tocking refined itself too; balance wheels morphed to pendulums which evolved to portable mainsprings and soon quartz and atomic accuracy came galivanting forth. Precision triumphed and rigidity reigned supreme.

There's an unsettling morbidity which hugs the clock face. Tragedies become immortalized in their frozen hands, exhibitions teem with the stopped watches of victims and traditions abound stopping clocks to mark a loved one's time of death, forever capturing the exact moment of their passing. The reality is, in most rooms we now enter, the ticking tocks on, eternally reminding us that time is running out. After appa died, I hated clocks even more; they tortured me with their constant reminder that things were moving on and that time waits for no one. But I wasn't ready to move on and their ambivalent hands slapped at my smarting soul.

So, for me, clocks had always ticked rigid and tocked morbid, swung sombre and chimed stiff and this made the comfort I found in that little lemon clock all the more surprising. It came to anchor me during my stay. Nightmares plundered my sleep, shaking me awake into a wide-eyed panic of sweat-drenched sheets, variations of the same scenes kept returning; amma pinned beneath a pile of panting soldiers, Ravi bent and bundled into a van, Ash bludgeoned to a pulp on her rug, appa's pistachio trousers. The darkness I stirred into took me straight back to the suffocating blackness under the floorboards and sent my heart bashing against my ribcage with renewed alarm.

But through the thumping and the pain came that shrill ticking noise, cutting through the panic with its grating hands. That little lemon clock was my guide back from the cliff edge and I'd cling on to that sound until my heartbeat synchronised with it. The rigidity had become reassuring.

Amazing how context can change one's perspective so drastically, isn't it, Shi? Take our dear friend the sloth. These tree-dwelling slowpokes have been vastly underestimated for far too long. Named after one of the seven deadly sins, early explorers considered sloths as stupid, bungled creatures that constituted the lowest form of existence. But if you watch sloths in their forest hangouts you realise slowness proves a winning survival strategy, with bodies designed to use up as little energy as possible while they sway silently between the branches. Take their necks; they actually boast more vertebrae than a giraffe's, allowing them to turn it 270 degrees to chomp leaves without moving a finger. Take their fur; teeming with algae, bugs and releasing no natural odour, it offers perfect camouflage to evade predators. Take their digestive prowess; the leaves they munch are racked with tough fibres and toxins which the sloth devours over months in its specialised four chambered stomach. Ok, I'll stop with the sloth fact flurry, you get the picture; appreciating something fully demands immersion in its environment. Immersion in Rosh's world certainly fostered a different perspective of him for me.

Rosh lived and worked with an unusually carefree air. He didn't take himself too seriously and he lapped up jokes and food with relish despite the weight of his past. He would talk for hours without breath if you let him, and with each laugh the humour wheezed and convulsed through his limbs, his entire frame shuddering to digest his delight. One evening after dinner, about a month into my stay, he picked up the smiling photo frame by the window and told me about what had happened to his family. He remained calm throughout, the only hint of discomfort being the slight tremor of his index finger each time he lowered his cigarette from his mouth.

Rosh's wife, Reeta, and his two-year old, Jenitta, died shopping for mangos in Puthukkudiyiruppu market. Reeta's father was a mango fiend and though sickness had swept in and stolen his appetite, his love of mangos remained steadfast. Worried about her father's deteriorating health, Reeta had travelled to Mullaitivu with Jenitta, and although she had asked Rosh to join them, she'd understood when he'd decided to stay at home to unwind and have a drink with his friends. She knew the stress of work, the war and the new strain of fatherhood was beginning to get to him. So, while the army obliterated Puthukkudiyiruppu market in their aerial attack that day, Rosh was back in Batti drinking heartily. As he spiced and gobbled a catch of juicy prawns, the market was strewn with charred hunks of human flesh. And as he bantered and smoked past sundown, Reeta and little Jen's bodies lay smoking silently amidst the mangos.

Before I could offer any sympathy he was off pottering around the kitchen, whistling one of his fishing songs as if we'd been talking about our favourite biscuits and not the grisly end to his family. Reeta and Jen had died almost ten years ago in the market attack so no doubt time would have played its healing role, but time dilutes pain, it doesn't wipe it out. Shouldn't tragedy demand some orbit of discomfort, Shi? Shouldn't we honour the victims with our lingering hurt? Perhaps. But in all honesty, I felt a swelling admiration for Rosh's approach. He had found a way to keep living and had locked up his burden of guilt and grief in a box. It wasn't that he'd shut his whole past away, he frequently shared funny memories of his little Jen and Reeta, but he'd somehow found a way to remember only the warmth, embrace the good bits and detach it from the terrible aftermath.

I figured it all came down to perspective. You know, not sulking because a beautiful erubadu tree has thorns, but delighting that the thorny thing has coral blossoms. We often hear talk about the glass half full or the glass half empty, right? Well, I've always figured that just depends on the action of the pouring. If you have a full glass of water and half gets poured out, then it's half empty. While if you have an empty glass and fill it halfway, then it's half full. This made sense when I looked at people around town; they were mostly glass half empty because they'd had their glasses vigorously shaken and the water poured out, some were fully empty, and hell, others were so traumatised that the glass had shattered entirely. Somehow Rosh's glass was always half-full and being around him helped to ground me in the present. He created the illusion of normality with his bizarre stories and chuckling fits to the point where living felt bearable again, and so as the weeks passed, I mustered the strength to peer at the books I'd salvaged and begin reading again. Sorrow-stained nostalgia flooded as I reacquainted with the pages, but it felt right, like I was welcoming back a part of myself I'd forgotten I needed.

As the months passed, I began to head out to my lagoon sanctuary once again. Sitting in the spot where I'd met Peri filled me with sadness, so I moved a little further down towards the swampy tangle of mangroves. Rain, shine, wind and sludge; no matter the weather, I'd sit there for hours watching the mini universe bustling away. Mangroves really are sublime, Shi. They're an inspiring kind of mess. They protect shorelines from floods, filter out pollutants, prevent erosion and their tangled root network offers a home to all sorts of creatures. Their tolerance is impeccable too. They can store four times as much carbon as rainforests and are the only tree species that can withstand salt water. Watching the life sprawling between the roots and branches, I resolved to channel the mangrove's tolerance; it was time to be more resilient.

Once more I found my focus drawn to the dragonflies and I became infatuated by their hovering. You see, Shi, dragonflies can move all four of their wings independently and when they hover, they flap their front and back set slightly out of sync which helps them to save energy. I hoped the longer I watched those hovering beauties, the better chance I'd have of learning their stillness.

It was near my new mangrove spot that I came across Tzu, a chunky water monitor I'd spotted along the opposite bank of the lagoon where the branches clustered thick with insects. Each day he'd appear in the same place, flicking his forked tongue, searching for whatever pic-n-mix morsels he could get his claws on. I've always liked water monitors; they have such prehistoric majesty and are the second heaviest lizards in the world after their Komodo Dragon cousins. They're fearsome carnivores too, with super powerful legs they use to chase down prey and serrated teeth perfect for severing tendons. Mr. Ananda once told me he'd seen one eating a baby croc.

When Tzu appeared he'd watch me intensely, and as we

stared at each other the whole lagoon circus seemed to slow around us. And do you know what, Shi? I found a real comfort in that gaze. It was so clear cut, no deception, no beating around the bush. Yes, there was no doubt he was eyeing me up as potential dinner, but he was also settling into the conclusion that it wasn't worth the risk. Sitting there watching Tzu, I couldn't help but think of the passage from appa's *Art of War* book, about the greatest victory requiring no battle at all. I realised I had to stop fighting with myself about things I should have done differently. If I didn't, my survival was itself a defeat.

One afternoon, on my way back to Rosh's after a particularly long staring contest with Tzu, it began to rain. Not your usual healthy drizzle or standard pour, but a thunderous release that came drenching everything in sight: appa rain. Saris scurried to shelter, roadside vendors packed up and darted for cover as the streets emptied in the onslaught. Before long it was just me, alone with the weeping skies. I stood transfixed, remembering the time Ash and I had been caught in a deluge whilst searching for shells on the beach, toes sticking in the wet sand, the rug held over our heads as the droplets thwacked on our carpet umbrella. As Ash bent down to retrieve a shell, the marigold petals in her pocket fell to the sand so we plunged to collect up the moist orange treasure, giggling and gasping in the downpour.

It was the first time in months I'd thought of Ash without images of soldier boots beating the blood from her fig tree skin flooding my mind. With the rain came a goodness, a brightness as vivid as her parakeet greens, and as I stood there, with the swollen clouds of her presence rising within me, the rain came sloshing around my ankles. In the gullies of water a tide of wrappers and twigs was swept along, and amidst them, like glistening jewels, a cluster of marigold petals danced past. Then, through the roaring water curtains, I heard appa's laughter. It washed through me so forcefully I couldn't help but laugh too, Shi. It surged right through me, a complete and delicious freedom swelling and reverberating through my tummy, lungs and throat. All the agony and anger was being diluted in the thunderous soak, each laugh and each droplet loosening the sludge of my grief.

As I stood there, laughing in the middle of the street, soaked to the skin, I was once again swimming in the skies with appa.

assassin bugs, scarred moon

Rosh would often return home with a few of his fishermen pals and they'd drink, joke and sweat until the early hours under a thick fug of smoke. Laughter and slurred stories would waft through my door splinters, but sometimes the chuckling stopped and a more serious tone gripped the air. This meant the war had reared its head.

Things were heating up in the north and tension throttled the curves of conversation. The army were ravaging the last Tiger strongholds in Mannar, Killinochchi and Jaffna. The Tigers were mounting a last-ditch attempt to claw back territory, using innocent civilians as human shields in the process. The army condemned the use of such shields but pummelled them with hot metal anyway. Frustration and bitterness clung to the kitchen chatter and a heavy silence lingered once they'd left.

Late one night, as I went to get some water from the kitchen, I found Rosh awake amidst a cluster of bottles, plates and brimming ashtrays. His friends had left hours before and I was surprised he hadn't staggered off to bed. He smiled wearily as he saw me and slurred a few words.

'Let's see how this pans out. Still a chance if you ask me.' He pointed to the chair opposite him. 'Come, sit. Tell me what you think. You're a clever girl, you tell me how this ends.'

I poured two glasses of water and plonked one down in front of him.

'It ends with you sleeping soundly in bed.'

He chuckled.

'I'm serious girl, the prachanai, how does it end?'

Quite the question to encounter on a four a.m. sleepy saunter. What was the point of pondering the end to something as inescapable as the air I breathed?

'Who says it ever will.'

'Ah, a cynic. Nonsense girl, it will end. Everything must end. Don't know when but it will.'

Rosh took a sloppy glug of his water, slammed the glass down and continued with replenished animation.

'The government have alienated us all. Fuel, food, plastic, cement, cooking oil, Chi! Look at us. How can they look at us skinny bastards and deny these embargos are starving us? They may have the manpower and the fancy weapons, but they don't have the commitment of the Tigers, they don't have their flexibility.'

He shook his head, half-laughing in disbelief.

'This is about dignity. We owe it to the dead to actually get something out of all this, no?'

He stared at me, waiting for a response.

'So, you think some rights can be agreed with the government then?'

'Don't be silly, girl. If we want justice guaranteed for Tamils, then the Tigers need to pull out all the stops and secure a separate Eelam. You can't win a game of chess without getting rid of some of the pieces. Separation is the only way, there's no shame in admitting that some people just don't get on.' He grinned excitedly at me. 'You should know this better than anyone girl. All those animals you read about, they stick to themselves, protect their own and they get on just fine. There's a reason you don't see elephants and snakes chatting away together, a reason leopards and monkeys aren't breaking bread together.'

Rosh took another sloppy glug of water and I thought about launching into a defence of wildlife symbiosis, championing the cooperation between species that allows ecosystems to thrive. I could have told him how egrets hitch rides on the backs of buffalos, picking them clean of harmful ticks and fleas. I could have told him how gravel ants protect the caterpillars that secrete a sugary fluid to nourish their colony. I could have told him how ostriches and zebras group together, harnessing both the zebras' fabulous sense of smell and the ostrich's eyesight in order to better sense impending predators. But I didn't tell him any of this. I knew nothing would knock his resolve, that no flurry of animal facts would penetrate the bubble of his thinking.

'I know,' said Rosh, feeling the need to address my silence, 'the Tigers have done terrible things, they're just as bad as the army, blah, blah, blah. It's messy, yes, but that's war. You've got to crack a few shells to make the best egg hopper, and just think how delicious that hopper will be. Imagine eating, laughing, and reading those books of yours with no more soldiers breathing down your neck. It'll be worth it in the end,

I'm telling you.'

He swallowed the last of his water, got up, steadied himself and staggered off towards his room. I grabbed a cloth and began dabbing at the water rings that blotched the table.

The assassin bug sucks its prey dry and then attaches the corpse to its back. Its new armour may offer protection, provide a shield; but who wants that morbid burden weighing down each new step?

I scrubbed the wood harder.

The bone house wasp is a fierce predator which stuffs the walls of its nest with the bodies of dead ants. The smell of the carcasses may ward off intruders but what of the stench inside? Who wants to live in a home built from dead bodies?

I stopped scrubbing and lifted up the cloth. The rings remained, stained into the wood.

❖   ❖   ❖

As the little lemon clock tocked on, an emotion I thought long gone began to rear its head. Hope. Night and day the feeling came scratching at my skin like prickly heat. I just couldn't shake it, the feeling that Ravi was still alive, still surviving somewhere, and from this hope resolve began to sprout. I needed to find my little brother, and perhaps where Ravi was, there too would be Kai. But where to start? When I'd spoken to Rosh about it, he'd laughed and said I was crazy. He told me to forget about it and that talking to anyone else about such things would have been a waste of time. Perhaps he was right. Beyond the gaze of the soldiers, people were too paranoid to discuss anything to do with the Tigers. Such conversations were a death wish and even if I could glean some information, the soldiers had us on lockdown so I couldn't very well go marching out of Batti and trapesing up north. All I could do was wait, wait until the situation changed, wait for some window to open that allowed me to actually do something, anything. And that window did come, opening up in the soggy folds of a grey January morning.

Rosh and I were slurping leftover stew at the table and hot, salty gloop filled my throat as the rain whiplashed outside. He had put down his spoon and was staring straight at me, his glare making my face itch.

'Everything OK?'

My words sent him blinking rapidly.

'I've been thinking about your brother, about what we could do. No, no, don't get your hopes up,' he said, quelling my excitement with a shake of his head, 'I've just been thinking about the best way to find him, the best shot you have.' He cleared his throat with a rasping wheeze and continued. 'You know the situation is getting worse here. It's changed things, it's hard to know what to expect anymore. Staying here in Batti may be no safer than heading up north. At least up there we'll have options.'

'Are you saying we should leave Batti?'

'Look, I have a friend who can get us away from here, we pay a small fee and they'll take us by boat up to one of the northern ports. No faff, no roadblocks, no checkpoints.'

'But it's too dangerous, isn't it, what about the army bombardments?"

'It's all slowing down again, there's talk of a new ceasefire, this could be the chance. There are people up there I know. They will help. Trust me.'

That last bit, trust, was what the whole matter ultimately

came down to. Rosh had helped me immeasurably, he filled my tum, put a roof over my head and coaxed me back from the brink. That said, before I settled into his neat conclusion, I set about bombarding him with a whole raft of questions. I grilled him for hours and suitable answers to all of my questions came wheezing back through tobacco stew breath. The boat would come in the dead of night. We'd meet it at the far end of the beach beyond the checkpoint where two drunkard soldiers were always snoozing. We'd be transferred to a bigger ship that would take us up to Mullaitivu, a stronghold of the Sea Tigers. Rosh had connections there, people who owed him a favour. They would help put the word out about Ravi. I hadn't told him about Kai, but as he spoke my hope grew and I just knew that it wouldn't be long before we were all reunited.

Things moved swiftly after that as the window for leaving was tight. Rosh had arranged for us to catch the boat the following week and as he set about tying up loose ends, I soaked up a couple of last sessions by the lagoon, etching the contours of my wildlife haven carefully into my mind. He'd also insisted we travel light so I headed up to the casuarina trees with a shovel and my bag of books, and in a kerfuffle of sweat and sand I buried the spines deep between the sprawling lattice of roots. I clarified my coordinates. *Eleven trees along (amma's birthday). Four steps south from the bent tree (appa's birthday). Two roots across (Ravi's birthday) and seventeen digs deep (the age when I'd first met Kai) Eleven, four, two, seventeen. Amma, appa, Ravi, Kai. Eleven, four, two, seventeen.* As I heaved clumps of sand on top, and marked the bent tree with an X, I reassured myself I'd be back digging them out in no time at all, with Ravi and Kai beaming beside me.

❖ ❖ ❖

We don't stop to marvel at our moon enough, Shi. Shame, because it's bloody marvellous.

Our satellite sprung to life as the child of a momentous collision that occurred when the Earth was still forming. An object, the size of Mars, called Theia struck the Earth's crust and the debris went spinning off into space. These whirling leftovers got caught in the Earth's gravitational field and were compressed together to form our orbiting moon. Beauty blossoming right there from the scraps.

Colourful mythology orbits our lunar neighbour in abundance. Native American Seneca tribes believe a wolf sung the moon into existence while Kenyan myths paint the sun and moon as squabbling brothers forced to be separated. Selene the Titan Goddess rides her silver moon chariot across Ancient Greek skies and in Inuit myths, a wicked moon god chases his poor sun sister, and with no time for him to eat he gets thinner and thinner as the month wears on.

Whilst tucking Ravi and I into bed as children, amma would tell us the tale of Ganesha riding home on his shrew one full moon night after an extravagant feast. As a snake slithered past, the shrew bolted and Ganesha went crashing to the ground, vomiting up all the tasty modaks he'd gobbled. The moon, Chandra, saw all of this and burst out laughing. Enraged, Ganesha broke off one of his tusks and hurled it straight at the moon, denting a crater into Chandra's skin and cursing him never to stay whole again. Ravi and I would gleefully re-enact this vomiting, laughing, tusk flinging scene from our beds, which amma didn't find amusing at all. She'd point to the dark patch on the moon outside, and in a tone as sharp as Ganesha's tusk, she'd tell us to see it as a warning to never relish in anyone's misfortune.

Appa, meanwhile, loved recounting his favourite Jataka tale on the Buddha's previous life spent as a white rabbit. The rabbit, along with his monkey, otter and jackal pals, resolved to practice charity on the day of the full moon. Thus, when an old man came begging for food, really the God Indra in disguise, the monkey gathered fruits from the trees, the otter collected fish, while the jackal brought a lizard and a pot of milk-curd. The rabbit, however, had nothing to give except measly grass, so instead offered its own body, throwing itself into a crackling fire the old man had built. Touched by the rabbit's virtue, Indra drew the likeness of the rabbit on the moon for all to see and learn from. As appa traced the outline of the rabbit on the moon with his finger, his smoky toffee mantra lodged into my fibres; 'He had nothing to offer but himself, La, and that was the greatest gift of all.'

I remember seeing the pictures of the moon in appa's encyclopaedia, the majestic green cloth tome he kept snoozing in his bottom drawer. Beneath the glow of his lamp, I'd trace the images of the scarred sphere as he talked through the names of all the craters, salt dips and ranges. I'd go skimming pebbles on the Lake of Dreams, somersaulting across the Bay of Rainbows and plunging into the vast Ocean of Storms. I'd run my fingers over the dark patches of the Sea of Tranquillity, the Sea of Serenity and the Seas of Nectar, Clouds and Showers, as he explained how those basaltic plains were formed by ancient volcanic eruptions, and how early astronomers had mistaken them for seas. I thought that was a pretty beautiful mistake to have made, poetic illusion rippling away through the centuries.

The night I left Batti, a full moon was beaming radiantly. Rosh and I made our way out along the beach and I told myself that somewhere Ravi and Kai lay sleeping soundly under the very same glowing face, that soon we'd all sit beneath it and finally hear those singing fish.

❖ ❖ ❖

We crept silently along the sand, following the slithers of moonlight to the army checkpoint at the far end of the beach. We crouched in the shadows watching for signs of movement. Nothing. We waited, studying the outline intently, the waves shushing louder. Nothing. We began to move again, stealthily hurrying past the checkpoint through the darkness, sand sliding beneath my soles, water rushing at my eardrums. Shapes, sand, water, shapes, sand, water; on we crept for what felt like hours. Then, there it was, in the distance a dark silhouette appeared against the water. We sprinted through the shallows towards the boat and Rosh urged me to climb aboard. Splinters pinched at my fingertips as I gripped the side and heaved myself over. Rosh thudded down next to me and squeezed my shoulder affectionately.

'First leg done. You did good, girl.' he said, 'You did good.'

Two women were hunched together beside us, staring down silently at the wood of the hull, their faces obscured in the folds of their saris.

'You rest here now.' said Rosh as he slid over towards a group of men at the far end of the boat. I watched as he picked up an oar and together they began to heave forward. The boat jolted, pushing against the waves, fighting its way through the surf, brine licking at the sides, sluicing over the edges and seeping into my clothes. As we pulled out further from the shore, the rocking smoothed and settled into a queasy rhythm. I watched the moonlight rippling against the water, thinking of all the marine life snoozing far below in the ocean's depths. The muttering of the men, the rolling of the oars and the sighing of the waves rushed at my eardrums and weighed down on my eyes as we swayed off into the darkness.

Rosh's voice lurched me out of my trance and as my eyes adjusted, I saw a large shape looming out of the darkness next us. He smelt of arrack and fumbled to light a cigarette as he motioned towards the shape.

'You see the big ship? Not long now. Get ready for moving over, should be there any minute.' He looked over at the two other women. 'You two as well, get ready to move.'

He flicked his unlit cigarette over the side and moved back to his oar. The ship grew closer, larger, sucking us into its orbit until the prow of our boat knocked up against its enormous metal hull. One of the men began waving his arms around and a rope ladder was thrown over the side of the ship.

'Come, come. Hurry!', said Rosh as he grabbed hold of the end of the ladder.

I struggled to stand as the boat rolled with the waves and clanged against the ship's hull; I stumbled over to Rosh and held on tightly to the side of the boat. The women went first, slow and shaking as they hauled themselves up to the chorus of Rosh's 'hurry, hurry, hurry!' When my turn came, I hoisted myself up with surprising speed but near the top, I missed my footing. As I peered down to find the rung, the ocean hissed and rumbled below like a hungry abyss. I shivered at the thought of plunging into its icy depths and gripped the rope tighter until my palms stung. Carefully, slowly, I climbed the last two rungs before being yanked over the side onto the deck. Before I could catch my breath, a muscular man pointed at the two women and barked at me to join them.

Rosh appeared next, scrambling onto the deck. The man didn't bark this time but instead took him aside. I could see their mouths moving and hands gesturing but I couldn't make out what they were saying, their words carried off and away on the salt breeze. From Rosh's shaking head, though, it looked like they were disagreeing about something. The muscular man reached into his pocket and pulled out a wad of notes. *Had Rosh not paid them enough? Had they raised the fare? Were they not going to help us?* The man counted out some notes and then handed them to Rosh, who stuffed them into his pocket. Two other men appeared beside me and the women, grabbed our bags, yanked us up roughly and began herding us across the deck.

Straddling the boat side, Rosh turned and stared straight at me. I'll never forget that look, Shi, not till the day I die. That look lunged like a dagger through my insides and impaled my heart. That look broke me. Every pore and crease of that look screeched betrayal.

part 5

frail flamingos, honeydew fix

The brain is good at shutting out darkness, Shi. We blink up to twenty thousand times every day but we rarely notice a single one. Why? Because our brain suppresses information about those moments of darkness to help us keep going. Same goes for our darkest thoughts. For the sake of sanity, we learn to block things out to spare ourselves from drowning in the torturous oblivion that rages between our temples. Imprisoned deep in the bowels of that ship, Shi, my brain got really good at this, it had to, there was no other way to survive. I have no idea how much time passed down there, shivering in that sour darkness where hope bled out and terror dripped from the walls. I lost track of everything. Even thinking back to the bowel room right now, Shi, I can feel my chest tighten and my temples begin to throb. So, I hope you'll excuse me if I skip ahead to when I was once again able to taste fresh air.

❖　　　　　❖　　　　　❖

The whirring of the propellers had slowed and footsteps, loud and urgent, came thumping down the corridor. Two of the other girls who I was imprisoned with scrambled back in panic as the bowel room door was thrown open. Hawk eyes scanned the room, locked on me and glinted. Panic clawed at my throat.

'You. Get up.'

I scrambled to my feet as the man's talons came digging into my forearm. The other women curled into the shadows and looked away as the man dragged me across the room and out into a musty labyrinth of corridors. We moved up and up through the body of ship until he pushed me out onto the deck. I'd never felt air that cold before, Shi, the ice breeze stabbed at my cheek, tore at my nostrils and scratched into my lungs. The man's talons twisted firmer as he tugged me towards the ship's edge where the rope ladder dangled queasily towards a spec far beneath.

'Climb. Now.'

I stared down at the roaring darkness, the wind lashing at my eardrums.

'I said now!' He barked, forcing my hand onto the ladder.

My palms ached as they reacquainted with the rope grooves, my whole body trembling as I descended into the blackness towards the dinghy that waited below. I was pulled down by my waist into the rubber belly of the boat and the sound of the motor tore through the fangs of the biting cold. As we screeched through the waves, I gripped tightly to the thin rope strung along the side of the boat, salt spray whipping my face, the wind slashing with every lurch, wet terror consuming everything.

When the sound of the motor finally stopped, fingers sunk

back into my arm and I was yanked from the dinghy and dragged through the shallows onto a pebble shore. Above me loomed the hulking chalk giants of Dover, jutting their sharp edges against the skyline. My mind flashed to an entry in appa's encyclopaedia. *The white cliffs were formed from the skeletal remains of planktonic algae that settled together at the bottom of the ocean and were revealed as the seabed became exposed over millions of years.* The pictures in the book had made the cliffs look serene, Shi, but up close they loomed harsher, a bleached graveyard towering through the blue dark.

I was dragged along beneath the cliffs, the pebbles shifting and receding beneath me until they finally gave way to solid ground. I was pulled across tarmac to a waiting van and bundled into the back as its doors gnashed shut behind me. The engine growled to life and a fug of petrol choked the air, its metallic sting forcing its way down my throat, filling my head with flashes of those charred bodies twisted through tyres back home. The voices of the men upfront blended with the drone of the vehicle and I desperately tried to picture appa transforming the racket around me into something more splendid, tapping his pen with the passionate thrust of the conductor's baton, whipping together the tyres, the voices and the engine into a new symphony, a new waltz. But there is only so far your imagination can take you, Shi.

How many miles from Batti was I? How many days had I been on that ship? I scrambled for some morsel of hope and pictured the marlins, leatherbacks and grey whales that went traversing the oceans, migrating tens of thousands of miles from where they started out, immersed in completely foreign terrain. They always found their way back, Shi, against all odds. I promised myself I would too.

When the van doors swung open again, hornet eyes pierced in through the mouth of the cage, hands clamped around my ankles and I was wrenched out.

'Move it. We don't want to keep Satyan waiting.'

I was dragged through a doorway and led down into a room that smelt of fried meat and stale breath. A hand on the back of my neck was forcing my head down, my eyes locked on a dirty threadbare carpet.

'What have we here then? Where have you come from ugly one?'

I slowly raised my head, as the grip on my neck was loosened, to see a man sitting behind a desk, staring at me. His eyes seemed to swallow up all the light in the room, the type of eyes that looked at you without letting you look in. On his right temple was a scar in the shape of the Kalu Ganga which threatened to burst with each throb of the vein beneath.

I stayed quiet and looked back at the floor. Growing up under the soldier's gaze had taught me that silence was always the safest bet.

'Mute as well as ugly ey? Good, let's keep it that way. Do what you're told, keep that mouth shut and we shouldn't have any trouble.'

'Orla!' he shouted, then cleared his throat and swallowed the phlegm with a grunt. A swollen lady with sweat puddles beneath her armpits entered the room.

'Take this one to the room with the old jogini, but get her stink cleaned up first. Can't have her stinking *and* ugly now, can we.'

Orla marched me into a room covered in cracked tiles,

handed me a towel, some pale scrubs and nudged me towards the shower.

'Get all the filth off,' she said, 'but don't waste the water.'

As she plodded back out, I stood staring at the faucet, unable to move, my mind lurching back to the ship and the day the man had come grabbing at me, his meaty sweat and grease bristled beard, the room with the tap and bucket, his eyes watching in the doorway, watching me undress, watching me dab the ice cold water under my arms, watching everything, disgust smeared all over his face. And when I was finished, with wet fabric clinging to my skin, how he had pushed me back into the sour darkness of the bowel room with the blunt ease of flicking away a cigarette stub.

I could hear Orla pacing outside. I stepped out of my rags, slowly turned the shower tap, took a deep breath and stepped under the flow. The current ran warm over my body, honey soothing my aching skin, dislodging layers of grime and sending brown rivers swirling down the sinkhole. As I was changing into the scrubs, Orla thumped back in, grabbed my chin and sniffed me up and down like a slab of meat.

'Good. Much better. Now come.'

She scooped up my old clothes, tossed them into a waste basket and just like that, the last remnants of my old life, my last connection to home, was thrown away. Tears swelled, Shi, but I didn't let them fall. That was a tsunami I knew I wouldn't survive.

I followed Orla down a corridor lined with doors, each the shade of clouds on the brink of bursting, her large frame waddling and wheezing up ahead. At the final door, after fiddling about with a ring of keys, she led me into a sparse room. Two metal bunkbeds stood against the side walls and a neon panel in the ceiling stuttered aggressively, illuminating a tired shrimp coloured carpet that reminded me of the pale flamingos, the frailest ones, who struggled to survive on the outskirts of my lagoon.

'The others are working, they'll be back soon. You sleep there,' said Orla as she pointed to one of the lower bunks, 'I'll bring something to eat later but for now you wait here. We'll get you started tomorrow.'

Before I could even process what she meant, she'd shuffled out of the room, the door locked behind her. The room was bare and cold with a fug of bleach that wafted with each swirl of the ceiling fan and a small, frosted window in the top corner of the back wall let through a dim shading of light. The walls were covered in a crusty psoriasis of salts that had bled through the plaster and a pipework python coiled around their base alike the sensation tightening around my chest. I settled down onto my bed and curled into the foetal position. After so long hunched on the floor of the bowel room, Shi, it felt good to at least have a mattress to rest my bones on.

❖　　　　　　❖　　　　　　❖

To be discarded by the one person holding you together, to be sold by the only person you trusted, how does your brain even begin to process that, Shi? How do you digest a betrayal like that? Whilst I was huddled in the shadowy bowels of the ship, my brain did a remarkable thing. It froze my pain before it could spread, iced it before it obliterated me. Imagine a piece of glass shattering into a thousand fragments, Shi. Now imagine the exact moment of the shatter completely frozen, all those jagged pieces suspended in time and space. Well, it was kind of like that inside my head. All the painful pieces were there but somehow my brain stopped them before they went slicing through me.

Acts of what we consider betrayal happen all the time in the animal kingdom. Take the ants and inga plant of the Amazon rainforest. As the young inga plant struggles to grow on the bustling forest floor, it faces countless herbivores pining for its leaves. To survive, the inga plant recruits the help of ants to protect it from such leaf eaters, letting the ants feed on a sugary nectar it produces at the base of its leaves in exchange. Now this protection-for-nectar arrangement works just fine until the riodinid caterpillar comes along. These caterpillars secrete an even more scrumptious honeydew nectar that is more nutritious and popular amongst the ants. So, in exchange for their honeydew fix, the ants betray the inga plant and grant the caterpillar access to its leaves.

Hunched in the pungent abyss of that vessel, with a sour sweetness curdling the air and clotting in the gut, shame swelled through all the gaps of my body. I was ashamed that I had been so trusting, Shi, ashamed that I had taken Rosh's blithe detachment from his wife and child as something to be admired rather than as a warning sign. Futility dripped from the walls around me and as I slipped in and out of sweaty delirium, the other women entombed there with me began to morph before my eyes. In that sulphuric darkness, each one of them began to appear like cave creatures.

The two young girls by the door became olms, their ribs protruding through their pale saris like the bumped curves of those blind white salamanders. Just as olms have receptors in their skin which can detect minute movements all around them, the girls were highly attuned to everything coming from just beyond that door. I always knew when trouble was due just from watching them. The two women Rosh had sold me with became cave beetles, the one with the lighter sari clinging so tightly to the other she looked like a swollen amber appendage on the other's back. The sobbing lady who rocked back and forth near the crates became a blind characid. Each time she shuffled to the pungent bucket we used as a toilet, her swollen eyes looked just like the deep ruby craters of the ghoul fish.

In appa's encyclopaedia I had always found the cave-dwelling troglobites spectacular in a distinctly unsettling way. Cut off from the rest of the world for millions of years, all sorts of eyeless, colourless creatures have evolved in the cavernous realms. Just like them, we too grew pale and accustomed to the darkness.

shrivelled spider, sobbing wolf

As I lay on the bottom bunk, in the harsh sterility of my new room at Satyan's, I listened to the gurgling of the pipes and imagined they were the sounds of the crocs back home in the lagoon. It almost felt as if I were back there, Shi. I could see the reeds swaying, feel the wet, spiced heat on my brow and taste the salty brine tingling on my tongue. The jangling of keys beyond the door broke the spell. Metal fumbled in the lock, scraped through my insides and seized my bones to attention. Orla's swollen frame appeared and behind her, two women trudged into the room wearing the same pale lime scrubs as me.

'Dinner in an hour.' Orla barked through pickled breath as she locked the door behind her once again.

Neither of the women acknowledged me. They trundled towards the bunks with the same caged creature eyes of the women on the ship, Shi, the same despair clouding their faces and pressing down on their bones. The older woman slumped down on the lower bunk opposite mine with a sigh, slipped off her plimsoles and began massaging the balls of her feet. The grey streaks in her hair glinted under the stuttering neon light like the feathers of a bedraggled old owl. The other woman, with milky skin and a nose that jutted sharply like the snout of an arctic wolf, headed towards my bunk and began to climb the ladder.

'You better not be another fucking snorer.' She scowled without making eye contact, the springs moaning above me as she settled. The three of us lay in silence, the mutual exhaustion swelling and blending with the sweat wafting from the owl's plimsoles, coating the room like rotting chutney.

Doors along the corridor winced and slammed while a metallic clatter made its way closer to our room. Soon enough Orla came thrusting three metal trays on the floor before locking us up once more. The owl and the wolf trudged over from their bunks and quickly devoured the greasy mush, shovelling it into their mouths like they hadn't eaten for days. I stared at my tray, watching the vegetable slop dribbling onto the scraps of staling kebab bread, the oil droplets oozing on the surface like boils.

'Eat. You'll need it, dear.' The owl said, without looking up from her tray. The wolf grunted indignantly between mouthfuls.

I dipped the bread into the stew and began to eat. The grease smothered my gums but at least it was edible, and it was certainly a hell of a lot better than the starchy gloop I was given in the bowels of the ship. That stuff looked like the bacteria-packed film troglobites eat, floating atop cave water like wet tissue, like its very flavour slurped away all other flavours. I would inhale the cinnamon scent from the old crates in the corner as I ate, willing myself to believe it was amma's cinnamon porridge sliding down my throat. It never worked.

The three of us returned to our bunks, sinking back into stale silence as the light slipped away from the frosted window. The springs winced above me before falling still, the sleeping breaths of the wolf filling the air in a slow pant. The older woman lay awake, stone still, staring at the slats of the empty bunk above her. It was reassuring to know someone was on watch. I thought of the hooting owls appa and I used to hear on our strolls, *the soft pulse of the twilight hours.* His voice rustled through my thoughts like the insects in the paddy fields as he explained how a flying owl was the symbol of impending victory for Greek soldiers. Lying in the bunk, in the chokehold of the gurgling python, I wondered what an owl that kept completely still meant.

With darkness still shrouding the window, Orla returned banging on the door, bludgeoning the silence with her fists. The owl and the wolf autopiloted towards her voice so I scrambled up to follow them. As Orla unlocked the door, I glimpsed other lime scrubs shuffling along the corridor, a stream of ashen faced women with eyes anchored to the floor. The owl and the wolf stepped out into the lime current and as I went to join them, Orla stopped me at the threshold.

'Not you, ugly. You stay here.'

Orla grabbed my arm and pulled me down the corridor in the opposite direction to the shuffling lime scrubs.

'Come, lots for you to do here.' She grunted, her fingers twisting into my skin as she dragged me to a supply cupboard and began shoving mops, scrubs and brushes into my arms.

I was put to work cleaning Satyan's place, moving from room to room down the corridor, in and out of the grey cloud doors, always under the watchful gaze of Orla. Each room was a similar barren metallic cell to ours, some with dirtier carpets, some with no frosted window at all. I mopped the floors, collected the trays and changed the sheets, the echoing scent of each of the nameless women still lingering there in the linen. Some sheets were speckled with blood; countless pillows were damp and salted.

Orla watched everything I did, studying how I scrubbed and folded while barking improvements in a tone that always made me flinch. Occasionally men would come down to talk to her, relaying Satyan's demands for 'the Romanian with the big tits' or 'the little blonde with the tight pussy' to be sent to his room when they got back from work.

While cleaning under one of the bathroom sinks, I spotted a tiny spider carcass shrivelled in the corner of its web. I wondered how many times its home had been broken, how many times it had to rebuild and start from scratch before it finally gave up and caved in. As I began to wipe the web away, the carcass rapidly animated and scurried behind the piping. An echo of hope flickered softly somewhere deep within.

I got used to the daily cleaning routine at Satyan's and blended into my surroundings like a cuttlefish, a pale lime shadow drifting from room to room. I scoured away with bitter intensity, until my palms tingled and the porcelain shone in surrender, and I'd lose myself in the motion of the sponge as I traced the shape of my lagoon in soap suds. Palms pressed against the cold tiles, I longed to adopt the survival tactics of the wood frog, Shi. I wished I too could hunker down in a secluded spot and freeze myself, stop my heart from beating, my blood from flowing and only thaw out when the brutal world around me began to warm up.

The nights wheezed on much the same. When the owl and the wolf returned from their shifts, we'd eat the leftover slop we were given and sink into exhausted silence. I found it impossible to sleep. My body writhed in feverish sweats which I tried desperately to suppress so as not to face a snap from the wolf above me. It's a strange thing, fever, feeling hot and cold at the same time, having an internal battle raging inside your own skin. As I shivered away, I felt like I'd brought the warzone with me, stuck between the white hot agony of my past and the bitter bleach reality of my present, neither dead nor alive.

One night as I lay there squirming, Orla came knocking earlier than usual. The owl made no attempt to move but the wolf autopiloted down the bunk towards the door and slipped out without a word. The silence in the room intensified. She returned a little while later, limping across the floor and wincing as she struggled to climb up her bunk.

'Are you ok?' I asked as she trembled up the ladder.

'I'm fine. Quit staring.' She said bluntly, without looking at me. 'You'll never get picked, you'll never know what it's like.'

As she settled down above me, I thought about how arctic wolves survive in their blistering terrain, how they have two thick layers of fur to protect themselves against the frost. They need to stay guarded, Shi, their survival depends on it. In the Arctic Circle, they also live five out of twelve months with no sunlight so they grow accustomed to total darkness, hardened to it.

Orla came banging at the door like clockwork a couple of hours later. The owl stretched and shuffled to the door, the wolf limping just behind her. As they slipped out into the pale lime stream, Orla's voice came barking towards me.

'You too ugly, time for you to do some real work.'

I scurried out and joined the scrubs, the corridor filled with the sound of arms grazing against cheap polyester. No one acknowledged me, Shi, all those caged creature eyes stayed fixated on the floor or stared out into nowhere. The faces began to blur. Sorrow swelled through the lime fog and a sense of gloom curdled thicker as we climbed the stairs.

The van spat me out at a night club where I was put to work cleaning the bathrooms. Sweat and perfume clogged the air and the beat of the music beyond the door was so boisterous it shuddered through my insides and tickled the back of my throat. As my eyes grew accustomed to the dim haze, the scale of the mess became apparent; sodden tissues clumped on the floor like tapeworms, matted hair sludge tangled the sinkholes and vomit crusted the tiles beneath my feet. Inside the cubicles it was even worse. It took a lot of effort not to slip on the urine-soaked ceramics as I went scraping toilet bowls scabbed with faeces and bile, and with my knees sodden, memories of the bucket on the ship came rising up with the stink.

The bucket sat there sloshing in the corner, the rotten stench oozing and squelching in sync with the rocking of the ship. Each visit to it was beyond repulsive, not just the grotesque reek which throttled the air and filled our lungs, but the indignity of it. I tried avoiding it for as long as I could, enduring the pain until my bladder was pinched close to rupture and I had no choice but to squat over the sloshing mess, clenching in sync with the lurching ship, leaking and dribbling for all to see. They gave us nothing for our blood , Shi. Some women tore off chunks of their saris to help soak the bleeding, others just let it trickle down their thighs and pool onto the floor. I remembered seeing the olm girl squat over the bucket, her legs quivering as dark clots plopped onto the surface. The ship lurched, she staggered forward, the bucket tipped over, and the rancid pulp spilled out over her feet, smothering her ankles and seeping between her toes. She started yelping and heavy footsteps plundered towards the door. Hawk eyes appeared and a man grabbed the girl's throat in his hand, slapping her hard across the face to silence her.

'Look what you've fucking done.' He grabbed her by the hair and forced her gaze downwards. 'Look at my fucking shoes, look at what you've done to them, you fucking animal.' He tightened his grasp on her hair. 'You wanna behave like an animal? Huh?' The girl whimpered under his grip. 'Then be an animal and lick it off.' He forced her to the ground, her knees buckling into the oozing brown sludge. 'You heard me, lick it off.'

The trembling girl began to lick the specks off his boots, retching as the waste sloshed around her palms and knees. We all turned away, sinking further into our pockets of darkness as hawk eyes shoved her aside, a reeking mess sobbing into the folds of her sari. They left it there with us, Shi, that vile rot seeping and crusting the floor. It didn't matter how hard you tried to look away, the smell of it forced you to see.

❖   ❖   ❖

After the shift at the nightclub, I was taken to an aggressively lit shop full of twirling chunks of meat. The air sweated with grease, lumps of fat sizzled on the grill and flies milled around a trough of salads paler than my scrubs. A chubby man with forests growing above his knuckles instructed me on my tasks and I set to work scrubbing chip fryers clogged with batter and disinfecting surfaces as the sour grease heat dripped from my brow. The two men guarding the meat skewers kept staring at me as I cleaned, muttering and sniggering in a tongue I didn't recognise. I knew their laughter was directed at my scar though, Shi, disgust doesn't need translation.

I got used to the vile cleaning-go-round, the same routine rolling on day after day. I ploughed on with the work and kept my head down like a lashed and aching mule. Scrubbing and de-clogging became the new dripping-ticking clock hands of my existence and as I toiled, I wondered about where the other women on the ship had ended up. I knew it must have been worse than the lot I was dealt. Sometimes, I'd catch my reflection in a bathroom mirror; a hideous but lucky face stared back. I found myself feeling grateful for the grisly stamp that kept predators at bay.

I knew I had my scar to thank for the fact Satyan never asked for me. The wolf wasn't so lucky. Sometimes she'd be picked several nights in a row, always returning with the same void expression, like her whole body had been sapped of life. One night, after she winced up the ladder, I heard her softly sobbing into her pillow, the bunk frame knocking gently against the wall with each shake of her body.

As she cried, I could once more picture the bowel room door swinging open, the heavy boots striding towards the woman at the back, the way she whimpered and begged him to leave her, gripping the crate as he tried to pull her away. I saw him stomp hard on her hand, heard her shriek like a bobcat, saw him bending down and grabbing her open jaw.

'You don't want to come with me?' He spat a gob of phlegm into her face, the droplets dribbling down her lips into her open mouth. 'Fine, I'll have you right here.'

He unzipped his trousers, parted her legs with his knees, and ploughed into her, impaling her over and over again. I tried so hard to escape it, Shi, scrunching my eyes shut as tight as possible. All I could hear was the crate thumping against the wall as he grunted; all I could see was amma's sequins glistening against the darkness of my eyelids.

With the wolf sobbing away above me, I knew there was no point even attempting to sleep. I focused on the gurgling pipes and stared at the underbelly of the wolf's mattress, tracing the stitched patterns that peeped through the slats like little clouds. I imagined myself lying on the lagoon bank beside Kai in the tropic heat, our shoulders touching as we traced the shapes of cloud tufts drifting up above us. I saw the amber glowing in his eyes as I pointed out creatures nestling in the mangroves, heard his laughter bubbling around us as we strolled through the jungles, his dimples glinting on a sunset picnic down by the beach. Even just the thought of holding his hand made me ache. There was so much I longed to do with him, Shi, so much I feared I'd never get the chance to experience.

'You ok dear?'

I turned to find the owl inspecting me from her bunk. I nodded half-heartedly and watched as she rummaged beneath her pillow. She pulled out a small napkin bundle which she opened out towards me, revealing a selection of colourful sweets as dazzling as a shoal of dragon guppies. I took a cherry and popped it on my tongue, my face contorting as the sour fizzing disco started to unfold. The owl began talking as she chewed.

'Mm, sweet and sour, just like the life of the Devadasi, servant of the gods. All sweet you'd think, the dresses, the jewels, the bangles, the beautiful dancing in the temples. But when you've been fucked raw and bloody by every flabby, crusty pig in town, passed around like a strip of gutka before you're even fourteen, that's when it's pretty sour.'

She looked directly at me, her gaze warm but urgent.

'You should be grateful for your mark, dear, good pig repellent. Better on the outside than in.'

The owl offered the bundle out once more. I selected a pink lace and began to wrap it around my fingers.

'When do I...' I trailed off and wound the lace tighter around my index finger.

'Go on, when what?'

'When do I get to go home?'

'Home?' She laughed, pulling at the strands on her head. 'Do you see these grey hairs dear? I've been here almost twenty years. There is no going home.' She began chewing on another sweet, the sour sugar dusting her lips. 'This is it, dear.'

velvet purr,
paradise bloom

Animals in captivity get bored, Shi. They nap, lounge and snack their way through but without stimulation, monotony comes yawning at their jaws. My days began to blur, the tide of chores broken only by slithers of dream escapism, but largely things rolled on as predictably as a dairy cow's chew. I tried not to think too much about my new reality. I did what I was told, ate my leftovers and stole sleep where I could before the early morning graft. One evening as I was finishing up my bread, Orla entered with an air of urgency. The wolf slid to the edge of her bunk and autopiloted down the ladder.

'Not you.' Orla stopped her and beckoned to me with a fleshy index finger. 'You. Come.'

I rose from my bunk and the owl reached out and gently squeezed my elbow. She didn't have to say anything, the tender strength of that squeeze said it all. I followed Orla out of the room and scurried along after her, following the lazy echo of her flip flops, past the bursting cloud doors and up to Satyan's office. Orla entered and instructed me to wait outside. *Is this how it was going to be? Was this going to be my first experience? Even if I was to find him, would Kai ever want to come near me again?* The door was left ajar, and I could hear a serious discussion unfolding in a tone too muffled to make out. I strained closer, desperate to grasp a few words.

'Impeccable English...might do...hard worker...won't talk...'

The room went quiet and Orla appeared at the door. She pulled me inside and forced me down into a chair opposite Satyan's desk.

'Long time no see, ugly. Better for both of us that way, ey.'

The Kalu Ganga scar quivered at his temple and he hacked up a gob of phlegm which he spat into an ashtray on the desk. I pinched my palms and stared down at the floor.

'You are a lucky girl, we have a special job for you. Oi, look at me when you're being spoken to.'

I raised my eyes and his piercing gaze shrunk me to the size of an Etruscan shrew.

'Something very special for you. Big responsibility. Think you can handle a step up, ugly?'

No clearly wasn't the answer he was looking for so I nodded softly.

'Good. You're very lucky. Not many girls get this chance. *But if you fuck this up for us there'll be big problems, ugly, big problems.* But you won't do that, will you? We'll be watching, no room for mistakes. Just a few hours each morning and you keep your mouth shut. Understood?'

I had no idea what he had in store for me but I knew I had no choice. I kept my eyes on the floor and nodded again.

'Good. Cross me and I promise that cheek of yours will be your best feature.' He chuckled to himself and turned to Orla.

'Right, now get this ugly one out of here and bring me one more to my liking. I've worked myself up a bit of an appetite.'

❖   ❖   ❖

The first morning I arrived at the house on the hill, the air was as crisp as the bronze leaves peppering the pavement. After so long spent scrubbing through the night shifts, Shi, I'd forgotten there was a world beyond the kebab shop kitchens, nightclub toilets and the frosted rectangle in our bunk room. Orla was chewing the gum behind the wheel of the car as I sat in the backseat gazing through the window at the world I'd forgotten existed. Everything was as clear as a salpa maggiore fish: the cerulean ocean up above, the marshmallow tuft clouds, the front gardens teeming with shrubs and petals, the pavements clustered with slices of lava, mango and beetroot that the trees had shaken off. Life swelled beyond the glass.

Orla killed the engine on a quiet street outside a house with an immaculate lawn and wisteria eyelashes that fluttered around huge glass eyes.

'Three hours and you are back in this car. I'll be waiting, not a minute later. Keep your mouth shut and don't mess this up. Now go.'

I opened the car door and took a deep breath. The air was fresh and cooling, like a glass of amma's sweet lime rushing down my throat. I stepped tentatively towards the house, its grandeur swelling the closer I moved into its orbit. My hands quivered as I reached for the doorbell, Satyan's warning ringing around my ears.

The lady who opened the door looked like she'd been cut

from a magazine, and as I stepped inside, I got my first proper look at Evelyn Clarke. She was thin, with high cheekbones and frosty eyes framed by a rigid candyfloss mane of bleached blonde. She wore a violet silk blouse with a cashmere shawl draped around her shoulders and heels that looked incredibly uncomfortable. She studied me for a moment, her frosty blues trying hard not to settle on my scar. Her face had no wrinkles or creases, but it was still easy to tell what she was thinking. You don't have to see judgement to feel it.

'You must be the cleaning girl?' She didn't wait for an answer. 'Right, come along, lots to get through. I'll prepare you a list of duties but a quick petit tour de la maison is the best way to start.'

She began clip clopping ahead in her plum stilettos, talking and pointing without pausing for breath.

'Pristine is the standard we're looking for. I need you finished up by eleven at the latest and I'd like you to focus on certain areas each day. Hallways, landings and bathrooms on Tuesdays, bedrooms and en suites on Wednesdays and lounge, study and morning room on Thursdays. No need for weekends, Michael and I are always entertaining of course and don't worry about the kitchen as our cook takes care of that. Right, let me show you where the equipment is so you can get going on the bathrooms. Pop the supplies back where you found them when you're finished.'

She paused and began fiddling with her pearl necklace. Her nail polish matched the colour of her blouse.

'Oh, and one more thing, I'd like you to keep out of sight when I have company.'

She locked eyes, desperate not to focus on my scar.

'Nothing personal, just the way I prefer it.'

A slight curl flickered across her lips while the rest of her face remained motionless. It seemed smiling was something Evelyn had forgotten how to do. I went over her instructions in my head, Satyan's poison bubbling in the backdrop, *If you fuck this up for us there'll be big problems, ugly, big problems.* I selected a few items from the cleaning store and headed towards one of the bathrooms Evelyn had pointed out.

What a house it was, Shi. I'd never seen anything so grand before; a decadent maze of hard-wood floors and soaring ceilings, fancy ornaments and ritzy furniture pouting from every angle. Thornfield Hall and Pemberley Estate sprung to life around me and a sharp pang of longing quivered up in my gut. Reading those stories in appa's library, I'd always imagined myself scribbling poetry by a roaring hearth or strolling through the grand green tapestry of the gardens. Not once had I imagined myself as a cleaner scurrying about with a bucket and scrubs.

❖　　　　　　❖　　　　　　❖

There was very little colour at Clarke Palace, it was all ivory throws, pastel greys, white sheets and pearly plush. Everything was immaculate, and in all honesty, Shi, I felt conscious that I'd somehow stain the fabrics just by standing nearby, like the very whiff of my skin would spoil them. The towels in the bathroom were the brightest of white, a white as pure as the wave foam that would break and bubble on the shores of Kallady Beach. I inhaled the sea salt soaps on the shelf and imagined I was back home with my toes lodged in the warm sand. The curtains on the hallway windows, with their delicate floral pattern, reminded me of the fabric of amma's best sari and appa would have loved the magnificent grand piano near the staircase. I imagined him poised at the foot pedals, stroking his fingers along the keys with that smile he saved for the best fossils and rainfalls. Wiping the dust frosting from the keys, it was clear no one had been near the piano for quite some time. In fact, the more I saw of all their countless beautiful things, the more I began to feel it was all for show; lifeless items to be admired but not touched. A gallery disguised as a house masquerading as a home.

As the grandfather clock in the hallway crept towards eleven, Evelyn came gliding back in a ripple of neat silk. She seemed satisfied with my work and quickly shooed me out of the house with an envelope that Orla snatched from me as soon as I got into the car.

'You did well then. Satyan will be pleased, might even give you a special treat,' she sniggered, as we pulled away from the house.

I stared out of the window at the whirring pavements and the bustling shop fronts, letting my eyes feast on lives being lived and savoured. Faces blurred and blended together. How I wished they would turn to the car, to see the face of Ravi smiling back or Kai's amber flecked eyes letting me know he was safe and well. Those fleeting moments made my heart yearn all the more.

❖ ❖ ❖

I kept up the pristine standard expected at Clarke Palace and handled every object with the delicacy of a dragonfly wing. I kept out of sight and was largely left to my own devices. When Evelyn went strutting off to her second home at the gym, an uncomfortable quiet came cloaking the house. Some silences are filled with warmth, expectation and the spiced afterglow of laughter, but the silence at Clarke Palace felt cold and empty, like an emotional void had settled deep in its lavish bones.

I would potter around getting on with my jobs, a mere shadow scrubbing about in the cracks of their kingdom. I rarely saw any of the other family members, but one morning, whilst I was doing the bedroom rounds, I crossed paths with the son, who was off sick from school. When I walked in, he turned to look at me, his pupils widening in disbelief as he quickly turned back to his screen. I moved quietly around him, collecting crusty socks, clothing bundles and the confetti of crisp packets that smothered the floor of his fusty den. As I cleaned, the sounds of his game erupted from the screen and with each tap of his controller he sent jets and tanks plundering into enemy bases. Just like that, one tremor of the finger and boom, mission accomplished, problem solved, hero victorious. *Where were the severed limbs, charred flesh and screaming mothers? What of the blood, guts and broken families?* Strange how he seemed so comfortable in his fantasy world of warfare, Shi, yet was unable to bring himself to look at the reality of it etched upon my face.

The resident of the house who enraptured me most went by the name of Leo; he created quite the mess, but I genuinely didn't mind cleaning it. He boasted big lime eyes, chunky butter paws and wore a dazzling marble coat of silver and onyx. One day, as I went to clean the study, I found him sitting on the windowsill staring out into the garden. Did you know, Shi, that when cats purr they are actually healing themselves? The sound is caused by air vibrations in the larynx, which help to strengthen bone and tissue growth. I scratched behind Leo's ears and as his soothing engine whirred up, I felt my own bones begin to heal and a calm settle over me like the hot syrup amma would drizzle over her bibikkan. I sat with him staring out at the squirrels skedaddling along the garden fence, the leaves trembling in the breeze and the sparrows flitting back and forth from their sun dial hangout. He was completely transfixed, thoughts twitching away on his tail. As we sat there staring, I longed to look up the different plants and flowers the Clarkes had growing in the garden, to sit with appa and watch the excitement glaze his face as he identified them. His words came echoing back to me from the day we had spotted the beautiful kadupul bud when out on one of our strolls. He'd leant down in the moist heat and explained how one night the bud would burst open to reveal a palette of paradise, a sweet white supernova soaring just above the soil.

'Same goes for you, La,' he'd said, 'you're a supernova rising. You've just got to grow into yourself; not grow up, but grow in.' he tapped on my heart with his palm. 'The future pigments are all in there right now, bright as can be, just need to keep nourishing them so your star can blossom into its own paradise. And remember, La, like this queen of the night flower, we only find our light in the darkest of hours.'

A pang of sadness lodged in my chest, Shi. Paradise had never felt so far away.

crumpled frog, swaying sycamores

Plato compared our brains to aviaries full of fluttering thought birds and said that in order for those birds to settle, we need to allow ourselves periods of aimless stillness. I really tried, Shi, I tried my best to keep still and calm. Lying in the bunk room I'd stare at the frosted glass window and try to imagine what was happening outside. But it let nothing slip through and looking at nothing in particular made my mind start whirring and my thoughts return to Ravi. I wondered what ceiling he was staring at, what food filled his belly and what thoughts were swirling around his head. I wondered if he'd gotten taller and what things those chocolate eyes of his were seeing. I wondered if he still laughed, still played cricket, if he and Kai would be looking after each other with thoughts of me filling their days. When my imagination lingered too long, jagged thoughts of Tiger Ravi crept in and I wondered if he cried, if he was hurting and what things his hands were being forced to do. I hated being alone in that room, alone with my thoughts because quite frankly, Shi, I feared what my quieter self had to say. I dreaded those moments of isolation and would anxiously wait for the other women to come wafting back in from their vomit-scabbed night shifts. Although we would still sit together in silence, at least it was a silence I could share with others.

The monotony of the routine dripped on as steadily as a dung beetle rolling its faecal ball and each day I hoped to find some form of deviation, something new, no matter how small. One morning, while cleaning the room of the teenage daughter, who I had never seen but had become intimately acquainted with, having spent several weeks picking up her underwear, I found two crumpled paper balls on the floor by her bed. I opened them out. On one was a scribbled poem, lamenting her annoyance at her father's refusal to buy her a new designer dress; it didn't even rhyme and there certainly wouldn't have been a place for it on appa's shelves. On the other was an outline of a frog perched in a puddle.

As I heard Evelyn's voice nearing, I quickly folded the frog and slid it into my back pocket. Once my duties were finished, and Orla had deposited me back in the bunk room, I carefully unfolded the paper and studied the frog's bulging eyes. I held the sketch close up to my face and imagined myself staring at a real life pug-snout by the mangroves, its skin glistening in the dew, the moist heat kissing my brow and the thrum of crickets whirring in the backdrop. For a flicker of a moment, it worked. I was home, Shi, back in my refuge, back on my jackfruit island. I tucked the frog discreetly inside my pillowcase, comforted by the little slice of home I'd discovered in the folds of someone else's trash.

Later that evening, in the window between the cold stew and the night shift, I could feel the owl watching me as I traced my fingers over the picture.

'That a toad?' She said as she sat up on the edge of her bed.

'It's a frog.'

'Same thing, no?'

'They're both amphibians but toads have shorter legs and bumpier skin. They also lay their eggs in long strands instead of a cluster.'

'Well, I've learnt something new today then.'

I felt the urge to keep talking so I handed her the picture.

'Frogs are really interesting creatures,' I said. 'Gastric brooding frogs swallow their eggs and regurgitate them as babies, and many frogs use their eyes to swallow prey. They push their catch down their throat by retracting their eyes into their head, a bit like a rubbish compactor. Gives a whole new meaning to feasting with your eyes. And did you know that hairy frogs can break the bones in their toes and push out claws when things get tense?'

'Now that is useful, I think we could all do with that skill around here.' She replied as she handed me back the picture.

'Do you have a favourite animal?' I asked, as I slipped the frog back under my pillow. I was keen to keep her talking.

'Hmm, I guess I have always liked giraffes.'

'Why giraffes?'

They're just...different...I guess. They can see above the bullshit we have to deal with.'

'Did you know their tongues can grow up to twenty inches long?'

'Is that right?'

'Yeah, the males use those long lickers to taste the urine of females. It's how they know if they're ready to mate.'

Her laughter filled the room just as amma's voice would chime through our hallway calling us all to gather for dinner. My mind drifted home. The scent of nutmeg steam wafting from her watalappam filling my nostrils and teasing my tummy to rumbles, the table brimming with delights and honeyed undu walalu glistening amber on the cooling rack, appa gobbling up coconut-salt aggala balls and pecking away at sugar syrup drizzled aasmi webs, Ravi bouncing around the table practicing his bowling technique, Kai arriving to hugs and welcomes and handing amma the flowers he had bought that afternoon at the market. But these images brought both warmth and sadness, Shi, and so I pulled up the bedsheet over my head, wrapped myself in darkness and waited for Orla to come summoning once more.

The next morning at Clarke Palace, I pocketed a small piece of paper and a pencil from one of the drawers in the study. Back at the bunk room, under the light of the frosted window, I began to sketch what I could remember of the giraffes in appa's encyclopaedia. It wasn't a great drawing, nothing like the drawing of the frog, but it was a pretty decent attempt. I folded it and tucked it carefully under the owl's pillow. Three days later I discovered a small bar of hotel soap tucked under my own pillow. I inhaled the fresh floral scent, sweet and clean like the wild pichcha budding in the breeze back home.

❖   ❖   ❖

In the Mount Everest entry of appa's encyclopaedia, Shi, I had read about a condition called hypoxia, which climbers suffer at high altitudes. The body gets starved of oxygen, the brain swells, vessels leak and you essentially feel like you're choking off into oblivion. You must act immediately. If you don't, you get stuck there and that's why there are so many bodies of climbers still littering the slopes of that famous Himalayan peak. It's hard knowing exactly when you need to act though, Shi. Sometimes you look at things and know that you should do something, but you just keeping thinking it through and before you know it the opportunity has moved on. Other times, impulse kicks in as fast as a spine tailed swift and you just act. That's how it was that Thursday morning at Clarke Palace.

I was busy dusting the piano when Evelyn waltzed past in her gym attire, looking pretty pleased with herself she flashed me a smile as false as the eyes on a lo moth's wings and sauntered off upstairs. It was then I felt it on my face, the breeze, the clean crisp feel of fresh air cutting through the cloying chemicals of the household's scented candle collection. I turned from the piano and noticed she had left the front door open, the solid oak shivering slightly on its hinges. I walked over to close it and stood for a moment on the threshold watching the sycamores swaying and jiving hypnotically in the breeze.

It was then I acted, Shi. There was no time to think, it just happened. I dropped the duster and ran. I ran until my legs burned. I ran until my sides split. I ran and ran and ran until my eyesight blurred and my lungs screeched at me to stop.

beaver teeth, hollow spines

That first night was a terror throttled blur, Shi. I had no idea where I was, what to do or where I should go. I just kept moving, eyes open, feet forward, pacing down the pavements, a confused and aching knot of fear and blisters. I knew my owners would be searching for me, Orla seething and Satyan's Kalu Ganga scar bursting its banks. Each corner I turned came drenched in hot alarm. Hawk noses bulged from faces, passing eyes stared and Orla's hands came snatching at every bend. Slowing down made the terror pinch tighter so I just kept on going; heart thumping, feet throbbing, streets bleeding all things strange.

As darkness swallowed, I limped through the neon intestines of a city swelling louder. I saw it all, Shi; the drinkers spilling out of pubs with foam burp laughter, phlegm throat coughs reverberating through the cold air, the sweaty thump of music seeping from guarded doorways, aftershave-soaked boys with reptilian sniggers, drunks dribbling piss outside shops stacked with bright liquor, mascara smeared faces staggering with dilated pupils and twitching jaws. On and on I stumbled, lost and dazed amidst the gum, smoke and sirens. Passing a shop lined with twirling meats, I froze. It looked just like the one from my cleaning shift but now full of life and with a fug of sizzling fat lurching on to the street with each exhale of the door. *What if the managers recognised me? What if they called Orla? What if one of the other cleaning girls was in there right now?* My head was a tangled labyrinth full of sticky dark tunnels with no escape in sight. Being alone with my thoughts was hard, Shi. Moving helped, forcing my feet down roads full of new distractions, but that still couldn't spare me from the triggers. They always appeared when I'd least expect it, sudden and crippling, trampling my chest like a buffalo stampede.

I kept going, Shi, I kept on walking and running and pacing onwards until I spotted a patch of green beckoning beneath a stuttering lamppost. But it wasn't real nature, the shrubs were stunted, choked with crisp packets and surrounded by little coffins cradling greasy bones; it was nature suffocated, throttled by the city. Still, I needed somewhere to lay low, a place to hide, somewhere to gather my thoughts. So I crawled through the jagged branches, the twigs grazing their hellos across my skin, and settled in amidst the bushes.

When you really miss something, Shi, it's incredible what your imagination can do. The weeds peeped up around me, sprouting like the branches of mini mangroves, and for a slither of a moment, I was back on Kallady Beach, the sea beaming through the lattice of casuarina branches like a jewelled mosaic. In the smell of the soil and the decomposing leaves was the scent of the fishermen's hot skin as they went toiling on the beach. In the amber glow of the hazy lamppost I traced the almond shape of Kai's eyes and in the flecks of broken glass glistening beneath I could see sand sparkling under a scorching papaya sun. I was back in the jungle snood with leopards lounging in steam canopies looped with lime plaits. I saw jewelled sunrises waking Adam's Peak, turtles hatching in golden Bentota sands and the rushing waterfalls of Nuwara Eliya. There inside those bushes, I could smell the damp green earth, feel the humid breath on my brow and hear the birdsong glittering the canopies. I could hear my home calling me, its ancient roots whispering loud and urgent. Problem was, Shi, I had no idea how to get back.

I couldn't hold on to those images, Shi, no matter how hard I tried. The night was bloated with the relentless pulse of prowling engines, bleeping buses and footsteps pounding pavements. The clamour spluttered and wailed, seeped through the branches and flooded my eardrums with the echo of those sobbing fruits from back home. I saw the faces of the homeless who'd huddled under the canopies, the weeping debris clinging to the remnants of their butchered lives. I traced their faces in my mind, remembered the whimpering of those mothers, and although oceans sprawled between us I heard their cries louder than ever, felt their tears stinging salt in my wound.

Nightmares came ravaging my broken sleep; a gigantic full moon dripped from the sky into a sloshing bucket and around it little girls laden with bangles danced in circles, crying and singing, laughing and whimpering. Behind them a lagoon bubbled thick like blood stew, glistening with sequins and peppered with ticking clocks. The moon began shrinking, the bucket overflowing. I crawled towards a row of cricket stumps, the gurgling grew louder, the ticking clocks more urgent, an amber light slipping further and further away.

As darkness softened into dawn, the waking city spluttered to life like a dripping haul of tuna, wriggling and writhing in one big heaving trap. Nestled there in that little fortress of litter strewn leaves, I imagined myself back in my childhood fortress, tucked in appa's study reading Dickens with a hunk of sweet kalu dodol. Dickens was the one who first introduced me to London, Shi, conjuring the fever fog of the city to life with atmospheric flourish. But no amount of Dickens could have prepared me for the bleak-twist-cold-carol reality that came biting beyond the page.

Two sparrows came pecking for crumbs near the bush and a phrase from appa's encyclopaedia pecked at my cortex. *Though sparrows are not water birds, they have been observed swimming underwater to evade predators.* I told myself I was doing just the same, head under water, holding my breath, surviving. Stomach pains came pinching harder and I knew I had to leave my shelter to seek some crumbs of my own, and so I walked on, pressing my blistered soles forward in search of morsels.

This is how I came to exist, Shi. Hours crawled into days and days into weeks, as I became a wandering stray drifting between doorways, hiding in alleyways and scampering between rubbish-choked bins. As the walls around me fell away, the walls within me mounted new heights. Some people stopped to give me coins, a sandwich or hot tea; I think my cheek helped stir some pity but largely I got by alone, scavenging what I could from the bags left outside restaurants and supermarkets.

I collected up empty boxes and used the cardboard to give me a little coverage at night, and as the darkness descended, and the neon came flashing, I'd crawl into my den like the bulbuls that crafted nests in the kumbuk trees or the hermit crabs who go moving into the shells of whelks, periwinkles and moon snails to protect their fragile exoskeletons. But Bulbul nests are shared, Shi, and hermit crabs aren't really hermits at all because they live in large groups. I, on the other hand, was completely alone, lost in a different jungle on the other side of the world.

On tougher days, I would wander the streets and picture myself as a Caribou traversing snowscapes in Canada, or as a Chiru antelope crossing the harsh Tibetan Plateau. I thought of how far they had to travel in search of food, of all the threats they faced from predators, of how much their hooves must have throbbed and stung.

When dragonflies migrate, Shi, they follow the rains. They take advantage of shifting weather patterns, gliding on wind currents, swaying from the monsoon rains in Asia to the downpours in Africa and back again for the next monsoon. When the rain came drenching the London streets I imagined them gliding through the droplets, flitting past my earlobes, wings glistening in the water haze. I would stroll with my face to the sky and let the droplets pummel me. When you are already crumpled, it feels right to be sodden too. When I listened close enough, beyond the flitting of the dragonfly wings, I could hear appa's symphony. The lashing curtains of water, heavy droplets plunging from gutters and the sloshing of car tyres. Rain puts on quite a show for those who have nowhere to be.

One day, as I strolled aimlessly through the rain, I stumbled upon a sanctuary of pocket fields with all sorts of sprawling wild thickets to hide in. With each step in that park, a calmness came seeping through me like sweet Ceylon tea and the boa around my chest began to loosen its grip. I watched dogs frolicking across the grass carpets, carp gliding ellipses in the fountain and a deer herd grazing under ancient trunks. I went peeping at mallards bickering on the honey green lake, shield bugs hiking over fallen leaves and squirrels burying their nuts amidst the mulch. You know, Shi, squirrels forget where they bury most of their stash, so inadvertently go planting countless trees. I've always liked that idea; thriving green havens found rising from what is lost, squirrels one day climbing the breathing pillars that sprouted from the gaps in their memory. Forgetting can be a beautiful luxury.

Under the drapes of dusk, when the night sky had slurped away the light and digested the day into its black velvet gut, I'd venture up to the building set like a milky blue topaz atop the sprawling green. I would wander around its base as the city glimmered in the distance like lightening bugs, my footsteps echoing in the cool dark, before making my way back down the blanket of green to lay beneath the foliage of a large oak tree.

Crawling up close to the gigantic trunk, I'd tuck my cardboard bedding between her roots and stare up at the swaying branches, the leaves quivering in the blue dark. It was easier to breathe beneath that tree, like her leaves were inhaling and sharing the burden of my pain, the roots soothing my aching body. I gripped her beneath my palms, feeling how deep she ran into the earth, reassured that the wind could move her branches all it wanted but it'd never shake her roots. I listened to her creaking limbs and traced her bark beneath my fingertips, admiring the scars worn so gracefully in the quiet wash of moonlight. Cradled in the arms of my beautiful friend, I wondered what appa would have thought if he could have seen me. It hurt to imagine his eyes settling on the dishevelled stray that I'd become. He expected a blossoming flower, a supernova rising, not a grubby bag of bones scavenging between bins and bushes.

I loved sheltering under my oak when it rained. I inhaled the downpour, letting it cleanse and stroke me drip by drip. It felt like I was part of that rain, Shi, like the droplets were plunging into the ocean inside my own skin. Back by my lagoon, I'd always wondered what a downpour felt like to the ras, barbs and killifish swimming near the surface. Given fish are about the same density as water, the vibrations most likely pass right through them. Sitting beneath the oak, full of the pouring sky, I was starting to understand the feeling.

When the birdsong came pouring with the dawn, I watched a glistening haze of gnats emerge in the sunlight, spiralling in delicate tufts around the decaying leaves. I thought of the new life they'd convert those dead leaves to and the breakfast snacks they'd provide for the rumbling bellies of beetles and birds. I'd sit and trace the patterns on my guardian tree, the way each branch from trunk to tip was a perfect copy of the one that came before it. I started to notice the same repeating patterns all over the park, on the spirals of pinecones, the veins of leaves and seedlings; each organism a canvas of smaller and smaller copies of itself. I liked uncovering the subtle symmetry, grounding myself in the enduring order nestled in the disorder.

Sadly though, Shi, just as the female mayfly gets a mere five minutes to grace this earth, my recharge in that park was cut far too short.

'Excuse me ma'am.'

The voice came startling me from behind. I swivelled around to find two police officers staring right at me. The boa tightened its grip around my chest. The uniforms, the boots, the batons; familiar dread went surging through my bones. They eyed me up and down and the female officer began to speak again.

'Ma'am, where are you staying at the moment?'

The boa coiled tighter, squeezing the last fragments of air from my lungs. *Would they lock me up? Bundle me in another van? Take me back to my owners?*

'Ma'am, can you understand me? Do you speak any English?'

Sharp flashes filled my head; the soldier boots at the checkpoints, the stamping in the hallway, Satyan's glinting eyes.

And so I ran, Shi. I ran and ran until their voices faded like smoke bush petals behind me.

❖ ❖ ❖

The fear of those uniforms had polluted things. They'd seen my face and I figured they'd come looking again meaning my park sanctuary was now off limits. So, I sunk back into the grooves of the concrete labyrinth and slowly began to adopt the habits of a beaver. Shifting between alcoves, I collected all the spare materials I could source and clustered them into my own little transportable dam against the world. Just as beavers boast self-sharpening teeth, my instincts sharpened amidst the nightly torment of drunks. Just as beavers have transparent eyelids that act as swimming goggles, and ears and nostrils that shut automatically underwater, I learnt to shut out the foul smells and sounds of the streets and keep my eyes constantly open. I embraced the jagged edges of my scar above all else. It was the core of what I was to the world, gnawing and steering me through the pity scavenge.

I found an alleyway behind a chip shop which I decided to make my temporary home. It wasn't visible from the main street and I could always find a decent supply of leftovers in the alleyway bins. But I wasn't there on my own. Besides the rats, a leash of foxes would come by each night, snooping for scraps in a whir of elegant snouts and bushy fire tails. With the city cloaked in darkness, my enchantment deepened in the silence. I began sharing my morsels with the vixen and her two cubs, and gradually their caution softened. Before long, the cubs were gekkering close by, the vixen inspecting me less intensely as they chewed. Scorned as a nuisance, foxes are far more interesting than people give them credit for, Shi. They can run up to forty miles an hour, use the earth's magnetic field to hunt prey and are the only member of the dog family which can retract their claws like cats. The vixen was entrancing, with eyes that looked right through me, dark and fizzing, full of my past. Those eyes knew. My consistency soothed her and I was careful not to make any sudden movements. It was comforting to have a bond based around focused stillness, and with the darkness still raging inside my own head, such stillness was an oasis for me.

But all things change, Shi, I had grown used to that. When the foxes moved on my loneliness began to swell once more. The darkness festered and the demons came clotting crimson in my mind. On the nights when my thoughts grew too intense,

I'd wander off and perch on a wall that overlooked an overgrown patch of rubble. I'd stare down at the tangle of weeds, litter and discarded scrap metal, marvelling at how nature could thrive in such conditions and endure our human folly.

It was there I spotted Rambu grunting his way through the pockets of decaying leaves, small and prickly like the rambutan stacks sold on the roadsides back home. I'd watch intently as he'd go about his business, doddering along, scouring for juicy slugs, completely immersed in his own little world, no place to call his home and not a care in the world beyond the moment to moment scuttling for his supper. Hedgehogs are fascinating creatures, Shi, they have not seventy, not seven hundred but up to seven thousand spines on their backs that are controlled by a network of muscles. Their quills are mostly hollow, comprised of a series of complex air chambers which make them light, but strong. Amazingly, they are actually born with these spikes. How does amma hedgehog cope with such a birth, I hear you ask, Shi? Well, the baby hog's skin is inflated with fluid so the prickles are kept beneath the surface. After birth, the fluid is then reabsorbed and the spines emerge in all their glory. Born ready to ward off threats, talk about a creature well adapted to our world.

It was there, sitting on that wall and admiring little Rambu, one crisp and still evening, that Joe Chops came trundling into my life.

Wonder Worms, Jeroba Ears

Many animals choose to live alone, Shi, snow leopards, skunks, polar bears, lionfish, orangutans, moles, you name it. But it's different when the solitary life chooses you. Isolation seeps into your soul, hardens into an armour and relying on no one but yourself stirs a caution and a strength that keeps you going, grounded, alive. When you have no one and live nowhere but within the maze of your own thoughts, contact with others starts to become pretty bewildering.

When I first saw Joe Chops he was picking up cigarette butts amidst the tangle beneath my lookout on the wall. He would pick each one up, inspect it closely and then drop it into the tin he was holding; a brown hooded creature hunting amidst the rubbish.

'Enjoying the show are ya?'

His voice made me jolt and I gripped the wall tightly to steady myself.

'I've seen ya here a few nights now,' he said as he continued picking through the rubble without looking up, 'oughta be more careful you know, fall and you'll do yaself some real damage from that height.'

He stooped to collect a handful of butts and in the pale light I could make out the dirt lodged thick in his palm creases.

'What exactly ya come looking for down ere then?'

I clenched my jaw, my mind quickly working through the best escape route.

'All eyes and no lip ey?' He looked up towards me, his face blistered, his eyes glistening green as an eclectus parrot.

'Oof, that's quite the scar ya got there. Is it a fresh one?'

I shook my head slowly. Pulling words up my throat felt like trying to drag a chewed leaf stem back up a giraffe's neck. I honestly couldn't remember the last time I had spoken to anyone, Shi.

'Ya hungry?' He began scrambling around in his pockets, cigarette chunks spilling from his tin. 'Silly question, course ya are,' he said as he pulled out a shiny purple wrapper and offered it up towards me. 'Here. Was saving it for later but reckon ya could use it more than me. D'ya like Freddos? More of a Twirl man myself but beggars can't be choosers ey.'

I still couldn't form any words or bring myself to move. I just stared, my whole body tensed like a huntsman spider. He shook the wrapper in his outstretched arm and grinned, his chipped teeth the same colour as his hoody.

'Tell ya what, how about we share it? Hungry work, this. Mind if I come up and join ya for a minute?' Without waiting for an answer, he offered up his tin towards me. 'Here take this while I scale this fucking thing.'

I placed the tin gently on the wall while he scrambled and heaved his way up beside me.

'Jeez Louise, this body aint what it used to be, I tell ya. I used to jump and climb these walls like a ninja, parkour and all, now look at me.'

He unwrapped the purple bar and snapped it in two, popping one half in his mouth and handing the rest to me. The chocolate caught whispers of streetlight and glistened in its shiny folded case. I began to nibble.

'Oof, I swear nothing beats chocolate sometimes. Hits ya where ya didn't know ya needed it. Nothing like a good Twirl or a Ripple dunked in a cuppa. Flake's a good'un too but halfa it crumbles off before it even bloody reaches ya mouth.'

He paused to look at me, one eye lingering a little too long on my scar.

'What ya been looking at down ere anyway, am I missing something?'

I scanned the tangled weeds in search of Rambu. No movement, not a whisper.

'Not much of a talker ey? Good on ya to be honest, better safe than sorry, don't know whose lurking round these corners. Streets are full of snakes, paedos and crazies these days. Still, there are some good folk, armed with good stories and snacks. I'm Joe, by the way, but everyone calls me Chops.'

I heard a rustling below and caught a glimpse of Rambu scuttling away. I pointed towards the movement and Joe's eyes followed my finger.

'Ah, fan of the night crawlers ey? Well, ya oughta come see my patch over by the park benches, plenty of birds and scuttlin' things down there, much more than this old heap.'

I gripped the wall a little tighter. He noticed.

'Don't worry, no funny business. Ya right to have your

back up but its strength in numbers out here, worth sticking together, warmth, safety and all that. Especially for youse ladies. Only me and a couple of pals down by the benches, Boudi's a sweetheart and Archie's a charming old nut. Should consider it. We're all good as gold, trust.'

That last word stung hard and Rosh's face flashed through my mind.

'Ey, no pressure, but the offer is there. We got some flasks of tea so ya more than welcome to come share. No harm in popping by to say hello, to the park creatures at the least.'

I continued nibbling at the chocolate, my taste buds jumping with sugary delight.

'Ya tried your luck at the chippie on the high road yet? Owner's a lovely bloke, always hooks me up with a free bag. That's why they call me chops, gift of the gab with the chippie owners. Ya see, it's my little superpower. Ever had scratchings? Crispy burnt bits covered in salt and vinny; oof, perfect when the cold comes creeping.'

Unfazed by my silence Joe sat sorting through his cigarette collection as he explained how he used to be 'the best bloody salesman' in a phone shop which went bust and how, after his flatmate had skipped town, his side hustles weren't enough to cover rent so he was forced out onto the street. My instincts stayed alert, Shi, but I have to say that it was nice to hear someone's voice again. It had been so long since someone had stopped to talk to me that I'd forgotten how much I missed the music of a story.

I'm not sure why I decided to follow him back to the park benches that night. I didn't let myself trust him, I'd learnt my lesson, but I also didn't not trust him, if that makes sense. I suppose I was beyond trust and care altogether. *Skunks are solitary creatures except sometimes they'll tolerate the company of others nestled for warmth in dens as a group.* So, once Joe had talked his throat dry, we slid off the wall and trundled through the streets to collect my sleeping clutter. Joe nabbed us some scratchings from a chip shop and with hot salt glistening from his lips, he nattered us all the way back to his patch on the fringes of a little park where two figures sat hunched in a bundle of sleeping bags and cardboard. Now they may have huddled by the bushes, Shi, but they certainly didn't beat around them. Before I'd even put my stuff down, a red-haired lady, with scabs on her nose that matched the colour of her hair, jumped to her feet and stared at me.

'Wowee, I'd love a scar like that. Let's 'ave a look, bet you make a killin.'

The elderly chap next to her, rocking back and forth cradling a bean can, began nodding in agreement. I smiled nervously as Joe stepped in.

'Now now, a little more respect for our new pal, what's her name.' Joe searched my face with his greens.

'Artemila.' I squeezed the word out in a squeaked echo. I hadn't told anyone my name in so long, Shi, that it tasted foreign on my tongue, like a stranger from another lifetime.

'She speaks!' Joe patted me affectionately on the back. 'Artemila, that's a good'un. I like it.'

He plonked his tin down, poured some tea from a flask and handed me a cup. I cradled it, letting the steam rise and tickle the hairs in my nostrils.

'Now where the fuck are my manners. Let me introduce ya Artemila. This gem here is Boudi,' he said as he squeezed the shoulder of the red-haired lady, 'Got her name cus she burnt down the cake shop she worked in after her prick boss tried sticking his hand down her skirt. Shame ya didn't have a chariot to ride through the flames ey, Bou.'

'Nah, just a shame he wasn't in when I lit it.' She chuckled to herself whilst munching on a biscuit, her sunken cheeks sloping further inwards with every bite.

Joe nodded towards the elderly chap rocking and smiling beside her.

'And this gent here's Archie, or Sir Archibald as he likes to be called. Look at that face, have ya ever seen someone glow so much in the gutters? If I could be half as handsome as this rugged fella in my old age, I'd be a lucky fucker.'

Archie grinned and tipped an invisible hat. He wore a tired blazer caked in grime but it was smart, a shredded echo of something once dapper, refined even. He began to rock faster, drumming his fingers on the bean can as he chanted.

'Glory BEAN to the Father, the Son, the Holy Toast. As it was in the beginning, is now and ever shall BEAN, Heinz without end! Om Mani Padme Hum! Hail to the BEAN of the lotus! Wa alaikum salaam! And peace BEAN on you too! Mitti me savva-bhúesu, veram mejjha na kenavi. May I have a friendship with all BEANS and enemy with none!'

'Bless him,' Joe whispered to me, 'not quite all there our Archie. Used to be some sorta genius professor back in Albania but started to lose it when he lost his family. As if that weren't enough, some racist geezer bashed his brains in with a brick one night cos of a problem with a takeaway order. Poor Arch, that really fucked him good. We found him under Hornsey Bridge, piss on legs, raki in hands, shouting Arch-ee-lay at the top of his lungs.'

Archie caught the whisper of Joe's voice and turned to chime in.

'Arch-ee-lay, Arch-ee-lay, Arch-ee-lay.'

'Yes Arch, that's it. Oh, reminds me, I got more lining for ya chamber of fly secrets.'

Joe unfolded a scrap of paper from his pocket and handed it to Archie.

'If ya ever see any dead flies about, send em Archie's way, makes his day. He's got a collection.'

Archie took out a shoe box from under his blanket, held it to his lips and began to hum. 'Black pearls, my pretties. My dark winged gritties. Things you've seen. Places you've been. Hush, hush, my travelling jewelled. Your secrets are safe with Sir Archibald.'

I was still very much on edge, Shi, don't get me wrong, but there was a comforting jolliness that hugged the curves of Archie's mannerisms. Being around humans again was going to take some getting used to but Archie's mumbling helped. He was like an old toy that still sputters fading chuckles when you squeeze its tum, reigniting a warmth lodged deep in the bones of your memory.

As Archie carried on humming to himself I settled my cardboard into place beside the bench and curled up in my sleeping bag. Boudi and Joe went on talking. I heard them but I wasn't really listening, like when you read a book and realise several sentences down that you have no recollection of what you just read. You follow the words but your brain is on autopilot, floating off elsewhere in the chambers of your mind, teetering in its own little void. I nibbled on the biscuits they shared and focused instead on scanning the surroundings for glimpses of the better kingdom.

It was a tiny park, more of a lawn really with a few trees and bushes lining the edges. I narrowed my eyeline and waited. Sure enough, beside the bench, I spotted an earthworm wriggling around in the soil. I watched it writhing and slinking, peach wet against the darkness, scouring for its mulch leaf supper. They might be seen as gross, Shi, but earthworms are mighty important guardians of the ecosystem. They help water flow down to the roots by making tunnels and breaking up thatch, they gobble up harmful parasites and they fertilise soil with their nutrient rich poop castings. It's no wonder Aristotle called them the intestines of the earth. Funny, how quick we are to judge those enriching the ground beneath us simply because they're mired in the dirt. I guess, Shi, that the most special often don't look that special at all.

As Joe's snoring began to rumble around us and with Archie mumbling on in the shadows, I watched Boudi fiddling about with a spoon and a lighter; a brown puddling bubbling up in the bowl of the spoon. She tightened a belt around her arm, took out a syringe, sucked up the muddy puddle and then plunged the tip into her arm. Her eyes rolled back, her arms fell limp and she slumped down on to her grubby floral bedding.

Archie rocked on, spiralling gusts of nonsense up into the darkness. It was reassuring to hear his voice, to know someone was around and on watch. But I wasn't going to rely on anyone else, Shi, my instincts were the only ones to be trusted. My ears stayed pricked like a jerboa, my nose poised like a bloodhound and my eyes wide like a tarsier through the night. Still, I sensed I'd found a suitable refuge for a while.

starling murmur, jungle fever

Chips and walking, those were the core pillars of my time with my three new acquaintances. Archie usually stayed put at the park benches but Joe and Boudi took me traipsing everywhere, pacing the pavements and collecting scraps and coins till our soles ached. I rarely joined in with their conversations, but it felt nice to be part of a group. I'd never had that before, Shi.

We got the odd hot meal at the day centre, if we were lucky, and occasionally a coffee shop would allow Joe and Boudi to use their toilet to wash. I never followed them in. Through the window I saw how the customers winced and stared at them like a circus audience gawping at show creatures. I really wanted to wash my grime-caked skin, Shi, but not as much as I wanted to avoid those eyes.

Whenever we reached a supermarket or a tube station, we'd sit down with our tins opened up before us, hoping for some passing charity. My cheek definitely helped with the coin flow, but I never made eye contact or 'shook my stunner scar' as Boudi kept telling me to. Instead, I'd zone out, staring at the blurred layers of legs shuffling past like a herd of antelopes traipsing across a grey savannah.

Joe, on the other hand, had very much refined his attention-grabbing technique. He'd dish out compliments tailored to each passer-by and write motivational quotes on cardboard scraps. With whatever landed in our tins, Joe and I would then trundle off to get more chips, or sausage rolls, or cups of tea. Boudi would always pocket her coins and tell us she was heading off to see a friend. Later on, when she returned to the park, she'd be sporting a fresh set of bruises, a wide grin and vacant eyes. There was an emptiness that seemed to fill her, or a fullness that emptied her, I couldn't be sure. On the evenings she wasn't injecting, I'd watch her picking at her scabs and scratching at the skin around her nails, tearing it raw and bloody. As the bitterest of nights crept in, I'd watch her hugging her knees, scratching and staring away at her breath dissipating into the darkness in front of her. It felt like I was watching trauma win; it was feasting on her carcass and whispering that I'd be next.

❖ ❖ ❖

Day and night blended into each other like anglerfish and the seasons came and went. Some police picked on us, others left us be. Some people taunted us, most stuck to pretending we didn't exist. Under countless moons, I propped my carboard by the benches and listened on the outskirts of conversations about the places the trio longed to see and the people they felt they could have been. I was grateful they accepted my role as a silent observer, never prying, never pushing me for more. Perhaps they didn't really care, Shi.

Yet, as reliably as Archie's beans and Boudi's bruises, those bench chats would always end up in the very same place with everyone wallowing in the sepia syrup-soaked sketches of their younger years. Joe's eyes would glaze warmly as he'd recount his tales of cheek and blunder with the lads and when Boudi wasn't as high as a griffon vulture, or as low as a Brewer's mole, she'd gush about her days in the bakery workshop mastering the perfect batter and buttercream spreads. Archie would slip into tender recollections of his childhood spent eating hot spinach and cheese byrek in his grandma's kitchen or of chasing frogs in the fields out back. The good old days were always there for them, a warm and welcoming refuge where they could rest their head and fill their tums, away from a present that wasn't so generous. I hadn't realised, Shi, that comfort could create such pain, that warmth could conjure such cold, that doom could cast such beautiful shadows. The hunger to go back to my lagoon, to appa's study and amma's spices grew stronger. My yearning to hear Ravi talk about cricket and to share stories of mantis shrimps with Kai grew fiercer. My heart ached for my island, Shi, while my bones throbbed constantly from the unforgiving cold and concrete.

One evening, on a routine stroll down memory lane, a cluster of starlings came darting and swaying in a murmuration above our benches. The conversation fell silent and we all sat mesmerised as the birds weaved, dipped, soared and drifted, beautifully untamed but orchestrated, chaotic yet ordered. Archie drummed on his can of beer excitedly as the murmur ebbed and flowed through the deep blue dusk. It felt like a reflection of us, Shi, for just as starlings sway hypnotically together to thwart peregrine falcons from targeting one bird, so there was a safety in our bench cluster. Starlings group to keep warm and exchange info on feeding areas, just as we clumped our sleeping bags together and listened to Joe's plans for the next deli bin raids. And, as we huddled by the benches with tea and scraps, there was an energy to our group which swelled beyond what any single member was offering, a pulse which kept us going through the bleakest of nights.

Though there was no magic carpet to cushion us, I know Ash would have fitted right in. I saw her in Joe's green eyes and heard her in Archie's tall tales. As I stirred between shards of broken sleep, I imagined her sitting there, weaving her necklaces, chuckling away to herself and scratching her birthmark intermittently. Some nights it felt like she was right there next to me, breathing on my skin as she hummed a Bhajan tune and walked her fingers across her open palm, mimicking little legs. At first I didn't understand but over time her seed lodged deeper in my head, a seed juicier than those pomegranate gems we'd gobbled together by Mr Ananda's stall. I knew I had to keep going, Shi, I had to make those steps forward and move on.

❖ ❖ ❖

As the oak leaves of autumn came falling again, they cascaded with a rash of red blisters pimpling their surface. They were a sore sight to look at and so was I, Shi. The rot and damp of the streets had seeped into my skin and mingled with my own congealing scent. I wore the pavements as much as they wore me and I took whatever slim pickings I could gather from the bags left outside charity shops. I convinced myself it was natural, that I was camouflaging with the streets just like a sloth, sweat and dirt cloaking my skin like the algae that brimmed from their fur. Every now and then I'd catch a glimpse of myself in the reflection of a shop window and barely recognise the wasting, grime-caked girl who stared back.

The test for self-awareness in animals involves marking creatures with a dot and seeing if they notice it in the reflection of a mirror. Orcas, dolphins, pigeons, magpies and apes have all noticed the dot and passed the test. Catching my own dire reflection in those windows, I don't know if I'd have passed. If Satyan and Orla were still looking for me, they'd sure as hell have struggled to spot me. I guess that was something.

Just as spangle gall blighted those autumn leaves, a rot crept into our group too. Our simple days of existing and lamenting soured and a rash began to itch in my soul. Boudi failed to return from one of her sourcing trips and Joe and Archie shrugged off her absence, convincing themselves she'd be back with fresh biscuits and bruises at any moment. But the days crawled into weeks and there was no sign of her. Archie and Joe began drinking even more, spiralling further into their pit of liquor and vinegar. I knew I could stay scraping through the days on sterling pity and copper coin insults with them but I couldn't shake that itch inside me; the niggling impulse to keep going.

So, I scratched the itch, Shi.

One night as the pair drifted off to sleep, with Joe's snoring rumbling as thick as amma's custard, I snuck off into the darkness. I've always hated goodbyes, not that I'd had many chances for them, and reaching the park gate I paused to take one last glance. They looked peaceful, their chests rising and falling like one huge snoozing nylon creature. As an ambulance whipped its wailing lasso through the crisp air, I began to walk, a lone wolf slinking off into the grey unknown.

❖ ❖ ❖

I wandered all over the place, Shi, a Peri stray reincarnate. My blisters hardened into callouses and my skin toughened with my resolve to keep moving. My cheek helped secure a pity sandwich or doughnut here and there and I aligned my rests near pubs at closing time to greet a steady surge of coins from the tipsy stumblers. I'd lay my sleeping bag down like a magic carpet, keeping my eyes focused on the mini mangroves peeping between the pavement cracks, imagining Ash and golden paws beside me, my coin tin a coconut husk teeming with marigold petals.

The world I encountered blurred and blended and when the darkness began to curdle in my gut, I would close my eyes and imagine appa whispering to me, peppermint toffee echoing on his breath, light cedarwood lacing the air. He'd point across the river: *'You see that obelisk over there La, they call it Cleopatra's Needle. There's a time capsule buried underneath it. Daily newspapers, fine cigars, and pictures of the twelve English beauties of the day all nestling there since 1878. Shall we go digging, La?'* By the Trafalgar Lion, he'd smile up at the sky: *'Look up, La, do you see Nelson's column? Just before its completion in 1842, the fourteen stone masons who built it did something pretty whacky. Go on, take a guess. Salute? Cheer? Sing? Even better, the fourteen fellows climbed up the seventeen-foot column and had dinner on the top. The great Banquet of Trafalgar.'* As I rested on the steps of the Piccadilly Circus fountain, he would chuckle away next to me: *'Piccadilly is a funny name, isn't it? Silly taste on the tongue. Apparently, it comes from a popular stiff collar, a piccadill, made by a tailor who lived in the area. Everyone flocked here to get their fine collars and the name stuck faster than one of ol' Anteros's arrows up above us.'*

Yet no matter how hard I pushed my imagination, I felt the absence of him aching louder than anything. I was filthy and alone, my skin covered with hives, my soul itching to get home.

With my mind stuck on Lanka, my feet went wandering into a different kind of jungle. The heaving bustle of colour and rhythm was overwhelming at first, but I soon found a comfort in those winding arteries and musty stable caves. Weaving my days through a simmering labyrinth of wares, flavours and traders, I once more felt the fever of the Batti fruit market folding its arms around me.

It was blissfully easy to lose yourself in there, Shi, and I found my face could slip by almost unnoticed. I still got my fair share of gawping stares, of course, but in there I was just one of many oddball ingredients, one thread in a splendid tapestry of weird. Each trader, each stall, each artery of that whole jungle market is etched in my brain with such detail that I can still meander through it in my daydreams. People of all different shapes, shades and scars existing together in chaotic symbiosis. Gossip scattering like seeds, hawkers squawking from polyester canopies and sweet cash pollen drifting from stall to stall. Melting into that shuddering maze, hidden smoother than a jungle cat, I began to observe the trader creatures clustered around its bends.

There was a lady who wore chunky gold rings and made delicious rotis. She called everyone 'sweet lime' and strutted like a bright Lankan junglefowl. One afternoon when she caught me watching her, she strutted over, shared a smile as vibrant as her feathers and handed me a roti filled with hot, sour chutney. My tastebuds danced back to Batti. The juice boys reminded me of toque macaques. They bounced around with floppy hair and pink faces as they squeezed plump oranges, bellowing 'Jugo de naranja fresco! Tan fresco! Ven rápido!' to all who passed. One morning, before the market shook to life, I found a freshly poured cup of juice in my watching alcove, beaming there like liquid carnelian. As I gulped it down, I felt the sunshine of home soaking and tingling down my throat. The owner of the record shop had slow loris eyes as big as the vinyl's pinned behind his till and he was always doused in musk aftershave. The musk deer secretes a distinctive odour from a gland that looks like a scrotum, Shi, and coincidentally the shop owner's loose neck skin looked just the same. The lady who ran the cake shop had a toddler who was desperate to help so she'd set up teddy customers for her to practice serving. It reminded me of the way meerkats teach their pups to hunt, bringing them dead scorpions to practice on before they grow mature enough to handle the live ones. Near the meerkat mum, a chubby man in a beret would sing songs while hunched over his ring collection, songs I'd later hear customers humming on the other side of the market. It reminded me of how humpback whales spread their melodies to be repeated by other whales far across the ocean. The crepe maker would often be singing those very same songs amidst the warm chocolaty banana clouds wafting from his stall. With his dangling beard plait and tactic of reeling in customers with sheer volume, he reminded me of the white bellbird.

There was no shortage of material to play with, Shi, problem was it just wasn't the same playing it without Ash. Yet there, deep in the bustling belly of Camden market, I found my safe haven. Past the beats and the colours, the woks and crowds, I'd slip down into the caves of the lower stables and escape to the secret universe of Cas's bookshop.

sipping gazelles, wounded horses

You know that distinctive old book smell, Shi? That musty, antique splendour that floods your nostrils and tickles the water from your eyes? Well, Shi, turns out there is a name for it; it's called bibliosmia. Inhaling the warm wood spice that rises rich from a page, I've often wondered what it is we enjoy so much about the scent. Maybe it's the permanence, the prospect of sweet and sour escapism or the whiff of adventure ahead. The reason old books in particular smell so nice is due to the breakdown of cellulose and lignin in the paper. As they break down, they release organic compounds that smell like vanilla, almond and flowers; a hint of amma's baking, a whiff of the petals near Peri's shelter, a slice of home.

Cas's shop was soaked with it. It was floor to ceiling of eclectic spines, soaring piles of paperbacks shrouding the floor into a tiptoeing maze. The shelves whispered, treasured tomes snored thick as buffalo curd and crumbling first editions muttered through dust stubble mouths. Atlases fizzed with bright eyes, encyclopaedias yawned in their jackets and memoirs slumped into one another like falling dominos. It had a flavour so thick you could taste it, spiced with possibility, full of escape routes spiralling off like pathways in a forest, teeming with the sense you could go anywhere, do anything, be anyone.

Like the long grass back home, the spines were alight with chatter. Anthologies sang softly in the corners, biographies babbled in their boxes and fiction classics nattered sweet and smooth as mango lassi. Insight swirled and danced in the shards of light and the floorboards sighed with each step I took deeper into that forest of reworked trees.

Books teemed all over the place; propping up lamps, under chair legs and the table beneath the till wasn't so much a table but rather several piles of hardbacks clustered together in a vague rectangle. I've always loved the way books stack together side by side, their very contours made to support each other like the sprawling roots of their ancestors. Above all their heads, a clock tocked lethargic breaths and a radio crackled softly somewhere amidst the glorious mess. Appa would have loved it.

On my first venture in, I was knocked back by the flood of memories. Nostalgia oozed from all the crevices, paper arms folded in and cradled me back to appa's study. I began to browse between the shelves, aware that the man with the silver mane by the till was watching me closely, but each time I turned to look at him, he'd turn away. It was a subtle dance amidst the book maze, like two gazelles sipping cautiously at a watering hole, both intensely aware of the other and poised in delicate alarm. There was one other browser in the shop, a plump lady skimming pages by a row of philosophy books, who winced a smile as she saw me and slid past with a scrunched nose. I couldn't remember the last time I'd washed, Shi, but I knew pungent didn't cover it. I was worried that the stench of my grime-caked skin was going to overwhelm the smell of the books and make the silver mane ask me to leave. Desperate to stay, I ducked towards the back of the shop, descended deep into the oak shelf shadows, and settled in amidst the messiest corner. It was dark, rich and humid with words, a pocket marsh separated from time and trouble, a refuge filled with splendid old friends who don't ask questions, quiet, bar the occasional slosh of the silver mane's flask, the creaking of his chair and the slick wet whisper of the pages as I turned them. Funny how books can conjure such silence in a room while they themselves blare bolder than kakapos and howler monkeys.

Cicero said a room without books is like a body without a soul and that one messy corner of the shop had a hell of a lot of soul. Other browsers came and went while I sunk deeper into the wild oak clutter of ragged, dog-eared and leather-bound jackets. There was a buffet of choice, a tantalising spread like the lunches amma used to whip up on a Sunday. Chunky stewing tomes and spines that flaked away like almond shavings. Old, new, spiced and crumbling fellows all bustling together; real breathing books.

I knew I'd found a refuge in that shop corner, Shi, and so I became a regular fixture there, returning day after day, creeping in as silent and still as the frosted spines that snoozed on the top shelves. I was petrified that if I crossed paths with the silver mane he'd tell me to stop coming and I couldn't handle that, Shi, I needed that corner. Every day, when the clock hands yawned towards closing time, a lowness began to curdle in my gut and thoughts of the night ahead began hissing. He would plod over to unhook a bunch of keys from the wall and when I heard their metallic jangling, I'd scurry between the shelves and quickly duck out of the door.

Back under the bridge by the canal, where I slept, I'd brace myself for yet another night closing around me as harshly as a hippo's jaws. I'd pretend the canal was my lagoon, the dripping water from the underbelly of the bridge was rainfall pattering onto luscious leaf palms, the drunken chants of pub goers the distant songs of the fishermen as they hauled in their catch. The night would crawl by and as morning yawned in, I'd stuff my sleeping tat discreetly under a bush and head down to the waking stalls of the market, waiting for the silver mane to trundle along with his satchel to unlock the door. I'd wait until he'd flipped the sign to open and as he shuffled off to his desk by the till I'd slip in and hunker down in the back marsh corner. He never approached or acknowledged I was there. There was a companionable silence between us, both of us aware of the other but content with the stillness.

In the afternoons there would barely be any browsers and a velvet hush would descend upon the shop. Each time the silver mane moved in his armchair the floorboards would sigh and spread a tremoring echo ache to the shelves. It felt like the whole room was sighing with him, an extension of his body, woven into his very fibres. Occasionally he would cough and take a large glug from the flask he kept on his desk, the peppery aroma wafting its way between the shelves. Although he kept his distance, Shi, I knew he was paying attention to me because each day the contours of my marsh would change. You see, whatever text I had been reading, I'd return the next morning to find my corner peppered with books of a similar ilk. Then one day, as I was crouched reading, I heard his chair creak, the room sigh and footsteps heading my way. *Was he finally going to ask me to leave?* I tried folding myself further into the corner, tucking my chin and knees close to my chest, making myself as small as possible behind the shield of a book. The footsteps stopped and as I peeped over the cover, I saw him standing right in front of me holding a chair with a plush tangerine cushion on top.

'This'll do you better.'

He plonked the chair down with a sigh and patted the cushion.

'Crack on, as you were. You know where I am if you need anything.'

No introductions, no shooing, no small talk faffing; just a chair. As he plodded back to his desk, I got up to inspect the new addition to the marsh and as I sank down onto that cushion, Shi, it felt like a throne. A rush of warm shivers thundered through me and my buttocks tingled in gratitude. Water rose up behind my eyes and my nostrils stung as I fought back the deluge. There in that musty marsh corner atop my tangerine throne, I felt the safest in as long as I could remember.

From my new cushioned vantage point, I could make out the books on the top shelves a little clearer. They looked glorious up there in their leather-bound robes, beaming down on the paper labyrinth below; Appa's *Arabian Nights* would have fitted in perfectly. One spine in particular caught my eye, a deep ruby cover with black stripes like the legs of a red-knee tarantula. As I sat wondering what world might be nestled in its decadent folds, the mane appeared again and this time plonked a stool down next to me.

'Mind if I join you?'

He sat down with a wheeze and ran his palm gently across the pale blue cover of a book he was holding.

'Do you know my favourite part of a book?'

His voice was gruffly soothing, like gravel soaked in monsoon rain.

'This bit, right here,' he said, as he tapped the book, 'before you've opened the very first page for the very first time, the bit where it could go either way. Might be a grand adventure ahead or it might be a big old anti-climax. Might leave a horrid tang in your mouth or a crackin' aftertaste that keeps you smiling for days. The raw delira and excira of it all still gets me even after all these years.'

He rooted around in his waistcoat pocket, took out a coin, flicked it up in the air and caught it, cupping his palm over it like the lid of a trapdoor spider's lair.

'It's like a coin toss. It could go either way, completely out of your control.'

He slid the coin back into his pocket and looked at me directly in the eyes.

'Don't you think some covers give it away?' I blurted out.

His eyes lit up like luminous opals.

'How do you mean?'

'Well, I think sometimes you know a story will be impressive just by the smell and feel of it in your hand.'

'In my experience, kid, the covers with the most wear and tear are often the very best.' His eyes settled on my scar and he took a swig from his flask. 'They're the ones who've seen and been savoured the most. It's a small tragedy in many ways, that the most damaged are the most interesting.'

He opened the cover and tilted the book towards me.

'You see, violence is embedded in a book's seams, its spine, its fibres. It has to endure the brute force of the clamping vice, the hammering of the spine and the splicing of the inlay corners just to be brought into existence.'

I could feel his eyes settling further into my cheek, lodging in my scar ridges. It wasn't pity I detected in his stare, but some other emotion, something I couldn't quite place.

I looked away and stared up towards the red-knee tarantula spine.

'Aha, a fine choice. Perhaps you do have an eye...'

He lingered with the sentence, searching my face for a name. 'Artemila.'

'And a grand name too. Well, Artemila, I'm Cillian, though Cas will do just fine'.

He placed the blue book and his flask on the floor, stood up and slid the wall ladder along to underneath the tarantula book. He climbed up and at the top, he blew away the dust frosting, tucked the tome under his arm and descended. Settling back onto his stool, he handed me the book, the deep creases in his face warming like hot toffee pudding.

'Quite the pick. A favourite old friend of mine. Should keep you entertained for a while.'

My fingertips tingled as I ran them over the embossed gold lettering: *Encyclopaedia of Natural History.* My heart swelled as I opened it and inhaled the decadent cosmos of images, graphs and anatomies that swirled between my palms. It was exquisite, Shi, and my mind slipped back to the first time appa had shown me his encyclopaedia.

It was a sweltering summer's night, one where no amount of tossing and turning could shake the moist fug as it smothered you. I'd snuck down to the light of the study and appa had scooped me up onto his lap. Handing me his cup of cocoa, he reached into the bottom drawer of his desk and pulled out a chunky forest green tome, its bronze lettering shimmering in the lamplight. Under the citrus glow, he opened the cover and began to flick through the pages; cathedrals, mountains, birds of paradise, ancient jewels, kingdoms, maps and insects all beamed back with slick gloss smiles as appa's cocoa warmed my throat. The past and the present collided there and then as Cas sat back and watched me read.

It's interesting, Shi, how read is spelt the same in the past and present tense, isn't it? We pronounce one differently but the spelling, the real ink flesh, is scribed the same. When we get lost in a great book, the past and present blends and blurs, consuming us to the point where the future doesn't get a look in. The story becomes both everything that is and everything that was, a universe of being and doing, been and done. And once we've read the book, it's never really cast to the past but rather stays with us, worked into the intricate mosaic of our present. In reading, you move forward but keep looking back all at once.

From that point on, Cas began to join me in my reading corner most days, bringing a stack of books with him and scribbling pencil notes in the margins as he sipped from his flask. Sometimes he'd ask me about the story I had my nose in but largely we dissolved into our pages and sat stewing through sentences. I'd start and end each day by crawling into the sumptuous embrace of the tarantula tome, but in between I delved into the paperbacks piled up around me. It felt good to consume pages like that again, Shi, slurping hot word soup which nourished me in a way I'd forgotten I needed.

Cas often muttered aloud the words he was reading, mouthing them without realising it. I liked this, the sound of his ink digestion, the melody of words settling and sinking in just beside me. I'd sneak little side glances at him and watch his knuckles whiten as he pressed his pencil to the page, see how his knee quivered, the way his forehead lines deepened and the way the wild white tufts above his eyes twitched as he scanned the words in front of him. You know when you finish a really good book, Shi, and that bittersweet emptiness comes creeping up on you, that warming sensation that's also a deeply melancholic one, a spiced sort of sadness? Well, that's how I sometimes felt about Cas as I watched him. I wanted to talk to him, Shi, but after spending so long alone it was like I had forgotten how to start a conversation.

One day though, while Cas and I sat reading in our own separate worlds he dropped the horse-shaped bookmark he used. As I stooped to collect it for him, the words just fell out.

'Why horses?' I asked, as I handed the bookmark back to him.

'Well, this place here used to be a horse hospital,' he said, as he ran his fingers along the bookmark, 'and stables for the horses that pulled barges along Regent's Canal...'

'Did you know that horses can run just a few hours after birth and they have long term memories that are on par with elephants?'

'Ha, is that so? Funny how history repeats itself. Guess this place hasn't really changed, still is a refuge for weird and wounded creatures.'

He turned the horse over in his hands, slipped it back in his book and took a swig from his silver flask.

'If you are interested, I'm sure I've got a history book on the area in here somewhere, let me have a looksee.'

As he went rummaging his vibrations sent a cluster of books tumbling off their shelf. I jolted, my jaw tensing at the thud.

'Hey, it's ok. Nothing to worry about. Those shelves have a lot to do. Just think of the weight of all those characters, all those worlds they have to hold up. They're bound to give way now and again.'

I watched as he reassembled the books and knocked on the shelf to test it. The reverberations of the wood sighed through my bones. Just like the shelves, Shi, we readers have a lot of weight to bear as well, laden with all those stories we carry with us. When we die, that vivid collection of characters living inside us, the cast conjured in the lab of our imagination, goes decaying too. When you think about it, Shi, it makes a single death like a massacre, a secret internal massacre that no one will ever know about.

❖   ❖   ❖

As the days rolled on, Cas and I slipped into a routine as vague as the walkways in the shop. At some point in the morning, he'd make us both a cup of tea and we'd sit reading in the marsh corner, him pottering back and forth to attend to the occasional browser. He always seemed strangely frustrated when someone entered the shop, like they were more of an inconvenient interruption than a potential source of income. I liked that about him; he never pandered to the customers and instead let the books do all the talking. As the clock hands crept towards twelve, he'd triumphantly close the book he was reading and potter off whistling into the market, returning soon after with a grin and a greasy brown bag of cheese toasties for us. I'd wait till he had sauntered off to his desk before ripping the package open and sinking my teeth into the sandwich, the molten cheese oozing and pooling hot sharp puddles of flavour onto my tongue.

Afternoons would roll into early evening and as the days passed I'm sure Cas began to notice my unease come closing time. He began shutting up later and later each day; fifteen minutes, then thirty minutes and sometimes even an hour. One evening, as I was about to say my goodbye and duck out the door, Cas declared he had something grand to show me. He bent down, hunting through a pile of books at the foot of his desk and came up with a large crumbling hardback with a magnificent rust bronze spine. He opened the cover, and as delicately as amma placed the nuts atop her bibikkan, he ran his fingers along the seam revealing layers of tattered paper in the binding.

'Do you see that?'

He lifted and turned the book towards me.

'Look closely. Do you see how the paper tucked in here has writing?'

I strained closer and sure enough, the scraps of paper curled around the spine were full of tiny, faded words.

'They're pages from another script, nestled right there in the skin of this story. History wrapped in history. Isn't it glorious?'

'What's it doing there?'

'Well, back in the day, they used older manuscripts to wrap new texts when they were short on binding materials. So, like this beauty here, we have all sorts of chunks of history secretly travelling forward through time, snoozing in the cracks of younger stories.'

He swallowed hard and handed the book to me. I perched on the desk and studied the binding carefully, running my fingers along the fragments until its contours were as familiar as my own scar. I wondered if any of the books in appa's study were secret carriers. I wish appa and I could have checked together, inspecting the spines for clues, looking for a secret that only we would have shared.

'You know, you could always have the room in the basement of the shop to sleep in,' he said, 'It's a bit of a mess but I reckon we could make it cosy for you.'

Rosh came blaring back into my head, his skeletal frame, the water ringed table, the smiling sheep clock, his eyes hungrily flickering under the casuarina trees. I dropped the book down on Cas's desk and rushed out of the shop.

gliding swan, forked tongues

That night at the canal I barricaded myself deep into my cardboard refuge, my thoughts blurring, the frost sinking its jaws into my skin. I tried convincing myself there were far worse ways to slowly die, like how the tarantula hawk wasp plucks on an arachnid's web to lure it out before stinging it with a paralysing serum. You know, Shi, the wasp then lays an egg on top of the tarantula before burying it alive in its own den. Then, the larvae eat away at the tarantula and feast on its live flesh for up to a month.

My thoughts were interrupted by two men who came staggering along the canal path, laughing and slurping from their cans. As they passed under the bridge one of them spotted my hunched frame, crumpled his can and threw it straight at me.

'Look at this poor sucker. Not got a fookin' thing to show for himself.'

'That ain't no bloke, thass a bird', the other slurred.

'Nah, I'll bet you a fiver it's a bloke.'

'You're on.'

My heart pounded against my ribcage and thoughts of amma came rushing up; the laughter, the yelping, the ripping fabric, the fingers pinning her down, digging into her flesh, pulling at her breasts, hands cupping her mouth as they violated her.

I smelt them staggering towards me, my limbs frozen, my torso curled like a pill bug. Why couldn't I turn my ribs into spikes like the gallipato newt or shoot blood out of my eyes like the horned lizard? Why couldn't I emit suffocating slime like the hagfish or impale threats with barbed quills like the porcupine?

I heard coat fabric crumpling and felt fingers gripping tight on my shoulder. Panic thundered through my body and I did what I had got so good at doing, Shi. I ran. I ran and ran until I couldn't hear their voices anymore. With my shelter left far behind, I crouched down in an alcove and shivered my way through the night.

The next morning, I was back at the bookshop as soon as the market gates opened, the very first soul in the jungle. When Cas arrived and found me pitched outside, we shared a look and I knew I didn't have to explain.

'Come on, let's get you sorted,' he said.

I followed him inside and watched him pick up a carrier bag tucked beside his desk.

"Got a few bits here for you.' He handed the bag to me. 'Thought you could use them.'

I peered inside to see a toothbrush still in its packaging, a bar of soap and a flannel. He nodded to the green door behind the till.

'Bathroom's there, feel free to use it to clean up if you want to.'

My mind flashed back to the ship; the tap, the bucket, the beard watching in the doorway. Cas crouched down to my eye level and softened his voice.

'Hey, only if you want to. No skin off my nose, completely up to you.'

As Cas settled down at his desk, I stuck my nose in the bag and inhaled. Fresh lavender swirled to my nostrils, my eyes watering at the floral fragrance. It was a freshness I'd forgotten existed, Shi. Seeing Cas's head buried in a pile of papers, I made my way towards the bathroom, slipped inside and locked the door behind me. I waited, listening, hoping not to hear Cas moving towards it.

Silence.

I slowly unpeeled my clothes, placing the wrecked fabric in a pile on the floor, and tiptoed towards the sink. Glancing up at the mirror, I jolted at the girl who stared back. The soiled cheeks, protruding ribs, the hair sprouting thick from under her arms. I didn't recognise her at all, Shi. The filthy stranger in the mirror started to cry, tears plunging down her cheeks, blurring her into a salt smear of brown and bones.

I began to scrub. Hard.

I scoured and rubbed and rinsed, letting the water run warm, smothering my blackened fingertips in bubbles of lavender, caressing each crevice, each fold of skin, until the dirt baked into my pores began to loosen and the London streets went pouring down the sinkhole.

Finishing up, I turned to my sorry bundle of clothes and as I lifted up my urine reeking hoody, there was a knock at the door. I dropped the hoody and stood there shaking, my naked body dripping with water.

'There's some clean clothes out here if you'd like'um. Nothing too great and probably a bit big but there's a few bits-n-bobs if you fancy them.'

Once I was sure his footsteps had trundled back to the desk, I unlatched the door and slid the pile of fabric inside. There was a vest top, a long-sleeved shirt, some plain cotton pants, blue jeans and a pair of red trainers. I quickly pulled on the clothes, the long-sleeved top like velvet against my skin. The trainers were a little too big but with the chunky socks he'd included, they fitted snugly.

I stepped out of the bathroom enrobed in my new comforts. Cas looked up from his desk and flashed me a brief smile. I returned to my tangerine throne and sat there letting my body adjust to the tender stroke of the fabrics, feeling my feet thaw as I admired the red gems on my feet. I placed my nose to my forearm and inhaled deeply, the scent of lavender blossoming from my own skin.

Things ticked along quietly in the shop for the rest of the day; teas were brewed, books devoured and toasties bubbled and dripped. I wasn't ready to open up to Cas, but I could tell he was ready to listen, I sensed it loud and clear in the little throw away remarks he'd make as I went browsing the shelves or reading quietly in the marsh corner.

'You know, ol' Heraclitus said we can't step into the same river twice, that everything is in constant flux and all that,' he'd say, 'but he forgets that each step you take in that river brings a little of the old river with you. The old water soaks your socks and clings to each new step.' Or 'Ol' Unamuno here really hits the nail on the head. Suffering isn't a problem to be overcome but an essential part of what it means to be human. I like that; something to learn and grow around rather than bury away.'

I had become so used to existing alone in the tangle of my own head, wading in a space that felt deeper and darker than where anyone could reach me. It felt like I was living between the lines, suspended between the sentences, trapped between the breathing, flowing ink. But that space is not empty, Shi, if you look carefully you can see the shadow of the words on the previous page and the outline of the words yet to come. You're stuck between the then and there, the past and future, and yet still detached from the present itself.

When Cas wasn't reading or sharing random quotations he'd be bumbling around in search of books and cups and pens he'd misplaced. Even when he was reading, he'd start chuckling to himself and saying how little he remembered of the story even though he had read it countless times.

'You ever get that?' he asked, 'Can't for the life of me hold on to all the details. Head like a sieve. Explored this story more than this whole damp country and love these characters more than me own pals but still can't blimmin remember what happens.'

When the silences descended too heavily, he'd sit back and fill it with his rambling.

'Did you know there was a real-life headless chicken? His name was Mike. Lived for eighteen months without a head.'

'What?' this time he'd caught my attention and reeled me in like a curious chub.

'When his owner went in for the chop, he missed the jugular vein and left the majority of Mike's brain stem intact. Enamoured by the survival of his would-be dinner, the chap decided to feed Mike milk and water through his open oesophagus using an eye dropper. Goes to show you really can lose your head and keep going, ey.'

A smile spread across his face like a sunrise peeping through monsoon clouds and I couldn't help but smile too.

As the day wore on, and it got closer to locking up time, Cas came over to my reading corner, shifting about with a nervous energy as he jiggled his flask.

'I hope I didn't worry you yesterday. I just wanted to make sure you were safe. At least let me show you the room.'

That's what all of his ramblings had been leading to. I didn't say anything, I just sat there watching as he started to clear away some of the books from the side wall. Paperbacks went crumbling away like cinnamon kokis to reveal a door in its full splintered splendour. Taking a handkerchief from his pocket, Cas began wiping the contours of the handle in small circular motions until it gleamed brighter than a rosemary beetle. Then, with a sharp pull of the bronze handle, he opened the door. What did I have to lose?

The door opened onto a narrow set of stairs which curved like a spout into a teapot of curiosities. As Cas flicked on the light, the teapot warmed to life, brewing with the aroma of intrigue. Artefacts sweated from every angle and as I followed him in, the stairs of the spout squeaked and whistled. The tangle of oddities seemed to heat the space, history steaming in all the crevices and condensing on the walls. A bronze armillary sphere sat beside precarious stacks of Tibetan singing bowls. A sextant compass beckoned you to adventure. A sack of conical flasks perched upon a gilded pirate chest. Small weighing scales glistened beside alchemy bottles which snoozed under a blanket of dust. An elaborate helmet beamed beside a magnifying glass perched next to an ornate brass telescope.

Forgive all the listing, Shi, but it's hard to describe the clutter of Cas's teapot without cluttering my sentences. Hieroglyphic prints and musical score sheets seasoned the floor beside tribal arrows that had escaped their quiver. A tangle of fishing rods leant drunkenly against a wall behind an old cigar case which spilled calligraphy seals and inks. Near the stairs, two intricately carved tusks glowed under a cracked Moroccan lamp. In the corner, satchels spewed clumps of envelopes like the contents of a leaking wound.

Being in that teapot felt like taking a stroll through Cas's mind. It was stuffed full but never fully still. A mind space brimming with intrigue, compelling and dusty, sprinkled with nostalgia and salted with neglect. The smells were oddly comforting too. The oaky book scent from his shop lingered there but it blended with other things; old coffee beans, cool brick and the comforting scent of dinners long gone. It was the smell of thoughts, ideas and the slight sour tang of a cynical mind in its element. With so much stuff teeming all around me, I was more painfully aware than ever of just how little I had. In a room of everything, I had nothing.

'What do you say then? It's got to be better than where you're staying now?'

I didn't have to answer, the awe glazing my eyes like fresh annasi dosi said it all. I settled down on the mattress he had brought in for me and surveyed the treasures cushioning me on all sides. A surge of comfort bubbled through me and quivered on my eyelids.

That first night, tucked away in the teapot of intrigue, lying on that mattress of woven clouds with my whole body shivering in gratitude, I thought back to when appa would tuck me into bed after a late night cocoapaedia session, how he would hush me and stroke my hair as I wriggled restlessly. 'Shh, La, sleep is just part of the story,' he would say, 'beds are bookends remember, the covers marking the beginning and end of each day, the gateways between a delicious stretch of stories on a shelf well lived, filled with promise and possibility. So, nestle in tight, La, time to go reading with your eyes shut.'

❖   ❖   ❖

Creeping down the whistling spout each evening after the shop had been locked up, wrapped up in the soothing bustle of the teapot room, I began to forget the feel of concrete. There were still whispering reminders of my life on the streets, though. The Moroccan lamp, standing on an old tea-chest, was the colour of Boudi's hair and the blankets Cas had given me were the same striped pattern as Joe's bedding. The scattering of dead flies brought Archie tumbling into focus and the more I looked at them, the more I thought Archie was on to something. Maybe they did know our secrets. Because of their high metabolism, flies experience time slower than us, that's why they're so good at dodging those rolled up magazines you try to swipe them with. Through those huge compound eyes, perhaps they see us for what we are, cruel humans swatting away at others with arrogant palms.

The longer I stayed amidst that tangle, the more my mind began to wander back home. The fishing rods against the wall became wild tufts of long grass and the damp scent of the bricks was the soil sighing after it rained. The musical score sheets scattered on the floor were carpenter ants scurrying for treasure and the spilling satchels were waterside shrubs bursting out into summer bloom. The magnifying glass reminded me of the one appa and I used to study insects in the garden and the alchemy bottles conjured the spice jars amma kept lined up by the hob. The jumble of dusty cricket gear brought Ravi swelling into focus. I wiped away the cobwebs from one of the stitched balls and held it tight, telling myself he was still playing somewhere, still acing his bowls and smiling as the wickets tumbled. I found a slither of peace in my little game, Shi, but it never lasted long. The reality that I was in a basement, on the other side of the world, would quickly come crushing like a rhino stampede.

Some evenings Cas would join me in the teapot for a little while, rummaging through the artefacts with bright eyes and eager thumbs. One evening he picked up the helmet and put it on, explaining, as he wobbled it around his scalp, how Kawari Kabuto were worn by Japanese Samurai warriors to frighten the enemy in battle. No two helmets were ever the same and many were inspired by animals: fish, cows, deer and rabbits. Another time, he began shuffling through some of the hieroglyphic prints on the floor, and after a bout of laughter he began telling me about the ancient Arabian quirk of human mummy confectionery. These mellified men were elderly volunteers who gorged themselves on honey until they died and were then coated in the sugary stuff in their sarcophagi. After being marinated in bee elixir for hundreds of years, they were then lined up to be eaten as medicinal candy, many believing that their bodies would possess miraculous healing powers.

Cas really was an expert distractor and thankfully there was no shortage of material around us. In fact, it was impossible not to get distracted in that teapot. A few seconds spent looking at one thing and you'd glimpse five other intrigues just beyond. He certainly had a knack for sensing my lowness creeping because smooth as a manta ray, he'd launch into a tangent or reveal some new oddity just as my grief waves came mounting. One time, when he found me staring silently at the cricket ball, he waltzed across to the old gramophone, slid a vinyl from its jacket and placed it on the turntable. As it crackled to life, the starch clouds in Cas's eyes glistened like fresh yoghurt.

'Welcome to the Carnival of the Animals.'

Strings plucked the air like hens pecking at grain, pianos raced like wild hooves before slowing to a steady tortoise crawl and a double bass came waltzing joyfully, stomping into the pot like an elephant. Cas tapped his feet along to the music, grinning wider as the rhythm folded around us.

'You know, Saint-Saëns was worried that people wouldn't consider him a serious composer if they heard this piece. He thought they would think it too whimsical and so he refused to allow any performances of it until after he died. The only part he released during his lifetime was Le Cygne, and it made quite the splash.'

We sat listening to the music uncurl and eventually, I heard the swan glide gracefully into the pot on a tide of slow cello and rippling piano notes. It was melancholic for sure, Shi, but in a strangely uplifting way. My body swelled with the symphony and my head filled with images of appa gliding between his shelves with open wings.

When Cas headed home later that evening, I put the record on again. I felt less alone by filling and sharing the teapot with the animals. One part in particular, *The Cuckoo in the Depth of the Woods*, struck a note I couldn't shake. The sound of the clarinet, chirping out amidst a dense forest of piano chords, calling softly as the world around it came swallowing. I lay down on the mattress and cradled the cricket ball, listening to the cuckoo beckoning amidst the cluttered darkness.

I went on playing that fauna carnival on loop, riding the movements round and round like a carousel. It was certainly better than the carousel in my head. I kept thinking of all the things I could have done differently, the things I could have done better. Over and over, I thought about how I could have distracted the soldiers in the house raid and kept them away from amma, how if I hadn't been on appa's shoulders that day, we'd have been further away from the lime motorbike, how if I had crawled out from beneath the floorboards earlier I might have been able to warn Ravi and Kai, how Kai and I could have been sitting together in the papaya heat haze cheering on Ravi as he took another turn at the crease. Those shoulda coulda thoughts came gnashing and frothing like a shark feeding frenzy and dragged me nowhere but down.

Memories actually start to shape the way you think, Shi, they start creeping into your present, serrated and viciously sudden, changing how you experience everything around you. The science backs it up. Our sensory experiences slightly alter the molecules of our neurons, shifting the different linkages between them. So, when you think about it, Shi, our memories are literally moulding our brains. I could deter and delay those memories as they went chewing my cortex with jagged teeth, but I could never escape them. Amidst the artefacts, tangled in the market, inside the books; reminders whispered everywhere. The good and the bad all came niggling and I started to accept that the ache of home was always going to be with me; no matter how much burying I did.

In the twilight hours, as I lay on the mattress conjuring my lagoon, I thought about Tzu. I imagined him appearing amidst the fishing rod wild grass, his tongue flickering near the bursting satchel shrubs. I longed for one of our staring contests. The *Art of War* passage bubbled up in my mind, about how the greatest victory requires no battle at all. But what if you can't stop the battle inside you, Shi, what if there is no end to it? What if it remains there, flavouring everything, jutting into your present like a dark forked tongue, like a sentence that has no end?

There are three ways to end a sentence, Shi. A statement ending with a full stop. An exclaimed outcry! Also, there's the question, right? I wish the sentences in my own life would end as neatly, boxed and tied up nicely like the mark which will follow these very words. But sometimes the sentences we endure are filled with such a weight that they seep into the next like an open wound; we can only use commas to delay them, to hold back the swirling, surging, rushing of emotions that floods deep and far. We must try our best to tie them up, of course, it's vital for our sanity and survival in the jungle of ink and blood. Still, sometimes having no marks or words at all feels more fitting, a deafening blank void swelling from chest to page.

quagga lost, magpie found

Seasons shifted, trees blushed their lime locks and blossoms came bursting in peach and butterscotch. I began to help out a little around the shop. It felt right to offer something in return for Cas's kindness and being useful made me feel less of a pity case. Besides, I needed the distraction from my own head maze. Those torturous streams of shoulda couldas were blaring louder and thoughts about Ravi were growing stronger by the day. Ravi alive and well. Ravi alive and cruel. Ravi dead and butchered. Each reality ticked and clicked around my head like a skipjack wriggling in the leaflitter. To avoid the mental torture, I focused my energy on neatening the shelves and set about cautiously thematising the paperback sprawl, filling my head with titles, authors and genres so the darkness had less room to seep through. In one section, while dusting off a few exhausted paperbacks, an old photo of Cas slipped out between the pages. A younger version of him leaning on a wall next to two taller men, all of them holding cigarettes and staring ambivalently at the camera. Behind them, you could see a lady caught mid laugh at something just out of shot; a background whisper of joy captured and immortalised there with them. It was a comforting thought, that beyond our immediate bubble, lie bright fragments of other lives.

As the sun kissed strokes of spring yawned brighter, little pieces inside me slowly began to thaw. It wasn't much, Shi, but it was something, like how the lick of dew makes the grass seem a bit greener. Some mornings, after sharing tea with Cas, I would take my chair out to the front of the shop and observe the jungle breathing. Occasionally, Cas would join me and mutter comments about the browsing faces between sips from his flask.

'Ah, the tyranny of choice. So many options, so little time. Always prettier, worthier, funnier, snazzier and tastier choices; always something better dangling just ahead.'

Other times he'd pick particular browsers and mumble nuggets of commentary. I remember one tall gentleman in a trench coat who caught his eye. We watched as he went striding purposefully between stalls, stopping momentarily before marching on to the next with the urgency of a hunting buzzard.

'Well, there goes a master of the coddiwomple if ever I saw one,' said Cas.

'A coddiwomple?'

'Yes, to coddiwomple is to travel purposefully in a vague direction. One of my favourite words. I bet you must have a few favourites?'

I paused and scanned the ink thickets in my head until one came bending to the front like the branches of Kottawa rainforest.

'Werifesteria.'

'Werifesteria hey, that's a good one. You've got me there. What does that mean?'

'To wander longingly through a forest in search of mystery,' I replied as my mind filled with images of appa inspecting fossils under his microscope, planting chilli seeds in the garden, grinning at a downpour, smelling flowers near the temple, chewing toffees at his desk. Brilliant bright little flashes of him surging all together.

'Are you ok Mila?'

I don't know why, Shi, but it was then I opened up to Cas, and once I'd started, I couldn't stop. The floodgates well and truly opened. On and on I went unveiling the golden years in appa's study, Ravi's cot and amma's kitchen. Round and round I went describing the lagoon, the paddy fields, the mangroves and the first time I had fallen into the pools of Kai's eyes. Down and down I descended into the Vesak festival, Sasni auntie's house, the raid, the cycling frenzy, my days at Rosh's, the bowel room oblivion and Satyan's pulsing Kalu Ganga scar. I told him everything and he listened intently.

Now, Shi, I suppose this is the part where I'm meant to say that it made me feel better, give you the gushy line about how cathartic and healing it was to get it all out in the open. Sorry to disappoint. It didn't make me feel better, it didn't make me feel lighter and it certainly didn't make me feel in control. I'd laid out my woes and was simply waiting for the flies to congregate. Not everything gets easier by talking about it.

Once I'd finished my outpour, Cas made no attempt to prod me on the details. He simply leaned over, placed his hand on my shoulder and squeezed tightly.

'When the darkness comes heavy,' he said, with the starch clouds watering in his eyes, 'try thinking of your memories as a castle. There are dark rooms, there's damp and hell, there are even vermin scuttling around. But there are also grand chambers and banqueting halls you can feast in. There are empty rooms too, not yet entered and ready to be decorated, waiting to be filled with memories yet to be made.'

There was a tension in his jaw as he spoke and a palpable strain coating all his features. I was used to sympathy, Shi, but it's a whole lot stranger when someone listens with genuine empathy. You can feel the difference in the room. It brings a weight, as if the air itself carries the burden and is straining and suffering away too. It's a heaviness that both revives and crushes you to nothing but peel and pulp.

In the weeks that followed, I began to sense Cas was avoiding me. He turned up late, kept leaving the shop for lengthy errands and headed home earlier and earlier each evening. Even when he was in the shop, he'd bury his face in his books and fiddle around with the documents on his desk. I gave him his space and retreated back to my marsh corner once again. Nestled there, I started to worry that I'd told him too much and that worry soon began to spiral into fear. *What if he went to the police? What if they dumped me straight back into the clutches of Satyan and Orla?* I couldn't go back there. I wouldn't go back there. Thoughts of Rosh's face began to fester in my mind like maggots in rotten pulp. Swirling in a hot stew of paranoia, I decided the only thing to do was confront Cas, but before I got the chance, Shi, in came the lady in the red leather jacket.

She entered the shop in a whir of zips and rouge, wiping her high-heeled boots back and forth on the mat by the door.

Peeping through a row of anthologies, I watched Cas rise from his desk and wave her over. Cas never stood up for customers, let alone smiled or shook their hands. Cas was gesturing towards the marsh corner as he whispered to the lady and panic began to rise in my throat. I gripped the shelf to steady myself, but the vibration sent a hardback sliding off and tumbling to the floor with a thwack. Both their heads spun towards me.

'Ah, there you are. Come and join us for a second.'

My muscles froze up like a myotonic goat.

'Come, nothing to worry about, got someone here who wants to meet you.'

The lady gave a little wave. I clenched my jaw tighter and forced my feet forward towards them, wading through a swamp of tension. As I neared, I noticed the lady was wearing a small dragonfly broach on the lapel of her red jacket. She smiled at me as warmly as a honey June sunset and held out her hand.

'Hello dear, you must be Artemila. I've heard a lot about you. I'm Rosa.'

I gently took her hand in mine and the warmth of her came flooding through my palm.

'Your friend Cillian here has told me all about your situation and I think we can help.'

I pulled my hand away and stepped back. Help? Images of detention centres and police officers raced through my head, the metal slats of the bunkbed slicing into my thoughts. Cas noticed my distress and gripped my shoulder firmly.

'It's ok, Mila, this is a good thing, promise. Rosa here might be able to get you back home.'

Home. The word struck hard, Shi. I had thought of nothing else but when Cas gave it voice, I didn't even recognise the sound.

'That's right,' continued Rosa, ignoring my recoil, 'I work for a charity that deals with situations like this all of the time. We regularly engage with embassies from countries all over the world and I am hopeful we will be able to source your birth certificate which will enable us to then get you a passport. We are trusted and they will work quickly with us to help verify you are who you say you are. Cas has filled me in on all of the details and we have already started to process the paperwork. I will need a picture of you...'

Her words began to blur, Shi, and I slipped off into the blank voids between them. It was all noise; I couldn't understand what was happening or why. The words kept spilling as she took out a phone and snapped some photographs of me. All the while I didn't feel like I was really there, I was lost between the lines, stuck between the spilled ink and the shadow of the words yet to come.

❖ ❖ ❖

Trying not to think about how Rosa was getting on was no easy task, Shi. As I'm sure you can imagine, when the bridge to your home and family hangs in the balance, it's pretty tough to cast it to the back of your mind.

'Best to keep our expectations down,' Cas had said after she had left, 'if nothing comes of it at least we tried, and you still have this place which isn't too bad for now ey.'

I focused on the simple repetitive motion of dusting, scrubbing and sweeping the shop, desperate to try and limit the mental space for my mind to wander. However, the thoughts would still find a way to seep in and glue themselves to the rhythm of the chores. Scrub left, Ravi alive. Scrub right, Ravi dead. Swipe left, Kai alive. Swipe right, Kai dead. Sweep forward, Rosa successful. Sweep backward, dead end lead. And so, to help keep myself distracted, and to stop myself from regularly pestering Cas for updates, I began to venture out into the market jungle a little more.

One morning, as I perched on the benches near the crepe stall, I spotted a dishevelled looking magpie pecking about for crumbs. As it hobbled closer to my bench, I traced the layered curves of its alula feathers running down to the coverts of its wing. Though magpies appear black and white, Shi, if you look close enough there's an iridescence that goes shimmering in between. As I lost myself in the myriad of colours, I was back once more with amma on a sweltering June day, her forcing me into a sari, tightening my hair into a bow and guiding me through the sullen faces who had gathered for a funeral in weeping huddles near the temple. A palm squirrel was scurrying about near the shrubbery and while amma and appa were caught in conversation, I wandered off to inspect. I got on my knees and crawled closer, studying intently as it twitched its tail and dug through the mulch for bounty. Amma was fuming when she found me, sari and palms covered in dirt, bow unravelled and hair clumped with twigs. Appa calmed her down, took me aside and wiped my palms with a handkerchief.

'I'm sorry, I didn't mean to upset amma.'

'I know you didn't La.'

He tapped my nose with his finger.

'You want to know a secret?'

I nodded like a wagtail.

'You've got magic there La.'

'Magic?'

'Yes, the way you light up around creatures, it's a kind of magic. Look at all these sad faces here, not everyone is as lucky as you, not everyone has that place they can recharge and escape to. It's a magic you must cherish and nourish, La.'

He leant in closer and lowered his voice.

'But maybe not in your best sari next time, ey?'

He squeezed my hands and winked, his eyes glistening like a morpho butterfly.

Watching the shimmering magpie beside the market bench, I found myself reflecting on how things weren't so black and white after all, and that if you look at things in a certain light, the subtle positives can be found there nestling. Perhaps I had a few iridescent feathers of my own.

❖   ❖   ❖

The days dragged on with no word from Rosa. Even when my mouth was shut, the inquisitive jam was smeared all over my features and I could tell it was putting Cas on edge. So, I buried myself inside the red-knee encyclopaedia to try and give him some peace from my eager eyes. I zoomed in on fossils, zoomed out to the solar system and delved into every nook and cranny in between. As I went reading about erosion, an old conversation with appa bubbled vividly to the front of my mind. We were inspecting his rock collection as a geode began to crumble away in my fingers. I had started to apologise but he stopped me.

'Don't be silly La, that's just the time old dance of weathering and erosion. Remember, all is not what it seems. When things turn to dust they do not end.'

'What do you mean?'

'When the rocks crumble down to debris, they flit off with the whistling winds and water as sediment to sustain life elsewhere. Dust to the untrained eye but really it's a trove of important mineral nutrients, a provider of new anchorage and growth.'

He raised his mug like a champagne glass.

'Salute to the sediment! Bringer of new beginnings, not just ends.'

Sitting there in the shop, I wondered if the weathering of a human heart worked the same way. As the wear and tear of life comes gnawing, what kind of new beginning could a crumbling heart of debris provide?

As I read on through the encyclopaedia, I kept spotting creatures nestled there that I'd never heard of, ones that no longer existed. Beneath a fading photograph of a quagga, the curling lettering noted their threatened legacy. That word, legacy, played on my mind. Le-ga-cy. I rolled the letters around my palate and let it tickle my thought buds until the word began to sound like gobbledegook. The longer I stewed over it, the more polluting the thought became. The western black rhinoceros, the Pyrenean ibex, the golden toad, the passenger pigeon, the Caribbean monk seal, the Javan, Bali and Caspian tigers; what of their legacy? What of the vaquita porpoise? Less than twenty of them left. The giant softshell tortoise? Only four of them. The Hainan gibbon, Franklin's Bumblebee, the Amsterdam albatross, the Santa Catarina guinea pig, the Chinese crested tern; the list of those teetering on the brink goes on and on. By the time you read this, Shi, some of them are probably already gone.

Slinking deeper into the grooves of my reading throne, plans began to flit like pipistrelles through my mind. No more running, no more hiding, no more suppressing. I knew I had to do better. At night in the teapot, I would hold on to the cricket ball and run my fingers over the stitching, thinking back to all of those nights when I had crawled into Ravi's cot, stroking his earlobes and listening to the sighing waves. I was his *lokku akka*, his big sister, and those toes and tiny fingers were still my responsibility to protect. My craving for home was growing more unbearable by the day and when the scar on my cheek started to make me nostalgic, Shi, that's when I knew it was getting really bad. I started to miss the way it used to sting, the way the humidity clung to its ridges and the way a sea salt breeze would prickle-whisper through its contours. With each glance in the mirror, I began to realise the piece missing from my soul was completely entwined with the crater on my cheek. For sanity and survival, I needed to complete the twisted jigsaw.

❖   ❖   ❖

On the day Rosa returned, I'd been organising the shelves near the front of the shop, watching the droplets of a downpour streaming down the window. The door opened and there she was. I had spent so long squashing my expectations, Shi, that I'd almost convinced myself that she had been a figment of my imagination.

'Hi Artemila, lovely to see you again. Forgive my bedraggled state, it's absolutely pelting it down out there.'

She wiped the water from her brow and began to pull a

folder out of her bag.

'So, I have some news.'

The boa tightened around my chest. She yanked a big brown envelope out of the folder and handed it to me.

'Take your time, no need to rush through it all now. Long story short, my dear, we're getting you home.'

I stared, stupefied, looking from her to the envelope and back again.

'Everything you need is in there, passport, certificates, references, all cleared by the embassy. We even have confirmation from the bank in Batticaloa that you will be given full and unrestricted access to your father's account when you return. So, you just keep that envelope safe, alright dear?'

I wanted to thank her, hug her, release the whirlwind of warmth rising inside me but I stood as still as a stick insect trying to digest what she was saying.

'Your flight leaves in a fortnight. I'll be coming to pick you up myself to make sure everything runs smoothly at the airport. You will be met by a representative from the embassy as well who will accompany you on the plane to make sure you have no problems with immigration when you land.'

It was time, Shi. Time to run towards the light and the waiting lens, left foot dipped in intimacy, the right one pounding the poetic.

◈   ◈   ◈

Leaving day arrived in a haze of light drizzle and strong tea. Cas and I sat together as usual on our reading thrones, sipping on our brews, waiting for the clock tocks to reach ten, when

Rosa was due to arrive. A fog of warm melancholia drenched the shop and spilled into my lungs with each breath. Isn't it strange, Shi, how time can race and stand still all at once, like some moments exist outside and beyond it. Rosa arrived fifteen minutes early, as we were halfway through another pot of tea. Fifteen minutes usually flew by in the shop but when it mattered, it felt like I'd been robbed of an eternity.

'So, today's the day then,' said Rosa, 'probably a bit of traffic given the weather so best to get on our way. You all set my dear?'

I reached for the rucksack that Cas had packed for me as he scrambled into his jacket and scarf. We locked up the shop and strolled slowly along the market cobbles and up the winding path to the car park. Rosa unlocked the car door and climbed into the driver's seat, leaving me and Cas alone for a moment, little droplets pattering perfect circles into a puddle near my feet.

'I've never been good at goodbyes,' he said, 'never really know what to say.'

Here it was, my last moment with the man who saved my life. I lunged forward and hugged him, the scent of the bookshop rising up through the damp of his clothes as the London tears whispered softly on his coat.

'Oh, I almost forgot,' he said, sliding the satchel off his shoulder. 'Don't know where you'll end up, but I'll sure as hell bet you'll be needing some reading materials along the way.'

He handed the satchel over to me, his starch clouds beaming bright and warm.

'Thank you, Cas. For everything.'

'All set then dear?' said Rosa, as she opened up the passenger door.

I was ready, but I wasn't. I'd waited so long for this moment that waiting just a little longer didn't seem to matter.

Cas gave me one last squeeze on the shoulder as I slid into the passenger seat and he slowly closed the door behind me. Rosa started the ignition, slipped the car into gear and we pulled away. I stared out of the rear window at the shape of Cas receding in the distance, watching as he dissolved in the watery haze. Droplets thundered heavier against the glass, swelling closer to the glorious appa rain, as the windscreen wipers waved a thousand slow goodbyes.

part 3

platypus rising, leeches thriving

Home. We use that word a lot don't we, Shi? Going home, missing home, problems at home; it's a word anchored to our lexicon like a limpet. Question is, what does it mean, what is home? Physically speaking, I suppose it refers to the patchwork of materials constructed around us into a shelter. It's fair to say we've got pretty creative with our shelter building over the years. From mammoth bone huts to hide tents, from mud bricks to stilt houses, from timber frames to machiya, from chateaus to yurts to caravans. Did you ever build a fort as a kid, Shi? You know, throw together a load of blankets and pillows into something cosy. In a way, I guess that's what all our shelter building is like. We love scurrying about and perfecting our little fort, even if we're messing up the bigger house around it, the only house that really matters.

Creatures have crafted some pretty remarkable shelters too. Cathedral termites build self-sustaining mega-cities complete with fungi gardens to feed their thriving metropolis. The caddisfly weaves itself a backpack casing of pebbles, sand and shells using silk it produces itself. Prairie dogs build warrens latticed with tunnels, listening posts and separate chambers for sleeping, pooping and nursing their young. Then there's beaver dams. They actually prop up whole ecosystems by creating lush wetlands which filter out toxins before they go gushing into the oceans. Pretty nifty stickwork.

It was only once I'd arrived back in Batti that I began to truly unpick what home meant. Everything around me felt both familiar and totally unfamiliar all at once, home and nothing like home at all. The bridge was still bustling, Gupta's chilli patch was still thriving and the lighthouse was still peeling away undeterred. Hot moisture came marinating my skin, tropical birdsong still pulsated through the swaying palms and spice clouds of cumin, cinnamon and cardamom came rushing to embrace my nostrils. Yet at the same time, so much had changed. For a start, there were bright-shirted-pink-faced tourists all over the place, sweating away outside huge new hotels soaring from the sand like termite mega-cities. Then there were the locals themselves. I barely recognised any of the faces by the sari shops, in the cafes or lying comatose under the beach foliage. They were all new, or I was new, I didn't quite know.

I'd never known my home without war, and as I meandered to the hotel that had been booked for me, I kept expecting the sky to erupt with bullet thunder or for a jet to go screeching overhead. Each corner I turned I expected to be met by the rumble of an army jeep or a body slumped under a blanket of buzzing raisins. Through the eyes of tourists it probably seemed perfectly peaceful; their camera lenses capturing a town boasting its wares, parading its prawn curries and smiling away on coconut-clad beaches. But there was something else beyond the lens, something that could only be felt.

Batti was trying to heal but it wasn't there yet. It was a wound still threatening to rip through the seal of a scab only recently formed. A sour tension was softly choking the place. The zeal of the warring sides hadn't just evaporated into thin air, it was still there brewing, waiting, animosity crackling like glowing embers after a fire. Even the humid fug of the air felt heavier, as if sodden with the weight of what had happened. We hear talk of homesickness all the time, Shi, but back in Batti, it curdled in its purest sense. My home was sick; suffering and scarred from the darkness that went before and the shadows that still sprawled under the scorching sun.

❖   ❖   ❖

The flight had been long and the questions at immigration squelched on and on like rotten durian pulp. I'd arrived late and checked myself into one of the new hotels, sluggish with jet lag and delirious from the old new heat. I lay down on the fresh linen and stared at the bleached wallpaper. But the longer I lay there staring at those clean-slate walls, the less refreshing they seemed. They felt more like a buffer straining to hold back the stains of the world outside, desperate to keep up a façade of renewal. It's hard to clean a canvas when the acrylics of war stain so deep and vivid.

I unpacked the few clothes I had brought and opened up Cas's satchel. He had gifted me the beautiful red-knee tarantula encyclopaedia and the weight of knowledge in my palms felt grounding. I held it up to my nostrils and inhaled the delicious, sweet smoke mist of the bookshop. I opened the cover and slid out the note tucked neatly where the seam met the binding. Cas's spoiled syrup voice emanated from the ink, waltzing in wobbly calligraphic curls and caramelising the room.

Artemila,
I hope this old friend here can form the first pillar of your own library someday.
Keep your head up and keep on exploring those grand chambers of your castle.
My thoughts are with you, inked and eternal.
Cillian

It was comforting to have a piece of Cas with me, a slice of the refuge that had propped up my own spine and that now felt so far away. How quickly things can change; I had gone from being a stranger in a foreign land to a stranger in my very own home. I thought of the box turtles who dig themselves an underground burrow for five months, stop breathing and lower their heart rate to five beats a minute, I thought of the marmots who hibernate for up to eight months a year, wondering if they felt disorientated too, returning to the world after so long spent isolated and removed. Eight years had passed since I'd been back in Batti, Shi, ninety-nine full moons since I'd been on my own soil and I felt far older than the twenty-seven years I'd accrued since I'd been gone.

On that first evening home, unable to sleep, I decided to take a night stroll through the town. Under the dusky mosquito thrum, couples were strolling past kiosk venders flogging choc ices while teenagers whipped up dust clouds with their footballing feet. It was all so different to the prickling silence that used to come coating with the curfews; so many people all mingling together, weaving in and out of restaurants and bustling at bars. Looking at all the eclectic faces smiling around town, unable to tell who was a lion or who was a tiger, it seemed people were perhaps beginning to embrace the platypus logic. With its duck-like feet, otter-shaped body and beaveresque tail, it really does epitomise how a combination of different elements can make something much more special.

I bought a fresh nelli juice and sat watching the bustling ebb and flow. Sleep began to weigh heavily on my eyelids and I drifted to memories of amma preparing fresh juice in our kitchen, chopping the amla, crushing the pepper and drizzling manuka honey into a beautiful, sweet salt fusion. I savoured the last sips of my drink and trundled back to the hotel.

The next morning, my first dawn back in Batti, I weaved my way into town between burping vans and purring tuk-tuks, bedecked with their lime and chilli offerings to the Gods. It was all so much livelier than I remembered. Music swirled from passing car stereos instead of the scuff clunk thud of patrolling boots. Bright fabrics and billboards beamed at every corner instead of camo lions prowling with metal snouts. Pigments burst from the pavements unshackled and unashamed. When I looked closely, though, I could still see the grief etched onto passing faces, slurping on them like chunky buffalo leeches. Once a leech opens up a bite wound, it latches on and secretes an anti-clotting enzyme to keep the blood flowing while they feast. Unlike the grief though, the leeches eventually let go.

A group of young schoolgirls came walking towards me, giggling away together as their mothers strolled a little way behind. Those girls had never known war, there was a whole generation now who had never lived through it and who would only have the memories of others to go by, a diluted kind of agony, marked but not scarred. They would never know the claws of curfew, the choking thunder of gunpowder skies, the thump of boots pressing into their floorboards. They would never see the burnt flesh twisted through tyres, hear the branches creaking with large rotting fruit or taste the metal tang of gunfire in their throats. They would never have to carry that unforgettable sickly sweetness in their bones. I flashed a brittle smile as the girls skipped past, their laughter echoing in the sunlight.

As I weaved my way toward Bazaar Street, I began to recognise a few of the faces. They were older now, wearier, but I recognised them all the same. I spotted Praba leaning against his cab, smoking and reading the papers and there was Mr. Kohan from the fruit market, whom Ash and I had nicknamed the moray eel. Mr Kohan was sitting on a bench in Gandhi Park, staring out at the water, chewing away on a pouch of salted seeds in his lap. He looked lost, Shi, like he was searching for something but had forgotten what. We exchanged surprise that we were both still alive, shared a few pleasantries but then the conversation shrivelled up quickly. The silence of our own company can be a peaceful thing, Shi, but when you surrender too far, there's always the risk it can swallow you. I sensed Mr Kohan was being devoured whole.

I left Mr Kohan to his solitude and headed to the exchange bureau where I was met by Mrs Ganeshan. She came out from behind the till and squeezed me tightly, telling me she was convinced I had died and how delighted she was to see me again. She never asked where I'd been or what had happened though, Shi, it was clear that she didn't want to dig too deep. The initial pleasant surprise swiftly dissipated into something more melancholic; her eyes kept drifting to my scar and it was clear my very presence was inflaming old wounds.

With everyone I met, the conversations quickly morphed into pained recounts of the war, the loved ones maimed and the disappeared relatives they'd been searching for to no avail. I asked them about Ravi and Kai, but no one knew of their whereabouts and from the pained looks on their faces, the pessimism oozed hot, loud and clear. Willing their own loved ones to be alive took all the hope they could muster and they didn't have enough hope to share round.

Thing was, Shi, I didn't mind hearing about their pain. I thought of those teary stew tragedies from before, the shuddering girl with the cheekbones, the sobbing fruits under the palm trees; in those days I was hellbent on blocking them out, distracting myself from the agony by tuning into anything in the world around me. But with my older feet firmly planted on home soil again, it felt wrong to keep blocking it out, to keep distracting myself from reality. So, when Mrs Ganeshan sobbed about her only son who'd been missing for eight years and sixty-three days, this time I really listened. As the tears soaked her chin and dribbled to the dust below, I realised crying is an essential condiment for the banquet of trauma. All the other distractions were still there around her, the fruits, the strays, the tuk-tuks, but I chose to tune them out. I chose to focus on her story because her hurt deserved to be felt. I unlocked the dark castle rooms, Shi, and pulled up a chair.

Having spent most of the day listening to so many trauma

tales, my scar began to sting. I needed to regather myself, so I left the centre and walked out beyond the lake roads to our family home. The very shape of the place was the same as I had always known it; the colour of the bricks, the contours of the door and even the herb patches out front. But there was a shift in essence, Shi, a different flavour to it. It was no longer ours; it was no longer mine. I let the memories of appa's study, amma's kitchen orchestra, Peri's shelter and my eighteenth birthday rush through and gut me raw. I had so many good memories nestled in the bones of that place, but the hurt consumed them all. It wasn't my home anymore.

In the front garden, I spotted a ruellia that had fallen away from its family, its petals quivering softly in the breeze. I remembered appa gardening on a warm spring morning, patting the soil down around his treasured anthuriums as I toddled out to join him. I'd noticed a bud that had fallen and shrivelled on the soil. Appa paused to wipe his brow, mud streaks splayed across his forehead.

'What's that look for, La? Could sour amma's achcharu with that face.'

I pointed to the bud.

'The flower? Don't be silly, La, that's something to celebrate.'

'But it's dead. It never got the chance to bloom.'

'Ah, but it does get the chance to bloom, it'll just bloom in a different way, through the soil, the roots, the burrowing creatures and the birds collecting décor for their nests.'

He put the spade down and crouched next to me.

'Look around La. Listen and breathe it all in.'

He pointed around the garden in a slow circle with his outstretched glove.

'Everything here has its place, all the moving pieces are working together in one big, beautiful symphony. May not be obvious at first but everything has its music to add. The leaves, the rain, the trunks, the birds, the buds, the bees, the ants; everything has its role. When one thing dies, it provides life for the other parts, sharing itself round in a big beating, breathing cycle.'

He reached out to smear a little mud on my cheeks as I giggled and protested.

'See, that's better. You've got to see, smell and feel it all, La, zoom out and see the whole mosaic. If you focus on one sharp note for too long, you'll miss out on the whole glorious symphony.'

He took his gloves off and scooped up a handful of soil, raising it to his nostrils to inhale.

'Smell the earth, feel the rocks, listen to the rain and chase the things that ignite you. That's all there is to it. Oh, and taste all of the things you possibly can.' His eyes twinkled like morning dew. 'Talking of which, I thought I spotted some of amma's kalu dodol in the kitchen earlier.'

❖   ❖   ❖

I left the house and its new residents behind and continued to walk. The presence of appa followed me everywhere. He was by the temples, the rockpools, in the birdsong and in the smell of the men's tobacco. I saw him in the shapes of scattered temple flowers, the contours of pebbles and the steam swirls rising from the teacups. Amma came thrumbling back with him. I felt her with each flash of a yellow sari and inhaled her in the spice pots bubbling from the restaurants. I tasted her in the sweet lime and heard her lost laughter sizzling in the pans along the roadside. In the fruit market, teeming with its colours, scraps and peels, I sat for a while in the spot where Ash's magic carpet used to be and breathed in the dust bustle view we used to share. The man running the stall behind, where Mr Ananda's used to be, was still selling pomegranates but they were nowhere near as juicy. I longed for Peri to be there by my side so I could scratch his ears and feed him a roti one more time.

I kept wandering, Shi, walking the roads where Ravi and I had cycled all those years ago. At the beach, I rested on the rock where we had once seen those spinner dolphins and ran my fingers gently across the RA and MI carving we had made. I wanted my baby brother with me more than anything, Shi, and in the hot breeze swirling past my eardrums, I heard appa and amma whispering their agreement.

Then came the lagoon, Shi, the return to my kingdom. I weaved my way through the long grass, the blades bowing and stroking at my shins, fizzing antennae of the universe bustling below. I crept down to where the reeds wore the water currents as the sun massaged moist kisses along the nape of my neck. The mangroves quivered in the gelatinous heat, their lime locks teeming with skiff, click and cedar beetles while the rasbora below rippled feverish whispers of my return. I settled down on the bank and inhaled the thrum of life into my lungs. Bulbuls warbled from the high branches as lizards scampered in the shrubs beside my feet. A huddle of cormorants were drying their feathers on the far side and everywhere, like sublime sugar crystals, the wings of young dragonflies glistened on the leaves. This buttered me hopeful, Shi. Rejuvenation was happening right there before my eyes. No matter how much cruelty and blood had been spilt in Batti, those creatures were going to carry on regardless, on and on, round and round in appa's big beating, breathing cycle.

As I sunk deeper into the grooves of my refuge I reminisced my favourite spots like height marks etched on a child's doorframe. I gazed at the mud patch where I'd spotted my first bull frog and the dip in the bank where I first saw a crocodile peeping out of the water. I retraced the branches where I'd spotted a huge crested drongo nest and the crevice near the mangroves where a dancing dropwing had perched on my knee for a full minute.

The more I think about it, Shi, the more I believe home is the space where you don't feel the walls. It's the place where the lingering essence of old memories cloaks you like a mist and where you feel the afterglow of your earlier self. Sitting there in my sanctuary of old, Shi, I realised that at last I really was home.

hungry vines,
sea-lion scraps

Do you ever pace back and forth when you're stressed, Shi? Polar bears, big cats and wolves do it all the time in captivity, repeating the same motion over and over to ground and calm themselves. With stress mounting about how I was going to find Ravi, I began to pace too. The shore, the corridors of my hotel and most of all, back and forth along the banks of my lagoon. I tucked into a meal here and there at the assortment of new restaurants but largely I paced and feasted on the creature comforts around my refuge.

It felt like I was being recharged, Shi, shielded from the one-hundred-and-one worst case scenarios running through my head. I watched the dragonfly nymphs by the water, skimming, shedding skin and gradually edging closer to their life in the skies. You know, dragonflies spend most of their existence as nymphs, moulting up to twelve times before developing wings in their final few months of life. It's a slow process that requires strength and patience, but one with an end result that glistens like no other. With each passing day spent with the maturing nymphs, my energy and resolve grew stronger until I could no longer put off the thing I'd sought so desperately to do. So, I moulted my last few layers of doubt and began my search for Ravi.

I started with the official routes, navigating all the channels and services I could find. I pleaded my case to countless receptionists, was ordered to fill out reams of forms but each time I called to chase up, the forms had been conveniently lost. I started writing letters to anyone and everyone with influence. Over cola and hot daal, I'd scrawl through the evenings, inking away like a squid, convincing myself that if I could just get one person to pay attention, it would make all the difference. After a lot of pestering, I managed to get a sit down with a regional MP. It felt like a breakthrough, Shi.

My palms wouldn't stop sweating in the cab ride over to the office and as I waited in that cool polished foyer, I felt hope begin to inflate inside me like a puff adder. The young politician was scribbling away at his desk as I entered, the air con lightly billowing the papers stacked on both sides. He greeted me with a handshake, his face autopiloting into a sharp smile that didn't venture beyond the borders of his lips, his posture as immaculate as his polished floors. He listened carefully to my story, served me tea in beautiful porcelain, nodded in all the right places and assured me his team would look into it. Problem was, Shi, I knew before the tea had even cooled that nothing would come of it. I'd gotten much better at spotting deception; gopher snakes and rattlesnakes may shake their tails and look the same, but only one strikes with a real bite.

Drawing blanks from the official pathways, I began reaching out to locals to see if they would point me towards any ex-Tiger fighters who could help. I took the Ganeshans and Praba out to dinner and made an emotional plea over chickpea curry. They warned me to keep my expectations down but eventually gave up a few names who they suspected had been involved in one way or another. I followed up immediately.

Unsurprisingly, most were unwilling to talk. All of them had lost so much in the war; limbs, children, livelihoods, and they were clearly paranoid about upsetting the Gemunu Watch soldiers and the Terrorist Investigation Department who still dropped by to check on them. But eventually, down by the jet ski rental, I met Arul. He was suspicious at first, arms crossed, brow furrowed, distrust wafting pungently with his head shakes. I bought him a beer which loosened him up a little but, in the end, he dished out the same standard advice. He suggested I head up north to search around the final siege sites because many of the Tigers who hadn't been killed or caught had melted into the towns around there. Every time someone mentioned going up north it plunged me back to the last time I'd heard that suggestion on my soil; that skeletal frame, the salt stew gloop, those eyes staring across the water-ringed table.

As much as I tried to resist them, Shi, thoughts about Rosh kept slithering into my mind as venomously as a pala polonga. I'd avoided going near his place at all costs; I didn't feel ready for what I'd find or perhaps what I'd find myself capable of doing. But after speaking to Arul that afternoon, I felt unable to avoid that rising acid in my throat any longer. So, I meandered down past the fishing boats and wound my way along to Rosh's old house. The breeze hissed at my eardrums as I retraced the familiar route, my muscles tightening with each footstep closer. It felt like I was wading through quicksand, Shi, my whole body battling against the direction I was pushing it in.

The house was almost unrecognisable. Thick weeds sprouted around the perimeter and crawled up the brickwork as if the earth were swallowing the place whole. The roof had slumped in on itself and vine creepers coiled around the gutted window frames. It had clearly been deserted for a while and it was reassuring to see nature thriving off the wreckage of past mistakes. I crept closer and peeped through the window of the room I once slept in. On one of the grubby walls, a pale circular shadow marked the spot where the little lemon clock once hung. The march of time really is a powerful thing, Shi.

Back at the hotel, I thought more about Arul's advice. I knew he was right. My best shot was heading northwards and there was no point delaying it any longer. Nothing was going to interfere with my white-hot determination to find Ravi and any residual bitterness frothing about Rosh would only add fuel to the fire. So, I unravelled the boa around my chest by its tail, rented myself a nifty little Honda Dio and began to make tracks up north.

❖　　　　　　　❖　　　　　　　❖

The roads were different to how I remembered them, Shi. Instead of roadblocks and army vehicles choking the highways, there were taxis, decorated vans and buses jampacked full of tourists. They were no longer tarmac arteries for fleeing but corridors for commerce and travel. As I passed through the towns on route, churning up hot puffs of dust with my bike, I noticed other changes too. New statues, shrines, stupas and Bodhi trees had sprung up, drenching roadsides as loudspeakers blared Buddhist chants into the streets. Sweaty tourists snapped their selfies near framed pictures of orange robed monks surrounded by lotus flowers and flickering candles. It was clear now who ruled the roost.

As I sipped cola and dunked string hoppers at the cafes along the way, I heard about army bases being built on Tamil cemeteries, bones dug up and dumped, Hindu temples being vandalised. I heard about artefacts being destroyed, places renamed in Sinhalese and textbooks cleansed to suit the Government narrative. Tamil discrimination hadn't ended when the war did, people just hushed up because it was better than having their tongues cut out. One conversation in particular caught my attention. I'd paused at a dilapidated little roadside café just past Mankulam to rest my muscles and fill my tum. The place smelt of cooking oil and body odour, salt grains scattered the tables and flies outnumbered the customers tenfold. Still, I was ravenous, so I slid into a booth and ordered a bowl of lotus root curry from one of the sticky menus. I watched the flies milling around lethargically as I waited; Sir Archibald would have had a field day. A few were circling the plates of two women who were sat at the table next to mine. As they chatted away, they kept swatting at them, but the flies persevered, dipping and ducking their way to the bounty of rice and curry scraps.

'No point wasting time heading there. Nothing to see.'

'But why not? It's enroute and I always loved visiting as a child. It's our heritage after all.'

'It's not anymore, Jaseena.'

'What do you mean?'

'Just forget it.'

'But I have such lovely memories of running between the domes and playing hide and seek there with amma...'

'Listen, Kandarodai is not the same anymore. They've wiped us from the history, so just forget it.'

A nauseous wave rushed through me at the mention of Kandarodai. Appa had once told me about the archaeological site there with such pride, raving about how it showed evidence of an early Tamil-Sinhalese tradition where Hindu and Buddhist practices had blended together. He'd said it was powerful proof that islanders of all religions could thrive harmoniously, like the ants inside the Gal Karanda plant he'd shown me in the rainforest.

The waitress soon appeared with the steaming bowl of lotus curry and the flies began to close in around my booth. I sat there, staring at it, stirring it round and round, watching the oil droplets refusing to mix with the water.

❖   ❖   ❖

After three weeks of scouring the north of the island with no new leads, my Honda's enthusiasm began to wane. It spluttered on with a modicum of dignity until one bad crater in Kilinochchi sent the tyre rupturing and the engine yelping into self-pitying moans too loud to be ignored. I wheeled it to the nearest garage where I was met by a sea lion hulk of a man sporting a thick moustache and a greasy oil cloth tossed over his shoulder. He inspected the bike for a moment, furrowed his brow and fiddled about as I listened to the nasal honking of his breath.

'Mm, tough one. You'll need to leave it here for a bit, pick it up in a few days' time.'

He winced unconvincingly as he ran his finger along the exhaust pipe.

'Tricky parts to source you see, plus we've got quite a lot on already.'

I was not in the mood to negotiate; I was covered in dust, aching all over and quite frankly ready for sleep. I scribbled down my contact details as my mind wandered to thoughts of a plush pillow to melt into.

'*Machan*, come get this bike.'

From behind the sea lion, a pair of legs working on the underbelly of an old Morris Minor rolled out on a board. The man lay some nuts and bolts down on a scrap of cloth, a bit like how amma used to arrange her kithul treats on the cooling rack, and he dunked the rest of his tools in a big soapy bucket. He wiped the oil smudges from his face and emptied his water bottle in four hearty glugs. Wiping his mouth with his sleeve, he strode over towards the bike. The sun was fading into a caramel sky and the soft light framed the striding silhouette beautifully, a peach halo spilling down behind his neck and shoulder muscles. Then the man's features emerged from the haze and my heart leapt like a klipspringer.

I couldn't move.

I couldn't take my eyes off his glistening amber lakes.

Kai was even more beautiful than I remembered, Shi. I'd rose-tinted him in my head long enough, but there he was, peach glowing, perfectly glazed and alive.

'Mila?! It can't be...'

His face contorted dramatically.

'I thought you were... how can you be...when did...where

have you...but I went back to Batti and they told me you were... I can't believe you're bloody alive! I guess we both picked up some tips from those Mantis Ali shrimp boxers, ey?'

My heart fluttered like the wings of a ruby-throated hummingbird. I couldn't believe he'd remembered our conversation from all those years ago. Overwhelmed with emotion and delirious with the heat, I lunged forward and hugged him tightly. I didn't care about what was appropriate, every fibre in my being wanted to hold him, so I did.

He smelt of oil and metal, strong varnish and hot soap. He mumbled something about not wanting to get me dirty before he gave in and folded his arms around me. We stood there wrapping our whole selves around each other, his heartbeat shaking me lightly with each little thump. It felt so reassuring to be enveloped like that, Shi. The grease, metal and wheezing sea lion faded away and it felt like there was nothing beyond me and him, our compasses synchronised, thump for thump, beat for beat.

lucky stripes, dancing eagles

Being with Kai again made me feel like fireworks and honey. His company soaked everything with a fizzing, soothing sensation and even grey pavements began glowing warm amber. He insisted he would fix up my bike himself but only if I let him show me around Kilinochchi. So, astride his superior steed of a motorbike, we did a little exploring. We went looping around Ambal Lake and riding up Kanakapuram Road, me hugging his firm torso as the fever of kiosks, billboards and tuk-tuks whizzed past in the blistering dust haze. It felt like we were flying, Shi, and I thought of how I used to watch the egrets and babblers flying above Ash's rug, wishing I could glide instead of having to try so hard to flap my way forwards. With Kai, it went beyond gliding. As the tropic hot life rushed past, we flew into an upward current and soared.

As our stomachs began to rumble, we picked up some string hoppers, curry and sambol from a little kiosk and dipped into a local park to enjoy the feast. The whir of excited kids echoed out behind us as we sat gorging on the flavours, side by side, just like all those years ago in Fort Park. I snuck little side glimpses at his face as he chewed, admiring the handsome features that he'd grown into. The curve of his nose, the twitch of his perfect lips, his sculpted cheekbones, the way his whole face melted into the warmth of his smile; all of it fitted together so beautifully. Entranced, I imagined it was how the female bowerbird felt when she saw a perfectly decorated nest or how the lady puffa fish felt when she saw her favourite symmetrical pattern etched in the sand.

That same enchantment from years ago came enveloping me like a rainforest mist and for a moment, Shi, it felt like no time had passed at all, like we'd been meeting every day on the same bench with our conversation fizzing on into the night. As we sat chewing away on the park bench, I noticed a palm squirrel scurry down the trunk with its eyes fixated on our hoppers. I tore off a piece and threw it near the bottom of the tree. The squirrel scampered down, cradled its bounty and nibbled away feverishly. As it finished, I threw another scrap a little closer to us, and another and another, until eventually it was nibbling away right beside Kai's feet.

'Would you look at that? Miss Mila Mowgli strikes again. They never get this close when I try to feed them. I think you have animal superpowers.'

'Hey, if I had animal superpowers, I'd be doing more than making hopper trails.'

'Ah, but maybe that's a cover. Can't very well have people knowing about your powers can you...' he said as he stroked his invisible beard.

'Maybe. Maybe not. I guess we'll never know...'

I winked dramatically and his abrupt giggle frightened the

squirrel away.

'So, go on, what's special about squirrels then miss Mila Mowgli? I know you're dying to tell me.'

'What do you want to know?' I said, suppressing a laugh. He knew me too well already.

'The best bits.'

'Well, just imagine seeing things from their perspective for a moment.' I pointed to the sprawling park, gently pressing the back of Kai's neck down to lower his eyeline. 'Look at the view they have.'

'Twigs and leaves?'

'Twigs and leaves to you maybe. For them it's a sprawling assault course for them to dip, dunk, hop and crunch through. Everywhere they turn, tree trunks offer soaring highways to the sky, with huge lattices of branching pathways to scamper, leap and scurry through. Bushes rustle with mystery, bins teem with bounty and the bushes glisten with secret hiding spots to bury their precious nuts.'

'You're selling it too well. Now I'm officially jealous of the squirrels.'

He leaned down further until he was lying belly down on the ground, gazing out at the assault course and bark highways. I joined him and we lay there together, watching intently.

'I reckon they must think the same thing about us.' he said.

'How do you mean?'

'Well, they see us eating all this good food, whizzing around on wheeled machines, darting all over the place. Must look pretty good fun to them.'

'Must look pretty weird too though. Why do those strange creatures keep putting their food in open boxes for all the world to steal? Why don't they climb the highways? And why-o-why do they make so much noise and wear all those funny cloths?'

'True... but things always look better from a different perspective, don't they? Beauty shows up brighter through a different pair of eyes.'

My face flushed hot and sensing my unease, he kindly filled the silence.

'Ah but we digress miss Mila Mowgli. Would you be so kind as to tell me more about squirrels?'

I circled my index and thumb around my eye like a monocle and pulled a posh face.

'Certainly, my good sir. Did you know that a group of them is called a scurry? Smart fellows too, detailed spatial memory for finding the nuts they bury and fake digging rituals to throw off the nut thieves. Some of them have even been known to chew old snakeskin then lick their fur to help them hide from predators. Quite something, I do say sir.'

He laughed out loud. It made my soul sing.

'Ah, but do you know why they have those three white stripes on their back, miss Mila?'

'I'd assume for camouflage sir. The stripes would blend with the dappled light on the leaf litter. Makes it harder for wild cats and birds to spot them.'

'Hmm very logical miss, I like your thinking. Definitely more sensible than what my amma told me.'

A sad smile lingered on his lips. I dropped the monocle and posh voice.

'What did your amma tell you?'

'It's not important.'

'Go on. You can't dangle the nut and then squirrel it away.'

'Simply punderful.'

'So come on then, out with it.'

'It's just the Ramayana myth. You must have heard it a thousand times.'

'Not told by you though, come on, indulge me.'

'Well miss, if you insist,' he cleared his throat triumphantly and mimed the opening of a book, 'according to legend, Lord Rama was busy trying to build a bridge to rescue his captured love Sita. The little squirrel was super keen to chip in and help so went scurrying off collecting pebbles, sand and all the small stones he could carry. Although he collected far less than the other animal helpers, Lord Rama was very impressed with the squirrel's dedication. The amount may have been minimal, but the earnestness was what mattered. So, the great Lord Rama picked the squirrel up and stroked its back affectionately with three fingers, leaving behind the three famous white stripes.'

He closed the invisible book softly and took a little bow as I clapped.

'I've always really liked that story. You know, the idea that it's not always about the outcome, but it's the intent and energy you put in that counts. Even if you don't fulfil the task or find the thing you're looking for, you can still earn your stripes in the effort. That's what I find so special about it, Mila.'

He paused to rest his voice on my name and raw colour surged through me, Shi. Funny how different your own name can sound in the mouth of someone you adore, how much richer and more flavourful it can feel.

We dragged ourselves up from the ground and made our way back through the park. Outside the gate, people were clustered around a vendor who was deep-frying jelabis and soaking them in sugar syrup. Kai spotted the excitement on my face immediately.

'Go on, you know you want to Mowgli.' He said, nudging me affectionately. 'Grab one for me too, I'll wait here.'

I hurried over to join the huddled queue of saris and shirts and as I waited, inhaling the sweet batter and rose water, I felt increasingly conscious that Kai was staring at me from across the road. At first I thought his attention must have been caught by one of the prettier women waiting in front, but as I turned to look at him, it was clear his eyeline was fixed on me. I figured my cheek must have caught the early-evening light in some ghastly way and the longer I stood there, the more uncomfortable I felt. The queue shuffled forward, I paid for my jelabis and took a quick bite. Fuelled by the chewy sweetness, I strode back over and decided to call him out.

'Why were you looking at me like that?'

Confusion contorted his face, his eyebrows furrowing.

'What do you mean?'

'You know what I mean. Why were you staring like that?'

'I wasn't. I...'

'You were. I saw you.'

His shoulders began to hunch as he went frantically spinning the silver ring he wore on his index finger.

'You know how uncomfortable it makes me feel, I'm not a freakshow. I thought you got that.'

'Don't you get it, Mila?'

'Get what?'

'I wasn't staring at your scar.'

'I saw you, Kai.'

'I was staring at you.'

This time my eyebrows did the furrowing.

'I was staring at you because I can't take my eyes off you. You're the only girl worth looking at on this island. You're the only girl that matters, Mila. So yeah, I was staring.'

'Kai, look at this thing.' I pointed at my cheek. 'Really look at it. There's no getting over something like this. It's here for good. This won't soften with age or fade with time, this is here forever.'

'Mila, will you just listen...'

'I'm not a naïve little girl anymore, Kai.'

'Mila will you just...'

'You deserve someone beautiful, someone who makes your heart sing to look at.'

He knelt down and began frantically undoing his laces.

'All of us are scarred, Mila. All of us. Yes, it's unlucky that yours is on your face, but it's just a scar. It's part of you, but it doesn't define you. Don't give it that power.'

He yanked off his right shoe and rolled his sock down, pointing to the lumpy space where three toes should have been.

'You see. We're all fucked up. But people don't go calling me two-toed Kaivan, and even if they did, who cares? Call me Emperor Twotoes. Sir Whereisyatoes. What does it matter? This isn't me, it just happened to me and that's that. I didn't ask for it or will it, it just bloody happened. Yeah, I can hide mine easier, but do you know what? I shouldn't hide it at all. I should parade it with pride and so should you. When I look at your scar, I see your strength, your pain and what you've overcome. You may be missing flesh, but your scar makes you the most complete person I know.'

There he was, beautiful Emperor Twotoes, kneeling sockless

in the dirt and delivering his inspiring little speech. A tide of warmth bubbled up so strongly that I had no choice but to open my mouth to let it out. Laughter erupted. Once I started, I couldn't stop. I just kept laughing and laughing and laughing, Shi, and boy did it feel good. My own laughter teased his out and before long we were both creased over and teary eyed. I was caught on a giggle tide of the toes, the heat, the jelabis and the pure absurdity of life. I was so caught up in it that Kai took me by complete surprise when he leaned forward and kissed me.

That stopped me laughing alright, Shi.

He tasted of spring, spice and watermelon. He held my neck softly, tracing the corner of my lips with his thumb. The kiss was a symphony that rolled and lulled all the other symphonies into one. The whirring carnival of the creatures, the refreshing downpour of the rain and the flavour harmony of amma's cooking; it was all there. I'd figured nothing could have matched the rose-tinted fantasy I'd crafted in my head, but there I was, immersed in amber tinted reality and it was so much better than I could ever have imagined. I lost all sense of where I ended and he began, as I dissolved into his amber lakes.

❖ ❖ ❖

As the day cooled off into dusk, we meandered along Kandy Road hand in hand, strolling our way through the fragrance of curry leaves emanating from a cluster of little restaurants. The simple sensation of having Kai's fingers interlocked with mine was such a rush, Shi. It felt so nice to be touched again, to be held, to be constantly reminded that he was real and right there with me. I thought of the seahorses who swim tail in tail to synchronise their movements, the elephants who entwine trunks affectionately and the otters who hold hands to ensure they don't drift away in the swirling sea. I couldn't bear the thought of losing Kai again and I found myself instinctively squeezing a little tighter on his hand.

We ducked into a little spot which was more like a garden porch than a restaurant, eager to fill our hungry tums. Despite all the commotion on the other tables, I couldn't hear or see anything other than Kai. I was lost in him, Shi, the good kind of lost, the kind where there's no need for direction or an endpoint, the kind where you are happy just to feel, inhale and savour the majesty of the moment. As he talked, I stared at the tiny scar dancing with each movement of his eyebrows, the twitch of his nose, the tremble of his bottom lip, the dimples that would appear every time he smiled; his whole face seemed to sway with the rhythm of his words. And while these little movements were going on, all harmonising into a mosaic feast, I found it impossible to look away from those amber lakes. Even amidst the clamour of the other customers, all I could focus on were those glistening pools. I remembered what I'd seen in his eyes all those years ago in Fort Park, how they looked like lanterns rising and falling above the water. This time it was different. This time I'd waded so deep into the water I could feel the amber all around me, like I had been suspended in time like those creatures from the past, forever preserved in resin.

From steaming banana leaves, we gobbled idli, daal and okra and then ordered ice cream to cool our talked-out throats. I loved how much he appreciated everything, Shi. Before he took the first bite of each course he would close his eyes and inhale, smiling in anticipation of the flavour to come. I knew amma would have loved that about him. I really wished he could have tried her food.

We talked about the good memories we had of Batti, about his family picnics on Bone Island and the cycling rides appa and I used to make through the paddy fields. We talked about the dazzling afterglow of sunsets by the shore, the scurrying sand crabs which emerged at dusk and the old fishermen chants of malu malu! that echoed far beyond the beach. It was so easy to talk to him that awareness of my cheek went melting away and when I did catch a glimpse of my own reflection in his amber lakes, Shi, the girl peering back looked almost normal.

'I always noticed you sitting there you know, watching the birds and studying things in the sand. You were my lucky charm.'

'Lucky charm?'

'Yeah, the catch we'd bring in always seemed bigger on the days I saw you on the beach. I don't know, maybe I was imagining it, everything just seemed better when you were there.'

I smiled warmly at him, his face blushing as he turned to scoop up the last of his ice cream. It was so nice to have someone to remember with, Shi. I'd spent so long reliving past moments on my own that I'd genuinely forgotten what it was like to share them. There's a big difference when you share memories, you can taste it, the warmth and flavour of the old scenes being conjured and inhaled in sync. I thought of the sea eagles who'd soar elegantly above the lagoon, how I'd watch them performing those graceful, synchronised dances to renew the bonds with their beloveds. With Kai, I could finally feel that grace.

We ordered some tea to finish the meal and tucked into a shared slice of bibikkan. The restaurant emptied around us and the call of the crickets thrummed louder until we were the last ones there. It was on those garden chairs under the cool breath of twilight, Shi, that I told him my story. I didn't hold back; I told him everything. Everything. It was strange, I wasn't worried in the slightest about how he would react. Maybe it was the darkness, the knot of hurt and pain we both had lurking there, but I felt safe with him, so at ease that everything came pouring out effortlessly.

He listened intently, the amber glinting sharper in his watery eyes. As I recounted the bleakest parts he leant across the table and held my hand, clenching it tightly as if he were trying to absorb the pain away. Then, as I told him about the creatures I encountered and the kindness of Cas, his face brightened. He interlocked his fingers with mine, raised my hand to his lips and kissed it softly.

'Sounds like you found your appa reincarnate in Cas, Mila.'

I felt the salt snakes rising and quivering on my eyelids. Kai reached out as I tried to turn my face away and held my chin gently in his hand. His eyes gleamed right through me, warming and enveloping me, stilling and calming me. Then, amidst the heat of our gaze, he crossed his eyes, scrunched his eyebrows and stuck out his tongue. I couldn't help but laugh, the snakes streaming down my cheeks as I chuckled. It was so refreshing to flit between the intense and silly so effortlessly. Each time the darker topics threatened to drag us down we'd grip the float of sweet hilarities and keep our heads above water, together.

I felt lighter around him, as if I were returning to an

innocence nestled deep inside me. I became the kid peeping gleefully in rockpools, gobbling lemon puffs on the lighthouse swings and skipping through the long grass in search of the carnival of crickets. Perhaps Kai and I were more like those immortal jellyfish we had talked about all those years ago, reverting back to an earlier stage together, thwarting the rules and the passage of time itself.

lightning bugs, darting drongos

Over the following days, Kai and I soaked up as much time with each other as possible. We met for lunch, strolled the streets and as the quilt of stars emerged we would dip into different restaurants to feast. After gobbling huge plates of mouth-watering kottu roti one evening, Kai invited me back to his place for tea. He'd almost finished fixing up my Dio, he said, and I should come and see it for myself.

'I've been adding some final touches to give you a little more oomph, but it should be good to go tomorrow. Nothing but the best for Miss Mowgli.'

I smiled back but felt a lowness creeping into my gut. As we weaved our way to his flat, I couldn't help wishing the bike was harder to fix.

Kai's flat, in the bluntest of terms, was barren. It was more like a big garage; cavernous with hard furniture, minimal light and scraps of metal all over the place. There was a mattress on the floor, a tool rack on the wall and a raised platform where my Honda was propped up, glinting much brighter than I remembered. I could see he'd gone all out for me.

'You'll be able to take on the worst potholes with these new beauties,' he said slapping the tyres, 'best in town I promise you.'

'Thank you, Kai, I really appreciate it…you.'

As he headed over to the counter to make a pot of tea. I perched on a metal stool and continued to survey his living garage. It clearly wasn't a nest for relaxation, it was a continuation of his workplace, another arena for him to busy his hands and keep his mind occupied with fixing things.

He brought the tea over, pulled up a stool beside mine and we sat sipping quietly. I noticed him fiddling with the ring on his index finger again, spinning the internal panel with the side of his thumb. Round and round he spun it, anchoring himself to the movement and staring off into the distance. Often you can learn a lot more by what isn't said, Shi, and those pauses of his were telling. As we finished up our tea, he stopped spinning the ring and turned to me.

'So, what's next then?'

'What do you mean?'

'Once your bike is ready tomorrow, where are you planning to head next?'

I explained my plan to keep scouring the towns around the final siege sites for Ravi, Mullaitivu in the northeast being next on my list.

'I really admire your determination, Mila,' he said, as he started to spin his ring again 'I get it, trust me. When you know they could be out there it's impossible to give up. I still find myself looking for my little sister. She'd be nineteen now and even after all these years it's hard to let go of the hope.'

'So don't let go of it.' I said, touching his arm.

'Anyway, so we're going to Mullaitivu?'

'We?'

'Yes, we, there's no way I'm losing you again Mowgli. I'm afraid you're stuck with me. Besides, I actually know a few units where ex fighters are housed down that way, so it makes sense for me to drive you. We can cover more ground that way, avoid the mosquitos and play some music as we go. It's a no brainer, I'll even let you DJ.'

'But what about your work?'

'Not a problem. I'm owed time off anyway and once we find your brother we can figure out the next steps from there.'

His optimism rushed through me like an ocean breeze. The chance to sink into a comfortable seat and stay paddling in those amber lakes sounded ideal.

'You're not alone anymore, Mila. We're doing this together.'

❖   ❖   ❖

In the moist scorch of mid-morning, we packed the car boot and started to make tracks towards Mullaitivu. The radio hummed softly from the stereo as the whir of street vendors, fields, faces, bikes and tuk-tuks smeared vividly past the windows. My attention, however, was glued to the inside of the car. Being with Kai was intoxicating, Shi. His fresh mango scent filled the vehicle and as he steered, the rhythmic tensing of his forearm muscles transported me back to how I used to watch him heaving fishing nets along the sand, his sweat beads glistening clear as quartz. Sometimes he'd turn the stereo up and begin goofily lip syncing along, his fingers drumming on the wheel and plucking at my heart strings.

Kai had a glow about him, Shi, an infectious light deeper than the amber in his eyes, a light that filled him like the bioluminescence of a moon jelly or the glow from a firefly's abdomen. Don't get me wrong, I could sense there was a darkness there too; I'd gotten used to the weight of trauma congealing and clogging up the air. But with Kai it was clear the warmth was winning out. Being with him felt like the moment the sun emerges through buttermilk clouds and begins to brighten up the sky, bursting through with shades of hope and light and promise.

Along the way we would stop off for cool drinks and snacks to keep us going. One time, when Kai had stopped to pick us up some nelli juice and rambutan from a roadside stall, three young women were crouched playing cards near the curb. As Kai turned back towards me, I saw him stop dead in his tracks as he caught the side profile of one of the women. His whole face flushed pale and the bag of rambutan slipped from his fingers. The three women stopped playing and turned towards him and as they did so, I saw the colour return to Kai's cheeks. He stooped to collect the scattered fruit and when he got back in the car he didn't mention it. He didn't have to. I knew what it felt like to glimpse your loved ones in the faces of strangers.

'Finest nelli for the finest lady,' he said, offering me one of the juices.

I reached out and squeezed his hand tightly before I took the cup.

Another time, when we stopped to enjoy some cooling mango lassi under a pandan tree, I watched Kai fiddling away with his eyebrow in the heat. Fingers cool from cradling the iced lassi, I reached over and stroked it, feeling the bump of the little scar etched in the slit.

'Where did you get it?' I asked.

'One of my happier memories. Me and my sister were climbing one of the palm trees just behind our back yard, racing to the top as usual. She was always beating me, so much lighter, so much quicker.' Kai touched my fingers as they rested on his eyebrow. 'But the day I got this I finally beat her. I was so excited to have won that I fell and bashed my head on the way down. But to be honest, what I remember most was her laugh. I danced around celebrating my victory with blood pouring down my face as she was creased over laughing her organs out.'

I loved hearing Kai open up to me. I knew he'd eventually tell me about the darkness, about what had happened to him when the Tigers came snatching, but I was in no rush. I wanted to give him the patience I was given in the bookshop refuge; some flowers simply take a little longer to open. The kurinji shrub takes twelve years to bloom and as for my island's talipot palm, well that can take up to eighty years to fully open its flowers. All pleasure demands patience, Shi, after all, and I had the patience of a thousand lifetimes for Kai.

Beyond our juice stops, we'd also pause at various cafes to stretch our legs and fill our tums with something more substantial. Sipping tea as the hot feasts settled in our bellies, Kai began to share nuggets of what had happened during the years we'd been apart. Usually there was a trigger, like the car engine that backfired and sent a flock of drongos squawking past our café window.

'Reminded me of the birds in the jungle, near the factory the Tigers made me work in,' he said, 'Every day when we started up they would go yelping from the trees at the sounds of the machinery.'

'The noise they make is their way of warning others of danger, they were just trying to help each other out.' I said, trying to ease him. 'Even little insects like treehoppers have their warning methods. They vibrate the stem they're sitting on to send out an alarm if danger lurks close.'

'If only it could work that way with us. Seeing the Sea Tigers set off on their suicide missions, Mila, I saw it the other way around. Their bravado drawing others closer to danger.'

At another café, where we'd ordered heaps of onion rice and brinjal eggplant, the same alarm came glazing Kai's face. He was staring at the shoes of a little girl who was sitting at the next table, completely transfixed on the glittery sandals swinging back and forth under the chair. I could see he'd slipped back into that empty space between the lines. We carried on talking but I could sense a withdrawal in him for the rest of the meal.

When we got back into the car, he began to fiddle with the stereo, clearly desperate for some kind of distraction. As the frequency fizzed and murmured between stations, his fingers begin to tremble over the dial.

'She was just so tiny, Mila. I can't unsee the pain in her face as she screamed for him. It haunts me every day.'

I reached out and pulled him in to my neck, feeling his wet eyelashes graze my shoulders.

That was the evening he opened up to me, Shi. He'd never before spoken to anyone about his time with the Sea Tigers, the ruthless naval wing of the Tamil Tigers, but there in that carpark, in streams of salt and radio fizz, it all came pouring out. Given you're very much mired in my story now, Shi, and

Kai is intricately bound up in my beating ink, let me share the broad strokes with you.

muddy monkey, jiving spiders

Kai couldn't remember much about the day he was taken, the day I turned eighteen, beyond the cable ties digging into his wrists, the sack thrown over his head and hours spent in darkness clattering around in the back of a lorry. When the engine finally stopped, and the sack was yanked from his head, his eyes adjusted to a boisterous training camp carved into the heart of the northern jungles, where he was set to work collecting scraps for the engineers working on the Sea Tiger boats. One such engineer, Harish, noticed how intently Kai observed his handiwork and decided to give him a chance cutting and welding the metal slabs. With lungs filled with burning metal and the oppressive jungle heat smothering on all sides, it was hard to breathe let alone work. Yet even in that sweltering pressure cooker, Kai's natural skill was obvious and Harish quickly took him under his wing as his assistant.

The Sea Tigers were excellent improvisers, Shi, experimenting with chunks of trains and planes and retrofitting weapons to ensure the little they had was converted to so much more. Kai was an expert at this innovation. Using scrap metal, he built lightweight wings for the stealth boats, helping to lift them out of the water on high-speed runs. He constructed a streamlined metal cage on old train rails, fitting it with an outboard motor to create the fastest one-man human torpedo the camp had ever seen. Steel hydroplanes, aerodynamic paddle boards, you name it, Kai went sweating away on them in that humid jungle factory. The metal screeched and spat between his hands, scorching his eardrums until nothing else could get through. He needed the distraction, anything to drown out the sounds that seeped from the nearby shipping containers. That's where the captives were herded to, Shi, shoved into those metal cages with trembling legs and blood trickling from open gashes. Screeching, yelping, begging, whimpering, shrieking, howling; the air swelled wild with the sound of souls being shattered piece by piece.

At night, as the sounds of the jungle took over, Kai would lie listening to the life thrumbling all around, the chirping, slithering, crumpling cacophony of the breathing tangle on all sides. When he peered at the silhouettes around the camp, at the sleeping men and scattered vessels, they looked like gigantic leeches, ghastly chunks latched and sucking away at the earth, draining everything dry.

As the days oozed and sweated into weeks, Kai was often joined in the evening by a young recruit by the name of Shyam, who would sit beside him at mealtimes, chatting away. He knew it was no good to form attachments, but he began to grow fond of his pink cheeked, baby-faced companion. Listening to him reminded Kai of an earlier time, of what it meant to be passionate about something, of the old shapes of hope and optimism which he'd left behind so long ago.

Eagerness aside, Shyam was too clumsy for engineering work, so he was given another special job by the commanders; when hostages had reached their expiry date, it was Shyam's job to remove the bodies from the shipping container and clean up the mess. As the war beast growled louder, he'd spend all day dragging bodies in his wheelbarrow and wiping blood and entrails in the damp heat, his enthusiasm trampled bit by bit, gut by gut, until he became a sad shell of a boy who barely spoke. When they ate together, Shyam simply stared and chewed, his eyes dimmed and his cheeks drained of colour. Right there in front of Kai, the keenest bean morphed into the boy of shattered dreams.

Kai threw himself into his engineering all the more. As he focused on fibreglass, joints and bolts, he was fed stories about the brutes in charge of the Lion's navy, their cruelty and the countless Tamil civilians they were massacring day by day. He was told how important his work was, how he was gallantly securing a future for his people and day and night he went twisting, welding, meshing, nailing and securing so tightly that no other thoughts had room to seep in. But it wasn't long before the work stopped altogether. The army had figured out where the jungle factory was and phosphorous rockets pummelled the camp, smoke plumes hissing through the thickets and slithering into throats, eyes and ears. The factory took a direct hit and pieces of metal splayed out in all directions, one wedging itself straight into Kai's right foot. As chaos erupted around them, Harish, in a flurry of panic, doused Kai's foot in arrack, ripped the shrapnel from it and bound it in an oily rag. As the metal snouts closed in, Harish dragged

Kai from the crumbling camp and hauled him away through a deep labyrinth of vines to find refuge in one of the local towns. Barely able to walk, let alone run, Kai's only option was to blend in with the locals and hope that none of the soldiers would spot him.

Limping amidst the hordes of refugees, Kai was there during the final siege of Mullaitivu, right there crossing the causeway in miserable surrender, trying not to look at the swollen corpses floating in the muck. He was there when they were herded into a vast holding pen, the last stop for those yet to be fully trampled. The cries of women and children pierced the hot air and disease ran rampant like the flies swarming to the banquet of open wounds. He was kept in that wasteland of filth for over fourteen months, Shi. Fourteen months of battered flesh, sixty-one weeks of gnawing hunger, four hundred and twenty-seven days of squelching agony and despair.

The soldiers would often come prowling through the crowds, yanking away those they suspected were Tigers. Kai would watch on as countless others were bludgeoned with gun butts, dragged away from their families and loaded onto buses to nowhere. A tiny girl with a button nose and sparkly purple sandals was sleeping right beside Kai when her appa was taken. When she woke, she kept calling for him, squealing and panicking, her face crumpled and soaked as she gripped at her stuffed monkey. Kai had wanted to soothe her, wipe her tears and comfort her like he would his little sister, but he missed the chance, Shi. The soldiers returned and the girl's cries echoed over their shoulders as they dragged her away, her little monkey left slumped in the muck. Kai tried desperately to focus on screwing more bolts and tightening more sockets in his head. Yet no amount of fixing could soundproof his thoughts from that little voice.

It was that little voice that really broke Kai, it shot through him like a bullet, lodged in his cortex and tortured him through and through, over and over, louder and louder. When he thought of all the boats his creations had helped to destroy, he began to think of all the little daughters left behind, all the little voices calling for their appas. He was the reason they'd never skip, sing, doodle or dance with their fathers again. He was the one who took away birthdays, marriages and first homes. He'd done that, his hands had crafted their misery, he was the engineer of their grief.

When Kai eventually got out of the squalor pen, he kept moving, heading west, bending north, pushing his way forward, step after step, road after road. He paused in a few towns along the way, some of which he recognised from family trips in his childhood, but it was never long before the triggers came stabbing and clotting into a restlessness that sent him chasing pavements and tarmac once again. Kilinochchi was different though, he'd never been there before and liked the fact that nothing felt familiar, so he picked up some regular repair work and stuck around. He wanted a clean slate, but it wasn't long before he realised that was impossible; the guilt kept twisting like a wrench and jolting him like a jump starter. No matter how many brake pads he fixed, fuel injectors he unclogged, and spark plugs he replaced, the little girl's voice kept on slicing through his thoughts.

As time crawled on, he learnt to live with his dirty slate. As his misery began to ebb slowly and steadily with the passing years, Kai came to realise that not everything can be fixed and it's okay to not be okay. With time tocking on indifferently, Kai came to place more value in the unfixed.

◈   ◈   ◈

Seeing Kai so vulnerable, Shi, sent my instincts blazing like cobra chillies. Seeing him so raw and unfolded there in that car, I was filled with the urge to take the pain away from him and absorb it into my own. It's a powerful tug, the urge to protect the ones we love. I'd studied the impulse aplenty in the animal kingdom, the way skink mates protect and nurture each other for decades or the way a black lace-weaver sacrifices its own body to ensure the survival of its babies. The way loom pairs stick together and fiercely guard each other or the way male fig wasps die carving an escape route from the fig flesh so the females can take to the skies. It's a powerful sensation, wanting to protect someone so much that you don't even consider yourself. Their well-being lodges in the front of your mind and their discomfort resonates deep in your bone marrow.

As well as the urge to protect Kai, I also felt an admiration swelling. I respected the way he kept going, the way he kept his head up and pushed on. Watching him shake the tears and begin to fiddle with the stereo again, I couldn't get over how impressively he carried himself despite all that pain. Agony is heavy, it hardens like a tumour, clots in your bloodstream and presses down on your spine, I knew this well. Kai rolled his shoulders back and began tapping along on the wheel, and as he did so I felt myself instinctively straightening my own posture.

Just ahead of us in the car park, a couple of rock pigeons were hopping about, one puffing its chest and following the other in circles. Kai pointed to them, clearly keen to divert focus away from the trauma lingering with us in the car.

'He's trying to woo her, right? I love it when they dance and puff out like that.'

'That's nothing, you wait until you see a six plumed bird of paradise wiggling and jiving for its mate. Oh, and the male peacock spider drums a beat to attract a female and then elaborately waggles around to show off his beautiful coloured abdomen. If she's impressed, she even does a wiggle dance back.'

'So, if she joins in it means she likes him?'

'Yep.'

'Right, better test the theory then.'

He swivelled the stereo dial to full volume and swung open the car door, letting the music pour out into the empty carpark. Then he leapt out, Shi, and began to dance. I watched him twirling around in circles, shaking his hips and swaying side to side in the gravel as he clicked to the beat.

'Come on,' he shouted to me over the music, 'what are you waiting for? Do I not get a wiggle back?'

I stepped out of the car and moved towards him, letting myself loosen into the music. We danced on and on, wiggling and spinning, unapologetic and free. It felt so liberating to just move like that Shi, to shake off everything and completely immerse ourselves in the present, swirling and melting into the buttercream folds of the now. The loose gravel in the car park sprawled around us, glowing in patches under the lampposts like the surface of some distant planet. We kept on moving, kicking up rhythmic dust clouds with our feet, just me and him, swaying together in our very own world.

zebra tails, snake charmers

As we drove into Mullaitivu, a sombre fog came rolling in thick and heavy, marinating the mood. The land felt haunted as we trundled through, the soil still throbbing from the final slaughter that had taken place there. Kai stiffened behind the wheel.

Carcasses of houses wept past the windows. Crumbling brick, bullet pocked walls and overgrown thickets crept around the structures, now ornaments of the war, battered husks lodged in the landscape, aching and reminding.

Kai's knuckles whitened around the steering wheel and the muscles tightened in his jaw. Not once did he glance at the houses we passed; he focused only on the road ahead. We let the unspoken pain hover between us and respected the trauma with our silence.

Veering off Beach Road, we trundled down a web of side streets before Kai pulled into a carpark next to a dilapidated housing block. A number of other cars, which had clearly seen better days, were scattered about and I could sense Kai fixing through improvements for them in his head as our tyres chewed the gravel underneath. Staring at the grubby concrete block, my thoughts raced with each thump of my heart. *Ravi could be here, right here, just metres away.* Kai sensed my tension, reached out and softly squeezed my hand.

'You've got this, Mowgli.'

We stepped out of the car and were hit by a wave of heat which blended with my nerves into a queasy hot cocktail, but I forced my feet forward on the momentum of Kai's reassurance.

The main doors moaned open into a foyer that smelt of bleach and stale rice. Behind a cheap desk in the centre of the room, a man was watching a video on his phone, rocking back and forth on his chair, chuckling away to himself. As we approached, he stopped rocking and a stern demeanour glazed his face.

'What do you want? You need directions?' His voice was thick and gloopy like date chutney that has been left out too long.

Kai stepped forward, whispered to the man and handed over an envelope. The man checked the contents and nodded.

'Take your time, machan, long as you need. Brace yourself madam,' he said as he turned to me, 'it's not pretty in there.'

We passed through another set of doors into a corridor clogged stale with sweat. A sour humidity clung to everything. Branching from the central corridor stem, a series of rooms with doorless frames sprawled out like dead flowers. Inside, men with worn faces lay sleeping on metal bunks, some muttering to themselves and others just sitting silently, staring into space. Heads swivelled as we passed by each room, vacant eyes seared into us.

It was hard to look away from the shaking men, Shi, all those vibrating bones together created its own kind of dark rhythm, a powerful pull that tugged on our own trauma and made each step feel like wading through mud. Kai could sense my unease. He reached out to steady me with a grip which felt like hope, like the first droplets of monsoon rain amidst a brutal dry season.

We waded through the abyss arm in arm, the air clotted sour with anguish, the stench of despair coating our skin and seeping into our pores. The more rooms we entered, Shi, the more those gaunt faces started to look the same. The sunken cheeks, dead eyes and emaciated frames began to blend and blur into ghost maps of grief, shadows of lives ended long ago. I had no doubt I'd be able to recognise Ravi, though, I'd never miss the crescent moon birthmark on his neck that I used to stroke while he lay in his cot.

We scoured the entire place, top to bottom, limbless to toothless, shouters to smokers. I peeped, combed and scrutinised every inch of it, but there wasn't a trace. Not a glimpse. No one looked even remotely like my brother.

As we got back in the car, I stared at the flecks of dust on the windscreen. Kai kissed my forehead and we sat there in silence. I knew it was naive to expect to find Ravi so quickly but part of me just thought I would, you know? Part of me was convinced he'd be waiting right there and everything would just fall into place. But reality came stinging once again and the cuckoo went on crying somewhere out of reach. Kai gently turned my chin towards him.

'Hey, remember that was just the first try. Let's take it day by day and piece by piece like that Ramayana squirrel, okay? One down, many more to go.'

But each stop was largely the same story, Shi. Staring eyes, sour rooms and shaking bones. Crumbling bodies, bullet pocked skin and overgrown beard thickets aplenty. Like the battered brick husks, they too were frozen in time, breathing relics of the war. Some were revved up, on constant high alert, like they hadn't been taught how to switch off from battle-mode, but even with them you could see their batteries were wearing down. On one occasion, in a scruffy bungalow near a patch of stagnant water, I came across a man who looked just like Ravi. Hope fluttered but as I dashed towards him to get a closer look, my spirits sunk to the depths of the trawler nets scouring the bottom of Lanka's oceans. I understood completely how Kai felt seeing all those girls who weren't his sister.

Mullaitivu polluted our lungs with every breath we took. We were tired, Shi, and certainly had no desire to go gobbling ice cream and feeding squirrels. Instead, we booked into a hotel and spent each evening there in the drab room, eating bland room service and watching mindless TV to try and numb our thoughts. When our eyelids grew heavy, we'd lie down together, Kai wrapping his arms around my waist and pulling me into his body. I breathed in his scent and let the warmth of his skin envelop my own. It felt so nice to be held like that. Just me and him, sad and together. It felt safe, Shi.

In the mornings, I'd tiptoe around snoozing Kai and wander off in search of breakfast. I discovered a little café not too far from the hotel and began autopiloting there in my dawn stupor. While they prepared the food order, I sat down at a table as sticky as a gecko's feet and zoned out to the hum of clinking cutlery and the sizzle of pans coming from the kitchen.

How long could I keep on searching? Would I ever feel ready to concede defeat?

An elderly couple were sat eating together, backs hunched over their table as they mopped ala hodi with string hoppers. I watched as the lady reached out for a napkin and the man pre-empted it, placing a tissue in her hand before she'd even raised her eyeline. A few moments later, as he reached for the saltshaker, she instinctively slapped his hand with a look which made him chuckle and relinquish it. I liked seeing their rhythm flowing so effortlessly, admired the way they moulded around each other with such ease. *Would Kai and I be like that one day? Would he come back to Batti with me? What would the future hold for us?* As they finished their meal and got up to leave, the old man placed his hand on the small of her back and guided her toward the door. I bet she'd had a lifetime of that little touch; I bet the grooves of her back had grown used to the contours of his palm. I thought of the way Kai held my chin and interlocked his perfect fingers with mine. I knew I could grow used to lifetime of that, Shi.

❖　　　　　　　❖　　　　　　　❖

On our final day in Mullaitivu there were only two locations left for us to visit. Our first stop was a boarding house where an Air Tiger's wife was rumoured to have taken in some fighters who had survived the detention centres.

We pulled into the driveway and I was immediately taken aback by how dainty it was; trim flowers, herb patches and a few rainbow wind spinners peppered the pathway that led up to a butterscotch door. It seemed more like a granny's cottage than an ex-militant hording house. We rang the bell and waited, the wind spinners twizzling lethargically at our feet. When the door opened, my granny image fizzled. A towering rake of a man with one eye stood before us, his presence sucking the very warmth out of the air. After taking an envelope from Kai, he led us through the front room and into a hallway, mutter-ranting under his breath.

'No point living like this...chi... they think they own us now.'

We followed him past a foul-smelling bathroom where two women were leaning against the wall, their conversation falling silent as we neared. Their saris were bedraggled and a scent of grease wafted from their matted hair. I felt dizzy, my head filling with cave darkness and the sloshing echo of bucket water.

'We should load the barrels again...dirty buggers won't see it coming,' the man carried on muttering, 'let's feed the soil... their blood not ours.'

He led us into what appeared to be study-come-kitchen. There was an empty pine desk in the centre of the room with a few plastic chairs scattered around it. At the side of the room, by a slim kitchen worktop, a grey-haired lady in a blue apron was brewing tea. The man dropped the envelope down on the desk with a grunt before mumbling his way back down the corridor. The lady turned towards us, her lips curling into a shape that didn't quite form a smile. She gestured to the chairs and we took a seat, watching as she meandered over, slowly sipping on her brimming mug. I stared at the little flowers etched on the porcelain; flowers just like the ones on Boudi's sleeping bag.

'Sorry about Jitto.' She gestured towards the corridor. 'More bark than bite. I've been housing him here since, ooh let me think, summer of '09 I'd say. My husband passed a few years back, so he insists on helping out. Pain in the ass but he means well. Was he talking about fighting again?'

Kai and I glanced at each other and stayed silent, which in itself gave her the answer she was looking for.

'I've warned him about that. Can't keep running his mouth off to any old visitor, can't be too careful these days as I'm sure you know.' She scanned our faces for a reaction. 'Anyway, enough about that. I assume you're here looking for someone?'

We both nodded.

'Well, take your time. I've got a fair few with me at the moment, about nineteen all together. Or is it seventeen now... not sure. Aiyo, my memory isn't what it used to be, I lose track of a lot of things these days. But sometimes it's better not to remember.'

She blew on the steam rising from her mug and let her words reverberate in the silence.

'Most of the residents will be upstairs. If you need me just shout for Sriti, and as I said, take as long as you want.'

She slid the envelope from the desk into her apron pocket and shuffled off towards the corridor. Kai stood up and held his hand out towards me.

'Ready then?' He said, as pulled me out of the chair and kissed me on the nose. 'Come on, let's do this.'

We headed up the staircase, our nostrils greeted by the scent of varnish, glue and body odour. In a big room near the landing, the source of the smell was revealed. A group of men were hunched around a patchwork of newspapers on the floor, piecing together dried out gourd shells, bamboo sticks and ribbons into pungi, the snake charming instruments tourists flocked to buy. In the corner, a couple of men were piercing holes in the bamboo sticks and two ladies were painting designs on the front of the gourds with black paint. Everyone was busy piecing together their own components but the collective trauma was seeping out like a thick miasma. I scanned each of the faces, inspecting the ghost maps with their sunken valleys, creased rivers and crater eyes that all stared the same shade of decay. One by one they'd lower their gaze and return to their work, sinking back into the rhythm of the abyss.

We moved on, checking each of the rooms in turn. I was used to the procedure by now; the peep, scan and scour routine before the inevitable sinking feeling came smothering. In the final room, after another bout of unfamiliar faces, I paused to collect myself before we headed back. I was trying to be stronger, Shi, but I couldn't stop the tide of deflation. Wrestling such a creeping sense of futility was, for lack of a better word, futile. Water quivered on my eyelids and I turned to the window. It wasn't that I was ashamed to let Kai see me cry, Shi, it was because I knew he'd want to soothe me and sometimes you don't want that, sometimes you just need to be sad. No solution, no fixes; just feel the sadness. Through molten eyes, the glass pane of the window rippled and the scene below wobbled. Amidst the blur, a figure in blue was sitting on a bench. I wiped my eyes and peered closer. The figure turned his face towards the house and my heart shuddered.

I raced along the corridor, down the stairs and out into the garden with the vigour of a ravenous peregrine, tears streaming horizontally across my face. I could feel it. Feel him. See the cuckoo. This was it.

As I neared the bench the face of the figure became clear.

Those ears.

That nose.

Those eyes.

Rivers streamed down my cheeks, soaking my face with their current. It was him. Unmistakably, undeniably him. Sodden, I buckled to my knees. It was him. Ravi, my baby brother, right there.

Consumed by the hot tide of emotion, I didn't know what to do. How do you greet your long-lost brother, your only living relative, the person you've been dreaming of for over a decade? I lunged forward and folded my arms around him. This was the moment I'd been waiting for, the moment I'd imagined so many times, the moment which kept me going in Rosh's house, in the bowel room, in Satyan's basement, on the streets and in Cas's teapot. The very moment I'd played over and over in my head, night after night, month after month, year after year. But before I could even inhale his hair, he began struggling to push me off, desperate to shake me away. I let go and stepped back. He clenched his eyes shut and began rocking back and forth, clutching his sides. I didn't understand.

'Ravi, it's me. It's Mila. Ravi, it's your sister, Mila.'

He continued rocking.

Had I got it wrong? I looked closer at his neck and the crescent moon mark was there, just as I remembered. His nose, his lips, his locks, his hands; everything was there, just as I remembered. But the man rocking there on the bench didn't recognise me at all, Shi.

torn dragonfly, swollen symphony

My brother was broken, Shi. I knew I was obscenely lucky to have found him, but it was a tainted kind of luck. You see the more I looked at that shaking, whimpering man whom Kai and I had brought back with us, the less he seemed like my brother at all.

Each time I had moved closer to the bench, he let out an agonising moan and dug his hands in his eye sockets. I was clearly distressing him. And that distress went both ways. It's hard to explain the unique hurt you feel when someone you love doesn't recognise you; when they see you as a source of intense discomfort when all you want to do is comfort them. It's like a slow prolonged plunging of a blade, a knife being shimmied around in a wound. Seeing Ravi look at me like that, straight through me like that, took me back to the days of amma and the bedroom shadows. My very presence was a source of agony all over again.

After hearing the commotion, Sriti came out with a potion of sleeping pills mixed in tea. We watched as she held his jaw open and forced him to drink, the liquid dribbling down his chin as he tried to shake free from her grip. As I knelt on the grass beside the bench, he began to stare at my cheek with an intensity I'd never experienced before, Shi. Young Ravi at least gave me the courtesy of pretending to look away but this new Ravi, he didn't care at all. He just kept staring, burrowing into it with his eyes as he sipped and rocked until his eyelids grew heavy and he slipped into a foetal position on the bench. My mind flashed to the last time I'd seen him like that, my childhood playmate curled up giggling in the sand, chuckling away beside me near a bag of empty kokis. It felt like a different lifetime, Shi.

Kai scooped him up in a blanket and placed him in a dazed heap on the back seat of the car while Sriti placed a pouch of extra pills into my quivering hands. We drove away from the boarding house, from Mullaitivu, and made the long slow journey back to Kilinochchi. Kai and I stayed silent for the entire journey. There were no words for us to share that would mean anything. My eyes stayed glued to Ravi the whole way, staring at each rise and fall of his chest. I couldn't get the sound of his whimpering out of my head, Shi. There are a range of chilling distress calls in the wild, the screech of the barn owl, the shriek of the cougar and the wail of the smoky jungle frog will all send tremors down your spine, but Ravi's soul-polluting melody of a wrecked being, cut deeper than I thought it was possible to go.

Back in Kilinochchi, we booked into a hotel and laid Ravi down on the bed. I stepped into the bathroom to splash cold water on my face and stood there letting my tears drip into the sink. Kai followed me in and wrapped his arms tightly around me.

'Mila, you've found him. Just remember, you've found him.' He began to pat my wet face gently with a towel. 'Now we take it slowly, step by step. Never let go of the hope. Remember you're a fighter, Mila, it's going to be hard, but I know you can do this. And I'll be there every step of the way, mantis fists at the ready.'

He folded me into his heartbeat and we stayed there like that for some time as I prepared myself to head back into the bedroom.

'I know you need some time alone with him,' he said, 'I'll come back in the morning, but you call me any time, ok? I'll come leaping like a mudskipper.'

After Kai headed out, I pulled up a chair beside Ravi's bed and watched over him as he dug his nails into his arms and clawed at his skin, twitching and murmuring. Seeing him lying there like that, his eyes closed, his body curled vulnerably, I caught a glimpse of my baby brother again and a wave of protectiveness prickled in my chest. I was overwhelmed by the urge to climb into the bed next to him, just like I used to, Shi, so I did. I slipped on to the mattress and drew in close to him. Each inhale of his breath sounded quipped and rushed, like he was struggling, panicking, lost somewhere, wherever he was. I reached over and stroked his earlobes to soothe him. I closed my eyes and for a split second, Shi, I was back in his cot again, holding my baby brother. It didn't last long. He elbowed me hard in the ribs and scrambled off the bed, withdrawing to the corner of the room where he wrapped his arms over his knees and began rocking again. If those were the aftershocks playing out on his body, I couldn't even imagine the inferno raging inside his head.

In the weeks that followed, things didn't get much better.

Ravi grew slightly less repulsed by my presence, but the rocking, staring and whimpering continued and at night he would shiver away in a sweaty tangle of blubbering and screaming. Screams that would make the devil bird shudder. Car engines backfiring, the shutting of a door along the corridor, a passer-by clearing their throat; everything startled him, and he'd dig his nails in tighter. Like so many of those wandering carcasses, he was on permanent red alert, fight or flight stamped right there in his retinas.

There were so many cracks in him, Shi, just so damn many of them. His hands permanently trembled and I found it hard to bring myself to look at them. I remembered how those very same hands would send wickets tumbling with a whooshing bowl. How they had picked eagerly through the rockpools beside me and how they reached triumphantly into the air with open fingers as he pedalled away on the lake roads up ahead. Those same hands, with all their potential and promise, now relics, cracked and crumbling. There was also a permanent wince etched on his face and the smile I remembered so fondly had been replaced by a grimace of quivering lips. Amma used to say his smile was the spitting image of her father's, appappa Nimal, and that whenever Ravi beamed it felt like her father was right there in the room with us. Watching Ravi's battered body rocking back and forth in the hotel room, I thought about how tragically history was repeating itself. Appappa Nimal's spirit revived in Ravi only to be bludgeoned and trampled all over again.

Ravi was nothing now but skin and bone, his body emaciated. Growing up, I'd always been envious of his physique. He had a strength about his movements, an ease and agility in the way he carried himself which clumsy bookworm me could only dream of. I remember walking through town with him one morning and passing a shop that had been ransacked the night before. The whole street stank of kerosene and there was glass scattered all over the pavement. Without even trying, Ravi bent his knees and leapt gracefully over the glass, walking on as if it were nothing. How I wished my body could do that, navigate space with such effortless strength and poise. While Ravi strode on ahead I had to tiptoe slowly around the glass, feeling the jagged, brittle shards cracking under my shoes. Looking at the Ravi trembling away in the hotel room, it seemed he'd morphed from the jumper to the glass itself; broken, brittle, shattering more and more with each step.

I wanted to know what had happened to him, what had turned my charismatic, sporty brother into this trembling wreck of man? Who had done this to him? What horrors had he endured? This is the part where you're probably expecting me to launch into a tangent on Ravi's story, Shi, waiting for me to cordon off his trauma so we can dissect it together. Well, I'm afraid I can't do that. This time I don't have a story to tell you. The story I'd thought about more than any other, the one I'd agonised over on dark ships, cold pavements and in oaky teapots, I simply never got to know.

I think that's a lesson in itself, Shi. Often you don't get to know the horrifying things war can do to people or about the things it makes people do. War strips and chews away everything you're sure of and vomits out a perturbing sort of uncertainty. It pushes people to places and situations you would never think possible, and it tests you in ways you can't even imagine. So, I never got to know what happened to

Ravi or the things he made happen. I never got to know if he was victim or murderer, predator or prey. All I know is that war doesn't end when ceasefires pop up or peace deals come a-scribbling. It simply moves terrain, morphing into a fiercer war right there in the head. And the mind is the worst kind of battlefield; darker, hotter and inescapable. The psychological wounds are never given as much attention as the visible ones, and yet they run far deeper. Memories of events go rippling around your head, tearing you up when you least expect them. And those ripples of the mind never stop.

People talk about PTSD as a disorder but really it's just a different order. To survive high intensity situations your labyrinth of synapses and neurons go creating new pathways and shortcuts in order to stay hypervigilant. But when the intensity stops, the shortcuts remain and you're left permanently on edge, condemned to eternal red alert. I spent many hours researching different conditions associated with surviving conflict in my quest to get Ravi some professional help. I read about the black dog of depression and wondered if we'd ever bring it under control for Ravi, but to be honest, it seemed like he was chained to a different kind of beast entirely, more like a black buffalo, a crocodile or a hippo. His trauma was not one that could be coaxed on a leash, but one that rammed, death-rolled and took chunks out of him, as he bled out into oblivion.

On rare occasions I'd catch him staring at the wall and not shaking at all. At first I thought he had calmed down, found a moment of peace, but I soon realised it was something else entirely. It wasn't a moment of respite but a moment of complete and utter emptiness. He was so drained from thrashing away with the thoughts in his head, from splashing away in the red currents and darting between those synapse shortcuts, that a wave of complete numbness would wash over him. He had no secret chamber, no sanctuary; he had nowhere left to retreat to. I knew that nowhere well.

The days in Kilinochchi blurred into each other with no real change in Ravi. During the nights I started to hear a few words spluttering through in his whimpering, but they'd always tremble out before I could piece them into any kind of a sense. Sometimes, I think words just can't carry the weight of experience; some feelings are too heavy to be held by tongue and ink.

Batti began to play more on my mind. I couldn't help but feel that perhaps Ravi just needed the right triggers to tap back into his former self, that maybe a familiar environment would bring it all rushing to the surface, that with the right smell, sound, taste or shape, my brother would suddenly remember me. I broached the idea with Kai.

'I think it's a great idea Mowgli. Can't hurt to try, right? When shall we go?'

'We? Kai don't be ridiculous, I can't expect you to just uproot the life you've built here for a plan that might not even work. We'll be fine, I promise, I can handle it.'

'Yes, we. I know you can handle it but how many times have I got to tell you, I'm not leaving you again. Memory of a goldfish, you.' He nudged me playfully.

'Actually, goldfish have pretty decent memories. They remember information at least five months after they're taught it. Chimps, on the other hand, forget things after twenty seconds.'

Kai started to laugh as he shook his head.

'Well, in that case, quit monkeying around and just accept I'm coming with you.'

'Chimpanzees are actually apes, not monkeys...'

'Mowgli!'

'Ok, ok, but what about work?'

'Not a problem, I can get a referral for another garage down in Batti. I know they're in need of workers so I can support us while we figure things out.'

'Kai I'm not letting...'

'Enough. It's not about letting, it's about wanting. Nothing to debate here.'

Even amidst the darkest moments, Shi, amber lakes had a way of showing me the light. That night, we strolled down to the restaurant and chatted through our plans over two fresh wedges of custard and cashew pudding. Three days later, we loaded up the car and set off for Batti.

❖ ❖ ❖

Back in our lagoon town, we rented an apartment in one of the new blocks near the beach. I could sense Ravi was already a little calmer amidst those bleached walls, or at the least, less resistant to my presence. Keen to reacquaint him with his roots, I set about hunting down some potential triggers, starting with the flavours of our childhood. I bought a fresh batch of the cinnamon kokis we used to love gobbling and he ate them, quite a few actually, but there was no semblance of recognition on his face. I sourced a few of his favourite curries, over-limed the sambol the way he used to like it and I even tracked down a kevum cake like the one Sasni aunty used to make for us. He ate everything I put in front of him, but nothing coaxed a response.

Next, I went out and bought some cricket gear. I placed the ball in his hand and watched him gently close his fingers around the stitching. He stared at it intently for a while and although I tried to convince myself something familiar was ticking over in his head, I knew he had just numbed out into nowhere again. It was heart breaking to see him so vacant like that, Shi, a total stranger to a passion that once defined him. He used to grip and swivel that ball with such confidence, spinning it round and round at the kitchen table like an extension of his own body. Now his fingers explored it like some foreign land, his wrists struggling under its weight. Had the passion been chewed up and taken from him? Or was it still buried in there, nestled somewhere deep beneath?

When I looked at the inferno in his eyes and the friction in his movements, it was clear there was a battle going on deep inside and this gave me hope, Shi, it meant that my baby brother hadn't yet been swallowed whole by the pain, that the darkness hadn't fully consumed him.

My trigger hunting was endless. I copied the impression of Mrs Pradeepa that he used to do on the beach; wagging finger, pout and all. He stared at me blankly. I took him to the rockpools and the patch where he used to practice bowling with appa. Nothing. I took him past our old house, his school and to the spot on the rocks where we had watched the dolphins. Nothing. Even as he ran his fingers over the faded carvings we'd made, there was nothing. Ravi's click moment never came, Shi.

I kept thinking I was just using the wrong key. He was in

there, deep inside, I just needed the right key to unlock the treasure trove of memories. Problem was, the more keys I tried, the more disheartening the whole thing became. I was starting to think that the locks had changed for good, or worse yet, maybe the place had been ransacked and there was no longer anything waiting on the other side. But then one damp afternoon, as I was beginning to worry that I had run out of keys, a lightbulb went on in my head. *The treasure. I had the buried treasure. How on earth could I have forgotten about the books I'd buried?* It all seemed so obvious.

In a surge of excitement I ran down to the beach with my rucksack and a spade. I raced along the sand and retraced the coordinates I'd etched into my skull all those years ago. *Eleven, four, two, seventeen. Amma, appa, Ravi, Kai. Eleven, four, two, seventeen.* I neared the edge of the casuarina trees, panting and lightheaded. Amma's birthday. *Eleven* trees along. I touched each trunk as I passed, gathering myself through deep breaths as I went. I stopped at the eleventh. Sure enough, on a slightly bent trunk, I felt a small, faded x. I swivelled south and counted. Appa's birthday. *Four* steps along. I made four slow, purposeful strides and bent down to clear the twigs from the sand. Ravi's birthday. *Two* roots across. I moved to the end of the root, the trees creaking, and the breeze whirring in anticipation. *Seventeen* digs deep, the age I'd been when I first met Kai. I rammed the spade into the sand and began to dig. Two, three, four. Bending, scooping, flicking. Eight, nine, ten. Heaving, shovelling, hurling. Thirteen, fourteen, fifteen. Sand spraying all over in a gritty whirlwind around my hot skin. Sixteen, seventeen, thud.

Yes. Something hard. Something solid.

In giddy excitement, I chucked the spade, fell to my knees and began clawing at the damp sand with my fingers. Soon enough, I felt soft plastic.

The bin bag.

I dug around it with frantic nails, heaved it out triumphantly and ripped apart the disintegrating plastic layers. They were there, they were all there, my favourite childhood elixirs; a little wet, a little cold but my old friends were there all the same. I clutched them close and breathed in their damp fragrance, inhaling the scent of home deep into my lungs. I loaded them carefully into my rucksack and scurried back to the apartment. Covered in sand and with arms throbbing from the dig, I still couldn't wipe the smile from my face, Shi.

'Where on earth have you been Mowgli?' Kai said as he opened the door to a sodden, grinning mess hunched over a gigantic rucksack.

'I've got it! I've found it!'

'Found what?' He said, wiping a clump of sand from my cheek.

'The key! You'll see, you'll see...'

I strode across the room and dumped the rucksack on the floor. Ravi was on the sofa staring into space. Unzipping the bag, I laid all the books out on the carpet and reached for his favourite, The Three Musketeers. He was watching me closely. I walked over and placed the elixir in his hands. He ran his fingers over the cover and studied the font closely. Then he looked up at me, blankly. I fumbled open the first page and pointed to the pencil mark where he'd written his name, waiting for something, anything to click.

Nothing.

I began turning the pages.

Nothing.

I flicked to the folded corners that housed his favourite passages.

Nothing. Nothing. Absolutely nothing.

Joints aching, cheek stinging, heart plummeting; I burst into tears.

❖ ❖ ❖

I'd grown used to the disappointment, Shi, and as the days trundled on I stopped pushing Ravi so hard to remember and began to slowly accept things the way they were. Kai helped, a lot. He was my anchor. Each time the sadness came welling up, he'd remind me that I was exactly where I should be; I'd found my brother, I was trying and that's all that mattered. And when those bouts of sadness became all-consuming, he'd walk me to my lagoon spot, hold me close and watch the dragonflies by my side until it passed. Gradually, I started to accept that I'd never get back the brother I knew. It was an incredibly hard pill to swallow but what other choice did I have? Accepting didn't mean giving up hope, it just meant recalibrating it.

I kept thinking of the young dragonflies, the ones who weren't so lucky. The ones who got picked on by frogs, birds and spiders while waiting for their wings to strengthen. No matter how much I wanted to protect them, I knew it was the cycle of life and there was nothing I could do to stop it. Some of those that had been knocked and damaged still managed to scrape through though, strengthening just enough to take to the skies, albeit with damaged wings that moved a little slower than the rest. Closing my eyes, those torn wings glittered softly near my earlobes and appa's toffee tea voice came warming; *At times like this, La, you've got to channel the patience of our pearl island. Friction transformed into beauty, that's how the pearl is made, that's what our Lanka does best.*

Life tocked on and we decided it was best to stay in Batti, for Ravi's sake, so we began to lay a few foundations. Kai picked up a steady job at the local garage, Ravi attended regular therapy sessions and I started to volunteer at the Eco Park near the lighthouse. The manager there was quite taken aback by my extensive knowledge of lagoon wildlife and before long he offered me a permanent job as a tour guide.

Kai and I didn't really have a plan, we still don't, Shi. For the first time in a long time there's no need to rush off elsewhere. There's no pressing desire to chase leads and there's no pressure to move on. We're comfortable, together and that's all that matters.

Don't get me wrong, we've talked a fair bit about future plans. Over hot suppers and through monsoon rains, we've discussed setting up a charity for sufferers like Ravi or expanding Kai's fix-up service to the impoverished northeast of Lanka. We've nattered about ways to help relatives of the *disappeared* and even talked about strategies to tackle human trafficking at the ports. Those paths are all there, ready for us to pursue, but for now, we're just here, co-pilots figuring things out together.

Of course, while life ticked on and I accepted Ravi's mental state for what it was, it didn't mean I stopped trying to trigger his memory. It just meant I'd got a lot better at coming to terms with the disappointment. Each failed attempt and expressionless response crushed a little less.

Just the other night, Shi, the night's sky was encrusted with the most beautiful full harvest moon I'd ever seen. It was huge, illuminating the darkness with its swollen glow. After we'd eaten dinner, I took Ravi for a stroll around the lagoon and surprisingly, he wasn't reluctant to join me. Watching the moonlight shimmering like silk on the water, I thought back to the full moon on the night I'd left the island and how I'd promised myself I'd be back watching another one with Ravi someday. As the water lapped softly near Kallady Bridge and the moist breath of evening kissed our skin, I turned to look at him. His cheeks shimmeréd beautifully in the wash of moonlight and for a moment it felt like I had my baby brother back beside me again.

I scanned the ground around us for listening tools. Spotting a chewed-up oar, I grabbed it, snapped it in half and gave one chunk to Ravi. He took it, and to my immense surprise, stepped towards the water. A little stupefied, I watched as he dunked it in and placed his ear to one end. Warmth surged through me. I quickly followed suit and joined him, oar to water, ear to oar.

As we stood there in the moonlit darkness, poised in hopeful stillness, craving a taste of the mythical realm beneath, I had what I would call a mild epiphany, Shi. Ravi's oar triggered it. Watching it positioned simultaneously in and out of that water, I realised I'd been looking at things all wrong. I'd always been seeing two worlds; the gritty cruel world of war, betrayal and bloodshed and the splendid world of nature to escape into. I'd separated the two neatly in my head to ensure I always had a sanctuary away from reality. But seeing that oar, perched both in the darkness and lunging towards the magical realm, and seeing Ravi, my broken brother straining to hear with it, I realised you have to connect the worlds if you want to live and not just survive.

Grief and hope are not locked in an either-or set up; they are as intertwined and symbiotic as the ants in the gal karandha plant that appa so loved. They are the beautiful blue Ceylon magpie with its head dipped dirty red. They are the rainfall that comes both wrecking and nourishing, the waves that come swallowing and soothing.

Darkness and hope need each other, thrive off each other and ultimately fuse with one another into a grand totality. Hope has to exist with the darkness, it's what gives it purpose. The majestic whale fluke, Ash's rug, Kai's amber lakes, Cas's marsh corner; they all emerge drenched with such meaning because of the darkness that surrounded them. Hope is power, the only solution for enduring the storm. And it's a power that spreads itself far and wide. It nestles in my creature muses and patters with appa's rainfalls. It swirls with amma's spices and purrs in Kai's engines. It's the flesh embedded around the shrapnel in my cheek; it is the mangled scar of survival itself. The oar has to straddle both realms.

Then it happened.

Almost perfectly on cue, something came rising.

I strained closer, the crickets and rippling water shushing into the backdrop. As soft as a whisper, sweeter than a siren, an ethereal hum came meandering to my eardrums and poured through me like mythic honey.

I turned to Ravi.

A flicker of a smile was curling across his lips and for the first time in as long as I could remember, my brother's eyes were aglow. On our pearl island, by that lagoon, under that bridge, there was nowhere else in the world for us to be. And so, we stood there, beneath the swollen moonlight, listening to the singing fish.

acknowledgments

Cicero, whose velvet purr thrumbled from my lap and kept me grounded through my scribbling nights.

Sean Campbell and the époque press dream team, whose creative eye, editorial prowess and nurturing confidence in my writing enabled this story to make it out into the world.

Papa, whose motorbiking, animal-packed tales of Lanka ignited a fascination that lodged deep and stained vivid.

Nana, for warming my soul with her island stories and for warming my tum with her rice and curries in the sun stroked kitchen of Cissbury Road.

My dearest mum, tigress bestie, who nurtured my wild heart and nature passion from the get go.

Dad, for the rainfalls, rocks and endless cups of the glass half full at the dock of the bay.

Shaun, Anthony and Hetty, for the love, drivies, forests and fizzio at Elm Park.

Io and Arty, whose unfaltering friendship and support boosted me the whole way and filled my lungs with AIR.

G, the supernova across the pond who warmed my heart and encouraged me beyond belief.

Kish- my CJ, my playmate, my inspiration to take life by the horns. Pocaribius eternal, pirate.

Poppy and Nisha, my soul tribe sisters from other Misters, for the soul food chats and lost rambles.

Lion, for the magic which caramelised my senses and helped spur me across the finishing line.

Mr Curry, for believing in my stories, encouraging me to never stop ink spilling and putting up with my young tomboy tiger antics.

Fuego, Peri and Pip, for the twilight bonding, cashew antics and fire bush tails that kept me grounded through the covid chaos carnival.